"WE HAVE A REAL PROBLEM NOW," AARON KURTZMAN ANNOUNCED

"It looks like Gary had a detonator failure and the secondary charges didn't fire. The bridge is still standing."

"Radio them to pull back," Hal Brognola ordered.

"I'm not sure that they can. They have a tank to deal with first," Kurtzman replied. "One of them got across the bridge. If they try to run, they'll be chopped to pieces."

"Another tank is trying to cross the bridge," Wethers called.

Brognola hoped against hope that the bridge had been damaged enough that it couldn't bear the weight of the T-72. But when an operation went to hell, hope was usually in vain.

"It made it," Wethers reported. "Now they have to fight two."

Popping two antacid tablets, the big Fed prayed to the gods of war for a miracle.

DON PENDLETON'S

MACK BOLAN®

STONY MAN™

Betrayal

A GOLD EAGLE BOOK FROM
WORLDWIDE®

TORONTO • NEW YORK • LONDON
AMSTERDAM • PARIS • SYDNEY • HAMBURG
STOCKHOLM • ATHENS • TOKYO • MILAN
MADRID • WARSAW • BUDAPEST • AUCKLAND

First edition May 1999

ISBN 0-373-61924-3

Special thanks and acknowledgment to
Michael Kasner for his contribution to this work.

BETRAYAL

Betrayal

CHAPTER ONE

Kaliningrad, Russia

"I knew there was a damned good reason why I should have stayed at the Farm," Yakov Katzenelenbogen muttered as an icy blast of wind sliced through his thin overcoat like a filleting knife. "I really do know better than to come to Russia at this time of year. I'm supposed to be a tactical adviser, dammit, not a field grunt."

He slapped his hands together to restore the circulation. "I'm getting too old for this."

Mack Bolan chuckled. Springtime in Northern Russia could be a bit brisk even in a good year. The people who were wringing their hands about global warming had never spent a spring in Mother Russia.

The town of Kaliningrad was an isolated outpost between Poland and Lithuania. Before the Germans lost it to the Red Army at the end of World War II, it had been called Königsberg. Along with the sudden name change had come a dramatic change in status. During the çold war, Kaliningrad had been a military headquarters and major logistical hub. Now that the Red Army was no more and its democratic successor a mere shadow of its former might, the military had abandoned the town. The facilities that had once serviced a horde of tanks and armored vehicles now maintained commercial long-haul trucks.

As a long-haul transportation terminal, Kaliningrad was a prefect place to conduct business, any kind of business. Most of it was legitimate, though. Now that Russia was open to Western Europe, trade was flowing, both in and out. Most of the trade, though, was going in, and little other than raw materials was coming out. Russia wasn't known for the production of quality consumer goods that anyone else might want to buy. The exception to that, of course, was military hardware. Russian weapons had always been in demand.

During the cold war, the Soviets had generously equipped the armies and air forces of their ideological allies around the world. There was hardly a Third World nation or People's Liberation Army that didn't have all the Soviet-made AK-47 assault rifles, RPG rocket launchers and MiG fighters it could use. The end of the cold war ended Soviet military welfare, but not the traffic in Russian arms. In fact more military hardware was leaving Russia now than ever. The difference was that the people responsible for the movement belonged to the Russian Mafia instead of the government.

The Russian Mafia was responsible for the most massive movement of military arms and equipment since the Gulf War ended. Dozens of arsenals had been looted and brand new tanks and aircraft were being written off as salvage as soon as they came off the production lines. While this black market material had shown up all over the world, much of it was simply disappearing. The fear was that this military muscle would show up on the streets on Russia's upcoming election day.

"There he is," Bolan said when he spotted their Russian intelligence agency contact, "over by that gray Volvo truck."

"I got him."

The right-hand door of the truck in question was halfway open, and they could see the logo of a French trucking firm painted on its side. The man talking to whoever was inside the cab looked no different from any of the other long-haul truck jockeys in the half-mile-long parking lot. He wore the quilted pants and jacket with scarf, thick boots and fur hat required to stay comfortable in Russian weather.

There was a fine irony for the two Stony Man warriors to be working with the SVR, the Russian state security agency. Not that long ago, it had been known as the KGB and had been the West's most dangerous and cunning enemy. Both Bolan and Katz carried physical and mental scars inflicted by their old opponents. It was true that they had given much better than they had received, but memories died hard. Regardless of what the President wanted, they weren't taking many chances with SVR Major Yuri Belakov.

So far, though, the Russian agent was working out well. Bolan and Katz spoke Russian, but with an accent, and they weren't as in tune with the culture as a native would be. Like it or not, to work this from inside Russia, they needed a Russian partner. The Russian Interior Minister had personally vetted Belakov as well as all of their other SVR contacts, so there was less chance of their getting someone who was on the payroll of the Russian Mafia. Even so, in Russia, one could never tell who was dirty.

Leaning against the door of the gray Volvo truck, Yuri Belakov butted the strong Turkish cigarette he had been smoking against the bottom of his work boot. One of the best things about the fall of the Iron Curtain was that he could now get decent smokes. For this job, though, he was stuck with smoking dried Turkish camel shit. Smoking a Marlboro while posing as a man of the working class was too dangerous.

Waving a farewell to the driver he had been talking to, Belakov casually walked over to where Bolan and Katz were waiting for him. Working with Americans was strange for him, too, particularly these Yankees. He had been briefed on what the commandos were in Russia to do, but not who they were.

"What did you find out?" Katz asked.

Belakov lit up another cigarette. "He said that he saw a convoy of tank transporters heading out of Kiev with T-72s on board."

The Russian's English was very American and almost accentless. With the death of the KGB, their

"Little Amerika" training center had been closed down. But, now that Western TV programs and videos were readily available, an agent didn't need the specialized training course to learn to speak like a native American.

"How did he know that they were T-72s?" Katz asked the obvious question.

"He did his national service in a tank regiment."

"Did he say where they were going?"

"East."

"That's the third sighting," Bolan said. "I think we're finally on to it."

The "it" in this case was a report that an entire Russian armored brigade had disappeared—tanks, ammunition, support equipment and all. Along, of course, with most of the officers and tank crews. Desertion was rife in the new Russian army, but that was ridiculous. What was even worse was that the information hadn't come from the military high command. In fact the commander of the military district involved firmly denied that he was missing any tanks or troops.

"Let's get out of the weather and make our report," Katz suggested.

Belakov looked around the crowded truck park. "Have you seen Gregor?" he asked. He had brought a second operative with them to cover his back while he poked around. With so many of the truck drivers moonlighting for the gangs, it was unhealthy to ask too many questions.

"There he is." Katz pointed his chin in Russian manner to their left.

The man walking toward them was over six feet tall and built like a bear. He was bareheaded, and his long coat was open in the front as if it were a spring day in Italy instead of Northern Russia. The man was in midstride when a pistol shot rang clear in the cold air and a patch of red appeared on his chest.

"Gregor!" Belakov shouted.

"Stand fast!" Bolan reached out and grabbed the Russian's arm to keep him from running to aid his partner.

Katz whipped open his overcoat to reveal the mini-Uzi hanging on a strap over his shoulder. Bolan's .44 Magnum Desert Eagle had appeared in his off hand as if by magic as the two scanned the truck park, peering under the trailers.

"I think he took his shot and ran," Katz said.

Belakov shook off Bolan's hand. "We'd better be gone too," he said. "Let me check Gregor while you bring the car around."

"I'll come with you," Bolan said.

As PERPLEXING as the disappearance of the armored brigade was, tracking several hundred missing tanks wasn't the Stony Man team's main mission. They were in Russia for a far more important reason. The man who had saved the fledgling Russian Republic in its infancy, President Boris Yeltsin, had suddenly resigned.

Unlike in the United States, the new Russian democracy was a "strong man" rule. Yeltsin had a second-in-command, but he wasn't an elected leader. He had been appointed by the former president and was little more than a figurehead gofer. There was no way that he could fill Yeltsin's leadership role.

Elections had been scheduled for May 9 of the year 2000, but they had been moved up and an incredible cast of wanna-bes had presented themselves to try to capture the brass ring of Mother Russia. Not since the waning years of the Roman Empire had there been such a high-stakes, winner-take-all, political free-for-all with the future of the Western World in the balance.

As everyone expected, the die-hard Communists were making a strong bid to reerect their glory days. In their corner were all the other forms of Russian socialists, ranging from radical Marxists to luke-warm British-style Laborites. Opposing that lineup was a mixed bag, including the free market buccaneers who had learned to reap the joys of unbridled capitalism, those who wanted to create an orthodox religious state and a racist "whites only" party. The real contenders, however, were the ultranationalists of the so-called Progressive Party and their backers in the military leadership.

Since the end of the Soviet empire, the once-proud Russian forces had fallen on hard times; their ranks were depleted and their weapons rusting for lack of money to maintain them. Unit morale was at an all-time low, desertion was rife, troops sold their weapons to buy booze, generals "rented" out their men as laborers—the list was endless. The once-mighty Russian Bear was almost toothless.

To gain the support of the military leadership, the Nationalist candidates had vowed that they would restore the military to its former glory. And, while that sounded good to the generals struggling to live on small pensions, it made the rest of the world nervous. With real peace in Europe for the first time since the end of World War II, a resurgent Russian army would again become a threat to the recently freed Eastern nations. No one wanted to see that happen, least of all the United States. That was why Stony Man was involved.

DAVID MCCARTER and T. J. Hawkins were at a political rally for a candidate from one of the pro-Capitalist parties. Neither one of them knew enough Russian to follow the man's speech, but if you've heard one political speech, you've heard them all. The fact that this one was being given in Russian didn't make it any different than what they would have heard if they had been in Texas or Paris. No matter the language, crap was crap, and all politicians were full of it.

The fact that they couldn't follow the speech let the two Phoenix Force warriors devote all of their attention to guarding the speaker. Their eyes were scanning the buildings around the small square below, always alert to the growing crowd. Democracy was so new to Russia that every rally and political speech drew large crowds. Everyone wanted to hear the words that would magically make their lives better.

"I'm going to go down and work the crowd," Hawkins said. "It's getting a little thick down there."

"I'll stay up here."

Hawkins exited the doorway of the two-story building and almost ran into a man holding an AK-47 at his side. Most of the candidate's security people were armed with 7.62 mm subguns, so this guy stood out. Moving a few steps back, Hawkins cleared his silenced MP-5 SD submachine gun for action and keyed his com link.

"I think I've got a live one here," he stated, lowering his voice to report to McCarter. "Right in front of our building, he's packing an AK and he badly needs a shower and a shave."

"Stay on him," McCarter sent back. "I'll check to see if he has any comrades."

When the gunman reached into his coat pocket and pulled out a ski mask, Hawkins knew he had a good target. The magazines for his silenced H&K stubby were loaded with 9 mm Glazer Safety Slugs. They wouldn't go through the man and hurt anyone else, and they wouldn't ricochet should he happen to miss.

When the gunman pulled the ski mask over his face and started to raise his AK, Hawkins beat him to the trigger. A 3-round burst took him high in the back. The ballistic cones of the Safety Slugs penetrated his clothing before opening up to spread their pellets throughout his upper-body cavity, pulping everything in their path.

Arching his back, the gunman groaned and fell to the pavement, his AK clattering on the concrete.

Nearby, another man, his ski mask only halfway down over his face, heard the weapon fall and spun, struggling to free his weapon from under his coat. Hawkins didn't give him a chance, either. This wasn't a game where fairness counted.

It was, however, a trickier shot. With the two people between him and the gunman, he couldn't just point and shoot. He did have a head shot, however, and took it. Snapping the subgun to his shoulder, he took aim and sent a single shot into the gunman's forehead.

The man's head snapped back with the impact as the pellets drilled into his brain. A fountain of blood arched into the air from the entry wound, and he slumped to the ground.

A woman standing close to him shrieked when she saw the spray of blood and pulled at her husband's arm. At that instant, Hawkins heard the crack of McCarter's scoped M-16 from the rooftop behind him.

At the sound of the first shot, the crowd panicked. Half of them went to ground where they stood while the other half frantically tried to flee. In the middle of a group of men, women and children who had dropped stood yet another AK-toting gunman in a ski mask. Even though he was exposed, he still tried for a shot at the back of the panicked candidate as he rushed from the stage.

Before Hawkins could attain target acquisition, McCarter's M-16 spoke twice, sending two rounds into the gunner's heart.

With no more targets in sight, Hawkins slipped his subgun back under his jacket and retreated into the building. Even though they had "get-out-of-jail-free" cards issued by the Russian Minister of the Interior and countersigned by the head of the SVR, the Phoenix Force commandos didn't want to spend a night in the local jail while their credentials were checked. McCarter met him at the bottom of the stairs, and the two men made their getaway out the back door.

By then, the square was almost clear except for the bodies on the ground—including the bodies of the failed assassins as well as the people who had been trampled in the scramble to escape. The warbling sound of European emergency vehicle sirens could be heard as the Phoenix Force warriors got into their Mercedes sedan and quietly drove away.

For a while, at least, democracy was still alive in this part of Mother Russia.

CHAPTER TWO

Moscow, Russia

While their teammates were busy reconning and foiling assassins, Rafael Encizo and Calvin James were in Moscow on a buying trip. At least they had convinced their Russian Mafia contact that was their intention. Now that Russia was no longer a training ground for worldwide terrorist groups, there were few Hispanics and almost no blacks in the country. The two men stood out in any crowd, and they would have a difficult time blending into the background to do the surveillance work. So, when Katz broke the Stony Man team into three teams for the first phase of the mission, he gave them the task of making contact with the Russian Mafia.

The two commandos were posing as buyers from a Mexican drug cartel wanting to place a large order for high-grade Afghan heroin. It was no news that the demand for the drug in the United States had skyrocketed, and new sources were hard to come by. The traditional producers in the Golden Triangle had fallen on hard times, and their output wasn't what it had once been. With the demand up and the supply short, it wasn't surprising that a Mexican cartel would be interested in what the Russians had to offer.

Nonetheless, in a country where they didn't speak the language and without the Executioner and the rest of Phoenix Force standing by as backup if anything went wrong, they would be walking a finer line than they liked. If they screwed this up, all Bolan and the other guys could do to help was to find their bodies and send them home for burial.

"Able Team should be handling this gig," Encizo grumbled. "They specialize in this kind of thing."

"They usually handle U.S. actions. And look what happened to them the last time they tried to do something like this over here," James commented, reminding him of a similar attempted buy in Prague that had turned sour. "They were damned lucky to have survived that one."

"That's what I'm afraid of happening this time," the Cuban said. "These bastards just don't know how to conduct business."

"If the minister's information is correct," James said, "they're doing a lot of business in this shit."

"That's not what I mean," Encizo replied. "They don't know that there's supposed to be honor among thieves."

"That's 'cause they're drug dealers, not thieves.

"Here's our man." James nodded toward the exit of the Metro subway station. "And he's on time."

"That's a good start."

AN HOUR AND A HALF later, Encizo and James got out of a Mercedes sedan at what looked like a deserted warehouse. Four AK-toting gunmen walked out of the building and positioned themselves on either side of the door, their weapons at the ready. When the two men approached, one of the gunners stepped forward. Without waiting to be told, the Phoenix Force commandos stopped and put their arms out to be searched. Both of them were packing pistols under their jackets. But, considering the roles they were playing, that was to be expected. It was also expected that they would be relieved of their hardware.

When the thug pointed at the briefcase Encizo had laid at his feet while he was frisked, he slowly reached down and picked it up. When he snapped it open and raised the lid, the Russian's eyes bulged. Even in the world of the Russian Mafia, a thousand U.S. hundred-dollar bills in neat stacks was quite a sight.

"Go in," the thug grunted as he waved the AK.

"YOU GUYS DID a good job," Gary Manning said when David McCarter and T. J. Hawkins returned to the makeshift command post that had been set up in one of the SVR safehouses.

"But any decent VIP protection detail could have done just as well," Hawkins replied. "The would-be assassins were thugs, not pros."

"It was routine work," McCarter said, echoing Hawkins's assessment. "A moron could have done it.'' As an ex-SAS operative, he was well-experienced in counterassassination work.

"And the worst thing is that we're being forced to react instead of act. We're never going to turn this thing around if we have to keep doing that. Plus, we're going to go into the bag ourselves if we're not careful. Any halfway decent VIP security team would have taken us out.''

"But,'' Hawkins pointed out, "since they were standing around with their thumbs up their asses and their minds in neutral, we're here to tell the tale. Actually I think they were bought off. That poor bastard candidate might as well have had no protection at all. Hell, it didn't even look like he was wearing body armor.''

"This whole thing is a scam.'' McCarter was thoroughly disgusted. "All of the political parties are so riddled with Mafia that we're never going to be able to protect all the candidates. We got lucky this time, but there's no way we can keep it up until the election.''

"What do you want me to tell the Farm?''

"Let's wait until Katz and Striker get back,'' McCarter said. "Did they give you an ETA?''

"They should be here before too long. And, speaking of leaks, one of their SVR guys got popped in the Kaliningrad truck park.''

"That figures,'' McCarter snorted.

"I've seen better CPs,'' Hawkins said as he stirred a spoonful of instant coffee into a cup of lukewarm water from the pot on the electric burner. "This place is a dump."

"According to the minister," Manning said, "he gave us the best safehouse he had available."

"Poor bastards."

Hawkins took a tentative sip and shuddered. "Speaking of poor bastards who aren't here to enjoy our luxurious accommodations, did you get an update on Able Team?"

Manning shook his head. "They're still tracking down those Russians who've been stealing high-tech gear and shipping it out through Canada."

McCarter snorted. "They should turn that bullshit over to the FBI and get their butts over here, we need them on this op."

BOLAN AND KATZ dropped Yuri Belakov off to report to the minister before they returned to their safehouse CP.

"Speaking as a certified tactical adviser," Katz stated as he walked into the communications room, "I certify that this mission sucks.

"Not," he said, turning to McCarter and Hawkins, "that you guys didn't do your usual bang-up job today. David, that was a good op. You got the bad guys and, better yet, you got the hell out of there intact. The problem is that you two can't be everywhere, every time."

"We were discussing that very point before you showed up," McCarter replied. "Since there's more of them than there is of us, we're going to step in it before too long. The law of averages and all that.''

The Briton leaned forward in his chair. ''What we need is a line on whoever's planning those hits so we can plan a preemptive strike against them.''

''There is that,'' Katz replied. ''But from where I sit, the bigger problem is that we're too scattered to be effective. You and T.J. are working VIP protection, Mack and I are chasing a missing tank brigade and Rafe and Calvin are trying to get a lead on the Mafia boss by buying dope. Any one of those tasks would be a full-time job by itself, and we're trying to do all three at once.''

''Do you want to talk to the minister?'' Bolan asked.

Katz nodded. ''I know the President has placed us at his disposal. But, sooner or later, we're going to have to have a talk with him about what's known as 'economy of force,' the concept of massing one's effort. The way we're going right now, we can luck out and be successful on all three of these fronts and still lose the war. We have to prioritize the mission if we want to maximize our results.''

''I couldn't agree more,'' McCarter stated. ''For one thing, we don't need to man this CP full-time. I want Gary to be our spotter and back-door guy the next time we go out. Had that candidate's security detail had their fingers out today, we'd have been in a serious bind.''

When they arrived in Moscow, Gary Manning had drawn the short straw and had been tasked with running Phoenix Force's CP while the teams were away. He was good with the sophisticated equipment that made the Farm only a quick satcom call away, but the inactivity was driving him crazy.

"I'll go along with that," he said. "Hal can wait for his updates like everyone else."

"I'll talk to Hal," Katz promised as he glanced at his watch. "In fact I'm going to do that now before we get involved again."

"Don't you want to wait for Rafe and Calvin?"

"When are they due back?"

"They didn't give me an ETA," Manning replied. "Their contact procedure was long and involved, and they didn't know how long it would take."

"I'll hold then," Katz said. "Hal's going to want to know how they did."

"I think we all do." McCarter was thinking back to the last time the team had tried to make a drug buy from the Russian Mafia. Rosario Blancanales and Hermann Schwarz had been ambushed and captured. "I don't trust these bloody Russian bastards."

"We have to try it, though," Katz reminded him. "We need them to get a lead on the big boss."

"I still don't have to like it."

RAFAEL ENCIZO and Calvin James weren't happy about the situation they were in, either. Like McCarter, they hadn't forgotten the disastrous ending to the Prague drug-buy attempt. This time, though, they hadn't been ambushed the minute they had stepped into the Mafia's turf. In fact they were being treated like celebrities. Their "hosts" were proving to be more than happy to make a contact with a Mexican cartel with a distribution network in both Florida and California.

"No, thank you." James put his hand over the top of his half-full glass of Finnish vodka.

The way the Russians were knocking that stuff back, he was surprised they could still walk across the room, much less carry on like they did. The old stories about the Russians being big drinkers were true as far as he was concerned. He'd always felt that he could hold his own with any man, but he'd had all the 180-proof he could handle and still shoot straight if the situation turned bad on them.

Encizo was also watching his vodka intake as he talked to the two men in charge. Since he was Hispanic, the Russians accepted him as the front man and James as the bodyguard without question. That was okay with him, but the Russians were acting like they had never seen a black man before. Three of them ringed James, and they hadn't taken their eyes off him all night except to refill their glasses.

"Okay, my friend," one of the Russians said loudly. "As the Yankees say, we have a deal."

"I am glad," Encizo replied, his hand automatically reaching out to cover his glass.

He'd been careful, but drinking vodka in a water glass was risking a quick trip to oblivion and he had to keep his wits about him. This wasn't over until he and James were back at the safehouse making their report.

"Now," he stated, glancing at his watch, "we need to go back to our hotel."

"You have a hot date?" the Russian asked, leering. "The girls at your hotel are ours too. Let me know which one you like, and I'll give her to you."

"No, thank you," Enciso said. "We're still trying to get over the jet lag."

The Russian frowned. "What is this jet lag? I do not know it."

Enciso sighed as he tried to explain the major drawback to international travel. He made a worst-case scenario out of it, and the Russians, who had never been further from Moscow than St. Petersburg, bought it completely. "So, my friends, we have to go now."

"Okay," the Russian said. "We don't want you to get sick from this terrible jet lag."

Outside the warehouse, the two Phoenix Force commandos were given back their hardware before they were driven away in the same black Mercedes that had brought them. Again, the driver took them on a circuitous route before dropping them off at the Metro station several blocks from their hotel.

"Where to?" James asked as the Mercedes drove away from the subway station.

"Back to the hotel, then we'll sneak out the back and go to the safehouse."

James feigned shock. "You don't trust our hosts?"

"Only as far as I can keep them in the sight picture."

MOST OF THE STONY MAN team were bunked down for the night by the time James and Encizo reached the safehouse. Only Katz and Bolan were still up.

"You guys have any coffee?" James asked. "I've got to neutralize some of that vodka."

"All that'll do is make you a wide-awake drunk," Bolan said, smiling. "Particularly with the stuff that came with this place. It's pure caffeine."

"I'll have some anyway."

"Over on the counter by the hot plate."

"We made the buy," Encizo said as he slid into the chair across the table from Katz and opened his briefcase. "A hundred thou worth of Afghanistan's finest with more on order."

"Did you get any kind of lead on the big boss?" Katz asked.

"My guy kept talking about someone he called The Lion, but I don't know if that's a nickname or a translation."

"It could be both," Katz replied. "I'll ask the minister."

"When do you see him again?"

"He's coming over to talk tomorrow."

"Good." Encizo stood. "I'm going back to try to sleep this one off."

"Sweet dreams."

"One more thing," Encizo said. "One of the honchos bragged that his gang also ran the girls at our hotel, so we're going to have to be real careful around there. Every one of them will be a potential spy."

"You know the drill," Katz said. "Pat them on the butts, but don't take them to your rooms."

"Bummer."

CHAPTER THREE

Moscow, Russia

The only way that an outsider would know that Josef "The Lion" Leoninski was furious was that his eyes were narrowed to slits. Other than that, the crime boss's demeanor was calm enough. To those who were part of his criminal enterprise, the so-called Russian Mafia, however, there were other more subtle signs that their boss was enraged. While his voice wasn't raised, the precise, bitten-off language he was using was more frightening than his shouting would have been.

"Who were they?" Leoninski snapped.

"I do not know." The man who had been in charge of the hit team at the rally spoke very carefully. As the sole survivor of the assassination attempt, he had a lot to answer for. And, when Leoninski was in this frame of mind, trying to cover your mistakes and shortfalls could be fatal. The Lion would forgive an honest mistake, but never a fabrication.

"They did not look to be part of the candidate's

security detail, and they were not firing standard-issue weapons. As soon as they had eliminated my team, they disappeared.''

Leoninski turned to one of the other men in the room. ''I thought we had an insider on the VIP security detachment.''

''We do,'' the man answered. ''The security chief himself. He gave us everything we wanted, but he did not say anything about any additional men being on the detail. This was supposed to have been a small rally in a secure town so only minimum security was laid on.''

Turning back to the hit man, Leoninski's eyes slitted even further, like a cat's. ''Leave him alone for now, but I want our contact in his campaign eliminated. First, though, I want you to talk to him and find out who those men were.''

''Yes, sir,'' the hit man replied, thankful to be walking out of the room alive. ''I will see to it myself.''

''Do that.''

As soon as the hit man left, Leoninski turned to his second in command, Valery Fyodor. ''This is not going to please the general.''

Fyodor was a polished Muscovite who had joined up with him in the early days. Leoninski was honest enough with himself to know that he did not have the inbred savvy to move unnoticed through Moscow's social elite, either official or civilian. He was a man from the fringes of the old Soviet empire, and he would always carry his outsider status with him.

Now that so much depended on his being able to work with the power elite of Russia, Fyodor was invaluable to him and his plans.

"Do you want me to set up another hit?" Fyodor asked.

"Not yet. I want to check on something else first. If Boris did see other than standard-issue weapons in the hands of the mysterious team, we need to check that out first. If someone in the government has called in outsiders, I need to know about it immediately."

Fyodor thought for a moment. In the current crisis, any political party calling upon, say, Western powers for aid would be seen by the voters as committing out-and-out treason. Even the government ministers would be leery of taking such a step. Except, of course, for one man, a man who had close ties to the United States. That minister had called upon the Americans before to deal with internal Russian matters, and he could be doing it again.

"I think I should have a close look at the Minister of the Interior," Fyodor said. "He's the only one of them who might have called in outsiders. And, if he did, they will be Americans."

"You said that Interior's the one ministry we do not have access to."

"Right now, that is so." Fyodor smiled. "But things like that can change if the right pressure is brought to bear. We've been trying to use bribes, but now I think we need to apply pressure."

"Do you have a target?"

"Let me go through my files."

"Don't take too long."

JOSEF LEONINSKI was a formidable man. His youth had been spent in Gori, his namesake Stalin's old hometown in the Georgian Republic. There, toughness, a quick mind and a streak of ruthlessness had made him the leader of the region's most vicious criminal gang before he was twenty years old. His nickname had been bestowed on him for the way that he dealt with anyone who got in his way. He had shifted his operations to Moscow, but he hadn't dropped the attitude that had made him what he was. If anything, it had only hardened.

His graduation to the big time had come when the Soviet Union dropped into the dustbin of history in 1991. In the chaos that resulted, opportunities abounded for anyone who had the courage to reach out and grab them. That so many of those opportunities were outside of the law hadn't been an obstacle to him. For all of its value, democracy also has its drawbacks, and one of them was that gangsters came with the territory.

The first of the many opportunities that he seized upon in the Russian capital were in the sex, guns and drugs arena. Those were the old standbys of criminal gangs, as they were the top three things that a newly freed people wanted as soon as they could afford them. The girls had been the easiest part of that mix. There was no shortage of young, sloe-eyed Slavic beauties who realized that they could make a month's pay in a night or two and that the fringe benefits of "the life" were great as well.

The guns were also easy. Russia had never been known for producing quality consumer goods, but their military industrial complex had always produced world-class weapons, particularly small arms. That they were well made, rugged, dependable and simple to use had been proved on battlefields all over the world. In the hands of various "freedom fighters," they had made their mark on more than one continent killing more people than the Black Death and Attila the Hun combined.

The drug part had been the most difficult to put into operation because of all of the competition from the established gangs. But, by recruiting several Afghanistan War veterans, he created a pipeline to the poppy fields of the Middle East. Heroin was the drug of choice in Russia, and he soon had all that he could sell. The best part was that most of the heroin in Afghanistan was paid for by guns that were purchased with the drugs in Russia. It was a win-win situation that was making him more money than anyone else in Eastern Europe.

Within a few months of his getting established in Moscow, Leoninski started to draw men to his organization. Nothing succeeded like success, and he was successful from the start. The word quickly spread that there was a new man in town who was a mover and a shaker. The word also went out that this new man shared his successes instead of setting himself up as a king. That alone brought more than enough recruits for him to pick and choose. Those who could work within the military-like discipline he imposed had done well. Those who wouldn't or couldn't were disposed of.

Now, though, it appeared that there were people on his payroll who thought that they could defy him and get away with it, and that wasn't something he was accustomed to. In fact the last man who had defied him had taken several days to die. Moving into the political arena, though, had proved to be a new experience for him. Politicians simply didn't have the honor and trustworthiness he expected from those who worked for him. He had never seen so many self-serving, lying bastards in his life.

Even though he was the leader of one of the world's most powerful criminal organizations, he never lied. Nor did he ever promise anything that he couldn't deliver. Like any intelligent man, he had always known that politicians weren't the best or brightest men in his country, Communist or not. He had always felt that, for the most part, they were weak, lying dogs. Now that he was on the inside, he was finding that to be more than true.

Nonetheless, the sudden resignation of Boris Yeltsin had almost forced him to get into politics. Though he wasn't a political animal, he was well aware of its value. Now that Russia was on the brink of extreme change, having the right men in office could make his plans much easier to implement. The wrong ones could cause him no end of trouble.

After studying the situation, he allied himself with

the Progressive Party, the ones the foreign press were calling the ultranationalists, and its leader retired General Pavel Zerinov. What was wrong with wanting his nation to regain its place in the world? Nothing. And, as his namesake had proved so well, nothing made a nation strong like a strong military.

With Zerinov as president, Leoninski's empire would prosper as no other criminal enterprise in history had. The general wasn't the most intelligent man in Russia. He was, however, handsome, well spoken and photogenic, a perfect front man. And that was what he would be for Leoninski. The Lion would call the shots, and Zerinov would make them sound like they were his own decisions. As long as the military got what they wanted, this unholy alliance would work well.

Leoninski knew that there wasn't enough money in all of Russia to satisfy him. But, when the election was over and he had his power base secure, he planned to move his operations into the rest of Europe where the real money was. An earlier would-be Russian crime lord had already set that process in motion before he met a mysterious death. He would simply take what was left of the earlier operations and expand them even more.

First, though, he had to secure the outcome of the election.

THE RUSSIAN Interior Minister read the report on the thwarted assassination and the death of one of the agents assigned to work with the American-based team in Kaliningrad. Part of his job was to oversee the SVR, and one of his agents at the rally had made a report on the outsiders' actions there. He was glad that the foreign team had been able to prevent another political death, but he knew that the seven of them couldn't be everywhere and stop every attempt. And, even if they could, the damage to the democratic process was being done anyway.

Already five candidates had dropped out of the race for Parliament and one of the presidential candidates had resigned. If this continued, only General Zerinov and the ultranationalists would remain on the ballot. And, if that happened, Mother Russia would become a Mafia whore. There had to be some way to save the country, but he was damned if he could think of it. The Americans had done such a good job before, but this was an entirely different problem, and he didn't fault them for not being able to make it right. It was a Russian problem, but the fledgling Russian democracy was simply not strong enough to deal with a criminal conspiracy of this magnitude.

The problem was that in a nation where the gap between the rich and the poor was growing too fast to even document, Mafia money spoke louder than democratic ideals. The fact that it was money gained by selling drugs, guns and women didn't matter to people who were starving. The Mafia paid well enough that it was easy for men and women to sell out their only chance to be really free.

Had everyone been starving equally, as had been

the case right after the Russian Communist Revolution, that would have been one thing. Now, however, the people clearly saw that the misery wasn't being shared. Too many people were driving expensive European cars, wearing furs and eating caviar while working families struggled to make do with public transportation, wore rags and ate cabbage soup. Not for the first time, he was ashamed for his country.

The minister had always been a closet democrat, and he had been secretly overjoyed when the Communist Party finally collapsed. Its brutal seventy-year rule had brought only tears to the Russian people for their hard work.

Like so many other Russians, he had hoped that the new democracy would finally allow the Russian people to take their rightful place in the modern world. That might still come to pass, but not if the Russian Mafia became the dominant figure in the election.

Glancing up at the wall clock that showed Washington D.C. time, he decided to make another call to his friend, Hal Brognola.

Stony Man Farm, Virginia

IN THE COMPUTER ROOM of the Stony Man farmhouse, Hal Brognola fumbled in his pocket and drew out a bottle of antacid tablets. Twisting off the cover, he shook several into his hand, then popped them into his mouth and washed them down with a gulp of room-temperature coffee.

After all this time, he was still undecided if Aaron Kurtzman's coffee tasted better hot or cold. When it was right out of the pot, it scalded the taste buds, lessening the impact at the price of blisters. But when it cooled, a film of oil formed on the surface. At least he had a clean cup this time; he had washed it himself in the bathroom.

"You want a refill?" Barbara Price, Stony Man's mission controller, stood in front of the coffeepot on the other side of the room.

He shuddered. "I'm fine." If the Stony Man operation was ever decommissioned, the EPA was going to have their work cut out for them. It would be easier just to designate the Farm's Computer Room a toxic waste site than to decontaminate the coffeepot area.

"What did the Man want this time?" she asked. For the second time that day, Brognola had received an emergency call on the secure phone from the Oval Office. Though his business card read that he was a Justice Department official, Brognola was the head of the Sensitive Operations Group, an organization that handled the nation's most clandestine operations. Since he answered directly to the President, he spent a lot of time talking to the Man.

"An update, of course," he replied. "I'd damned near give up my federal pension if I could get him to understand that these operations take time."

"There's been three candidates assassinated now," she reminded him, "so I guess it's understandable that he's nervous. He committed us to helping the Russians, and he doesn't want to look bad.''

"Three or thirty, it doesn't really matter. Striker and Katz can only do so much, so fast."

"Able Team isn't moving much faster," she said. "And I'm starting to wonder if we're not wasting them up there. If we cut them loose, we could send them across the pond to reinforce Phoenix."

Brognola thought for a moment. "Do it. Pull them out as soon as you can. I've got to do something to get the Man off my back."

"I can have them on the way by tomorrow morning," she replied. "They're closing in on that suspected Russian Mafia hangout right now, and we can turn that one over to the FBI and ATF after they're done with it."

"Make sure that you warn them about the arms cache they have there," he said. "I don't want them to go waltzing in and get their asses blown away."

"I'll give them our mission file."

"Make sure you sanitize it first."

"Give it a rest, Hal," Price said, smiling thinly. "We've been doing this for some time now."

To ensure the iron-clad security that made the Stony Man operation possible, they had to keep themselves a long arm's length from all other federal agencies. They often cooperated with the other Feds in the course of a mission, but it was always done on the Farm's terms and only their terms. The blanket of executive privilege they operated under was

Kevlar and provided a bulletproof cover for the Farm's activities.

Even so, they always had to make sure that anything they shared with another federal agency had been "sanitized." All traces of the deep-cover sources they had used to develop the background information had to be erased, as well as any traces of the Farm and the President's involvement in matters that couldn't endure the glare of publicity. It was something the Farm crew was good at doing.

"I'm going to call the minister and let him know that we're sending him reinforcements."

"I just hope that he's stopped up the leaks in his office by now," Price said. "I don't want to have to go through that drill again."

"I think he's had that lesson burned into his brain." The minister was a good man, but even though he ran the SVR, his internal security had been proved a sham at least once before. But learning that his own wife had been a Mafia spy had rocked him to the core.

Price withheld comment. Sometimes she felt that Brognola took too much on face value. She knew that the minister was sincere and hardworking, but that didn't mean he was the best man for the job. Considering the situation in Russia, though, she didn't know if anyone could really do anything to get it under control. Even so, she knew the effort had to be made. A criminally controlled, ultranationalist government would be more of a threat than the old, nuclear-armed Soviet Union had been.

CHAPTER FOUR

New York State

As Barbara Price had predicted, Able Team was moving in on the element they had been tracking, a U.S. version of the Russian Mafia. The target for the day was an upstate New York hangout of a Russian immigrant gang known to be linked with the shadowy Russian Mafia. Like many of the Russian criminals who had moved their operations to the States, they specialized in stolen vehicles and high-tech gear while they ran a few girls and peddled drugs on the side. It was a good mix and never failed to make money for them, a lot of money. What made the Russians different than all of the other drug dealers, car thieves and pimps in the U.S., though, was their tie to the Mother Country.

Unlike the traditional Italian Mafia and the drug cartels that had caused so much death and destruction in America, the Russian Mafia had a political rather than economic agenda at its core. They were the overseas financing and technical support arm of the Russian Mafia in its quest to dominate the future of Russian politics. High tech equipment not available in Russia was being stolen and smuggled across the border to Canada and loaded onto Russian freighters.

As he moved through the woods, Carl Lyons looked like a SWAT team extra in a *Terminator* movie. He wore full-coverage body armor over his woodland-pattern camouflage suit, and his assault harness was loaded to capacity with the tools of his trade. The only thing missing was a Kevlar helmet, but he hated to wear headgear. The ex-LAPD cop was loaded for bear, he had the tools to make the kill and he was likely going to need them.

Hermann "Gadgets" Schwarz was also armored like his partner, but he was wearing his Kevlar helmet with the body armor. For the expected fight, he was packing an M-16/M-203 over-and-under assault rifle-grenade launcher combo. The bandoliers of 40 mm grenades draped around his neck were loaded with high explosive rounds. When they reached the target, they wouldn't be playing around. Not with this bunch of hoods. They'd be going for the kill.

The Russian gangs in the United States had been well trained in their homeland. Living under Communist rule was a good school for violence. Even the Latin American cartels had nothing on the Russians when it came to pure viciousness. This wasn't going to be one of those numbers where a warning shot would cause the bad guys to drop their weapons and give up. A firefight was definitely on the program today, and they were ready for it.

Rosario "Politician" Blancanales was also suited up, and had included the helmet. Along with his personal weapons, he had an East-German-made RPG-7 antitank rocket launcher and half a dozen shaped-charge-warhead rounds for it. While the RPG was an older, foreign-made weapon, it was difficult to beat, particularly in a situation like this. Their target was a barnlike structure at the end of an unpaved road, and their information was that it had been armored on the inside with steel plates and concrete. The RPG warhead was able to penetrate twelve inches of steel-reinforced concrete.

"Talk to me," Lyons growled over the team com link when he got within eyesight of the target. The trio had moved in on separate paths to keep anyone from rushing out the back and getting away.

"I'm up," Schwarz replied, swinging his assault rifle combo into firing position.

"I'm ready," Blancanales said as he raised the RPG launcher to his shoulder.

"Let's do it," Lyons snapped. "Pol, you lead off."

"Got it covered."

Blancanales peered through the rocket launcher's sights and took aim at the main door of the building. Keeping the door centered in the sights, he gently squeezed the trigger. When the rocket's prop charge fired, it kicked the 85 mm round out of the launcher with no recoil. Twenty feet out of the launcher, the main charge ignited and drove the deadly antitank rocket into its target.

Even though the door was armored with a half-inch steel plate on the inside, it didn't stand a chance. The RPG's shaped-charge warhead was designed to blast through six inches of hardened steel armor plate, and the door's armor was only cold-rolled plate. It might as well have been tinfoil for all the protection it offered against an RPG rocket.

Not only did the blast of the shaped charge blow a hole in the door, the force of the detonation tore it from the frame and sent it flying into the building. Stepping out from cover, Schwarz raised his assault rifle combo and sent a 40 mm fragmentation grenade through the opening, following it with two more.

He heard screams from inside, followed by orders bellowed in Russian. Unlike in most American gangs, the Russians always brought military-style discipline to their endeavors. Firing ports opened in the building's walls and AK-47 muzzles jutted into view. The firefight Able Team had expected was about to commence.

Taking another RPG rocket from his chest pack, Blancanales calmly loaded it into the front of the launcher and thumbed down the firing hammer. One of the nice things about the weapon was that it didn't depend on fragile electronics to function. The rockets were fired with a percussion cap like any round of pistol or rifle ammunition and were just as reliable.

Lining up the sights on one of the AK firing ports,

he sent the second rocket streaking on its way. This time, the detonation peeled away a section of the building's sheet-metal siding, revealing the steel plate behind it as it punched through. The place was a fortress, and he only had four rockets left.

"Carl," he said over his com link, "that armor plate goes all the way up to the roof beams."

"Roger," Lyons sent back. "We're finding that on this side too."

The return fire got a little too intense, so Blancanales moved to the left to try to find a more productive target. When he was under cover again, he sighted through the blown door into the building. When a massive, rounded, white object against the far wall caught his eye, he knew he'd found the key to the castle. The enemy had put their propane tank inside the building instead of safely outside where it should have been. Bad for them, good for Able Team.

"Guys," he sent over the com link, "I've found the answer. They have what looks like a two hundred and fifty gallon propane tank in there against the back wall. I'm going to take a shot at it."

"Geez, Pol," Lyons sent back, "hold on until we can get outta here."

He was well aware that of all the nonnuclear explosives known to man, fuel and air mixtures were the most powerful. Aerial-delivered FAE—fuel air explosive—bombs had been used in Vietnam to cut helicopter landing zones in the triple-canopy jungle, and, during the Gulf War, they had decimated Saddam Hussein's vaunted Republican Guard divisions in Kuwait. Sending a rocket into that tank could take them out as well if they weren't prepared for the blast.

"I'm holding weapons cold," Blancanales said. "Get under cover quick."

When Lyons and Schwarz sent the all-clear a few seconds later, Blancanales raised the launcher to his shoulder again. The open doorframe wasn't all that big a space to aim through, but it was big enough. The magnifying optical sight on the RPG gave him a clear shot to the end of the tank. He had four rockets left and knew he'd hit it with one of them.

Holding a good sight picture, he squeezed the trigger. The instant the rocket left the launcher, he flattened himself on the floor of the forest. If he'd had the time, he'd have piled dead leaves on top of himself for protection from the fireball that was coming, but it was too late for that now. He did clamp his hands over his ears to try to save his hearing from the explosion, and he opened his mouth to ease the pressure that was sure to come.

The detonation of the warhead was immediately followed by a flash that lit up the woods for at least two hundred yards. This propane tank was small compared to the blockbusters the military used, but the effect was as if several hundred pounds of TNT had gone off. The sheet steel armor plating that had shielded the Russians from Able Team's small-arms fire contained the blast for a microsecond and funneled most of it upward.

The blast was deafening, and, even with his hands protecting his ears, Blancanales was stunned for a moment. When he looked up, only one wall of the building remained standing on the concrete slab.

The other three walls, as well as the roof, had vanished along with whatever remained of the men inside and the vehicles they had been working on. Scraps of sheet metal littered the branches of the trees that hadn't been blown over. Smaller pieces of wood, paper and what might have once been gangsters added to the chaos. From the air it would have looked like God had emptied a giant garbage container in the woods.

"We really needed to know what they had in there, Pol." Lyons was breathing heavily as he spoke over the com link. That was as close as he had ever been to an FA explosion, and it hadn't been pleasant.

Schwarz clicked on the com link. "We can just call in one of those ATF forensic units to comb the woods for evidence. I'm sure they can piece it all back together."

Lyons snorted. "Let's get the hell out of here before someone comes to see what all the noise was about."

"And the cloud of smoke," Schwarz added, looking up. "Don't forget that. And, it's going to start raining pieces of Russians before too long, but I guess that's good for the environment. They're organic, you know."

"You're sick, Gadgets," Blancanales said.

"It's true though."

"You're still sick."

"I'm just trying to do my bit for Mother Earth."

"I'm sure she appreciates it."

Virginia

IN A MOTEL ROOM in Arlington, Virginia, rented for this purpose, Stony Man Farm Security Chief Buck Greene ran through the pile of applications on the desk one last time. Choosing new blacksuits for the Farm wasn't an easy task, and the level of security surrounding the interview process made it only more difficult. But that was why the system worked as well as it did. Unlike most security force operations, guarding Stony Man required more than a bunch of overweight, retired street cops or MPs hanging around the Farm. Being a blacksuit was more than a nine-to-five or even a graveyard shift situation. The guards were on duty twenty-four hours a day, and, when they weren't working the land during the day, they were patrolling the grounds at night.

A task like that required more than three shifts of men who went home when they weren't on the job. To a man, the blacksuits were single, divorced or widowers. A man with a family he had to spend time with wasn't a good candidate for the job. They worked on-site in a thirty-day-on, thirty-day-off and thirty-day-on standby rotation. It wasn't the life for a married man.

Each twenty-eight man crew worked a twelve-hour day and wasn't allowed to leave the Farm during that thirty-day period. On the fifteenth of each month, half of the crew was rotated out and half of a new crew came in. This allowed an overlap so that the new crew could come up to speed with any changes that might have taken place since their last tour of duty.

After going off duty, each crew was given a thirty-day R and R, or I and I as the blacksuits called it—intoxication and intercourse. When they came off that, they went into a standby phase at another location an hour away, where their movements were restricted, but they weren't locked down. On standby, their job was to be ready to reinforce the Farm within an hour of any alert. After thirty days on standby, they went to the Farm for their on-site duty tour.

It was a rough life, but the pay was good and each blacksuit knew that he was making a real contribution to keeping his country more secure. After Stony Man, Brognola always found the "retired" blacksuits high-paying employment as a reward for their faithful service. Oftentimes active servicemen were rotated in for a tour of duty.

The security chief didn't have to interview men for his force very often and, when he did, he was very careful about who he chose to join. One ringer, just one, could destroy the nation's most secret organization. Along with the usual federal background checks, he ran all the candidates through the FBI's and CIA's systems. When that was done, those who were left were given lie-detector and other psych tests. Those who survived that step, had their military skills tested in a three-day exercise conducted by the Army's Delta Force. Then, and only then, did he talk to them himself.

As Greene went over the remaining applications, he lit up his postlunch cigarette in preparation for the final round of interviews. He had six applications in front of him, and he only needed four people to fill his vacancies. He, and he alone, would decide who would make the cut, and he would do it based on his gut feelings about each of them. What it boiled down to was did he want to put his life on the line beside the applicant in a firefight. It was as simple as that.

Waiting until the cigarette had burned down to the filter, he butted the smoke, rose and walked to the door connecting his room with the one next door and opened it.

"Dillert!" he called out.

One of the candidates stood and walked toward him.

"Have a seat."

AT THE END of the six interviews, Buck Greene sat back and savored an unscheduled extra cigarette with a cup of coffee. All of the candidates were good this time, and he didn't have a bad feeling about any of them. More and more, that's the way the selection process had been going lately. All of the questionable candidates had been weeded out before it came to his final interview, and now it was all up to him.

Butting the smoke, he picked up the first file on the pile, James T. Gordon, currently a U.S. Marshal. He had a good rap sheet based on almost ten years of federal service. He wasn't a top-of-his-class kind of guy, but he had never been far from it. His home background was solid, the son of the great American middle class. Sometimes he was concerned when a candidate's parents were too left wing, but Gordon's insurance salesman father was a registered Republican and his mother was a Democrat. Neither one of them had been involved in radical causes or fringe nut groups of either side.

His federal training scores were good, and he'd had some good live-fire experience with the marshal's service. He'd been in two shoot-outs in his ten-year service; that wasn't too much to make him think he was a top gun, and it was better than his being a virgin. Making a final gut check, Greene signed off on James Gordon's application, put it aside and reached for the next one.

When he had made his choices, he gathered up his material and locked it in his briefcase. Before he informed any of the men of the results, he always ran them past Hal Brognola, as more of a formality than anything else. The Justice Department officer had never down-checked any of his choices.

Grabbing his jacket, he headed for the door to make the trip back to the Farm. Brognola was on-site, and he wanted to get his approval on these candidates so he could bring the new men onboard as soon as possible. He didn't like to have blacksuit vacancies at any time, but certainly not while there was an operation going on.

It was true that the action was taking place overseas this time, but that didn't mean that he could afford to relax his vigilance at the Farm.

Not now, not ever.

CHAPTER FIVE

Stony Man Farm, Virginia

Aaron Kurtzman and his Computer Room staff weren't exactly sitting on their hands, but almost. This was one of those missions where cybersleuthing wasn't playing a large part of mission support. This was an old-fashioned hit-the-bricks operation where eyeballs and gut instincts were trumping Cray mainframes and wizard programming.

Nearly everything they had on the target had been provided by the Russians. Kurtzman had put Hunt Wethers to working the edges, particularly looking for evidence of renewed Russian Mafia activity in Western Europe, but that was it. Kurtzman himself was trying out a new program for translating the long-dead Hittite language, and Akira Tokaido was looking for evidence of plagiarism in acid rock music. Beyond keeping the communication connections open and taking reports, the Computer Room was like a tomb.

When Barbara Price wandered in, she automatically stopped off at the coffeepot for a shot before going to Kurtzman's workstation. "Anything new?"

"Nothing," Kurtzman replied. "When's Hal coming back?"

"He said he would be spending the night in town."

It was a good thing that they had independently decided to cut Able Team loose to go to Russia. The minister had called the Oval Office, and the first topic on the agenda had been reinforcements. Brognola had been able to tell the Man they were on the way.

Pulling up a chair, Price leaned back holding her cup in both hands. "What's your take on this?" she asked.

Yakov Katzenelenbogen might be on the Stony Man roster as the official tactical adviser, but she had learned long ago that Kurtzman's evaluations of a situation were more often than not pure gold.

"Well—" he turned his wheelchair to face her "—I think that we're urinating into the wind, as T.J. would say."

"I think he says 'pissing'," she said.

"Whatever." Kurtzman grinned. "I'm not sure that it's going to work out for the minister this time. For one thing, our guys aren't calling the shots. Using them as VIP protection teams is a waste of good manpower. The SVR should be taking care of that so our guys are free to do what they do so well."

"The minister said that would send the wrong message to the Russian voters."

Kurtzman snorted. "What does he think the voters are going to say if they find out that Americans have been involved with the election? Our guys will be lucky to get out of the country without being lynched. You know how I hate political missions, and this is probably the worst one we've ever been asked to take on."

She had to agree with him; mixing politics with military action was always asking for a disaster. Theoretically Stony Man was only to be called in to set things right after the politicians had completely screwed it up. When something absolutely, positively needed to be taken down immediately, the action teams would do it and do it well. But they couldn't do that if they were playing political games.

"I guess we just have to stay loose in case they need us."

"We're so loose, we're about to flow out of our goddamned chairs."

Price laughed.

JIM GORDON WASN'T surprised when he got the official notification the next morning that he had been chosen for the mysterious security-force job and was to report for duty immediately. And why not? His background was that of the perfect American. According to the record, all the way back to grade school he had been an outstanding young man, and everyone had always thought that he would go far.

The problem with Gordon's perfect background was that it was a fabrication. It was an elaborate fabrication to be sure, backed up with reams of paper, electronic data, photographs and even hometown newspaper articles. Should anyone care to look, all of that material was there to be sifted through. But there was only one problem; it wasn't the story of his life. It was the life story of a man named Jim Gordon. His real name was Dimitri Spatkin, and he had been born in a small town not far from Leningrad in what had then been the Soviet Union.

His real father had been an officer in the KGB, not a State Farm Insurance agent in Eugene, Oregon, and his mother had been with the Bolshoi not the PTA. There had been a real Jim Gordon, and maybe there still was; he didn't know. All he knew was that the summer when Jim Gordon graduated from high school, Dimitri Spatkin crossed the Canadian border at a small town in British Columbia and drove straight down I-5 to Eugene, Oregon. That trip had been his final examination in an education process that had started when he had been six years old.

His KGB father had placed him in a special school outside Moscow with the mission of his becoming a deep-cover agent. Most spies didn't start their training when they were six years old, but he wasn't just any special agent. James Bond didn't have a thing on him.

That special school he had been sent to was in a highly restricted area known to KGB insiders as Little Amerika. This was a highly classified operation that took Russian children and made replica Americans out of them. This was done in a years-long immersion program in a town that expertly duplicated small town America down to the Juicy Fruit wrappers in the gutters and the McDonald's on the corner. Along with learning perfect, idiomatic American English, how to steal bases and recite the Boy Scout oath, the students learned what was known as tradecraft, the skills of being a spy. Upon graduation, Dimitri Spatkin was ready to take his place in the United States as an American, completely indistinguishable from any other young man his age.

After spending a month in Eugene, Oregon, he had moved to Portland to take a summer job before starting college. At Portland State University, Gordon studied law enforcement and, upon graduation, applied to become a federal marshal. His grades and letters of recommendation had been excellent, and he had been accepted.

It was in his second year of service in the U.S. Marshal Service that the Soviet Union collapsed. This came as a stunning blow to Gordon. For all of his life, he had trained to become a KGB secret agent. His entire life, as had the lives of his father and grandfather, had been devoted to the ideals of Soviet communism. His father had served in the KGB during the cold war, and his grandfather was a veteran of the "Great Patriotic War" as the Russians called World War II.

Fortunately for him, this earth-shaking event occurred while he was on a two-week leave at a beachside resort in Mazatlán, Mexico, with his girlfriend. They had been in the sports bar down the beach from the Mazatlán Riviera hotel when CNN broke in with the news. It had taken every bit of self-restraint he'd had not to throw his beer glass at the TV set.

His first instinct had been to disappear in Mexico and try to make his way to Cuba. As it was the last stronghold of communism in the West, he could pursue his career there. But doing that would negate all of the work that had brought him to where he was now. To honor both his father's and grandfather's service to Mother Russia, he had to continue to carry out his mission. To do anything else would negate the sacrifices they had made in the war against the Capitalist Imperialists. They had devoted their entire lives to the workers' struggle, and he could do no less.

The question was, though, what could he really do? His mission had been to become an American and wait in place until he was ordered to act. He knew of other deep-cover agents who had lived out their useful lives without ever being called to duty. Now, with the fall of the rightful government of the workers, he would never get such a call. Unless he disappeared, he would have to remain an American, something he loathed above all else.

Back at the hotel, Gordon got drunk that night. This was something he rarely did, but he had developed a taste for tequila while he was in Mexico. When he woke the next morning, his girlfriend was gone and a note on the desk told him that she was returning to California. She had a thing about men getting drunk and yelling like her stepfather had done, she wrote.

Seeing the note, he knew that he had made a serious mistake. A deep-cover agent could never afford to step out of character like that for any reason. Mexico would be the excuse this time, but he could never allow it to happen again. And, as far as the girl went, he had become entirely too comfortable around her. He had enjoyed the easy sexual morals of the Americans, but in that path lay danger. He knew too well the pitfalls of sexual attachment. The girls in Little Amerika specialized in that aspect of tradecraft, but the boys had been trained in it as well and had practiced on the girls. In the future, he would cut out the women except for one-night stands and put the energy into his vengeance.

As he nursed his hangover with strong coffee in a cabana beside the pool later that morning, he decided that he would stay on as a federal marshal and look for the chance to dig deep under America's defenses and find the one place where his skills could do the most damage. His search led him to where he was now, a security guard at America's most clandestine action base and the perfect place for him to extract vengeance for his old homeland.

JOHN "COWBOY" KISSINGER was the sole lord of his domain. As the Farm's weaponsmith, he oversaw the weapons training and outfitting of both the action teams and the blacksuits. If it could cause murder and mayhem, he had it on hand.

He was doing routine maintenance on one of the workbenches when the door opened.

"I'm one of the new guys," a man said, putting out his hand. "Jim Gordon, late of the U.S. Marshal's Service. I was told to come here."

Kissinger took his hand. "The name's John Kissinger, but they call me Cowboy around here."

"I was told that I have to see you for weapons and equipment issue."

"That's a fact," Kissinger replied. "What are you qualified on?"

"Nearly all of the standard issue—the MP-5, M-16, M-92, MAC-10, Uzi, M-60 and various sniper rifles. We never standardized on them."

"We use the Winchester 70, the M-23 and the new Springfield Heavy Barrel around here for the long-distance work."

"I haven't fired the Springfield, but I've used the other two long guns."

"Great. I'll be able to get you up and running in no time."

"Where'd you get the AK-74?" Gordon asked when he saw the Russian assault rifle laying on one of the workbenches. It had been coming into service before he left Little Amerika, and he was very familiar with it.

"I've got a room full of the most likely foreign stuff the teams might run into. They need to know how to use them in case that's all they can get their hands on. We also issue them for some of the more deep-cover jobs when we don't want the bad guys to find any evidence of outside operatives.''

"Know your enemy and confuse them.''

"That's it.''

"Where are they anyway?'' Gordon asked. "The teams, I mean.''

Kissinger didn't usually answer questions like that. The blacksuits were only briefed on field operations when they had a need to know. Sometimes when Able Team was operating in the States, the blacksuits were put on alert in case the mission exposed the Farm to retaliation. Usually what they didn't know, they couldn't inadvertently leak. But, since this guy was a new guy, he was naturally curious.

"Able Team is working a Russian Mafia hit in the northeast and Phoenix is in Russia.''

Gordon was shocked to hear that, but he knew better than to ask any more questions. He was a master of intelligence gathering through casual conversations, and the technique was slow. Trying to learn too much too quickly could put him in jeopardy.

"With that kind of action going on, it sounds like I got on board at just the right time.''

"Russia, Pakistan, Colombia, it doesn't much matter where they are for the security force around here,'' Kissinger said. "Rarely does a mission affect what goes on here. To be perfectly honest, being a blacksuit can get pretty boring. Day in and day out, all you do is make your rounds, do your boots-and-blue-jeans job, eat and sleep. It's been a long time since we had any excitement around here.''

That was about to change if Gordon had anything to do about it.

''Okay,'' Kissinger said. ''Let's get started on this. I want you to be checked out on at least the MP-5 and the Beretta 92 today so you can start tonight.''

''I'm qualified on those two weapons,'' Gordon replied, frowning.

''I'm not doubting your qualification,'' Kissinger said. ''But around here, we do our own just to make sure. Since there's so few of you guys, if the shit ever hits the fan, we need the best shooters in the country protecting us. And don't feel bad, I even requalify the guys we get from Delta Force and Blue Light too.''

Gordon shrugged. ''If that's the drill, let's do it.''

''We'll start with the Beretta.''

IT TOOK TWO HOURS for Kissinger to run Gordon through the weapons qualification course. The new blacksuit had wondered how it was going to be done because he had not seen any firing range on the grounds. The short-range work had been done on a hundred-foot indoor range. The rest of it had been done on a weapons simulator. But this wasn't like any simulator he had ever seen before.

For one, the weapons were loaded with live ammunition so the recoil could be taken into account.

Not only did the hologram target images, computer-generated, move in 3-D, they fired back, and the computer made adjustments for Gordon's weapon trajectory. It was so real that after the first few seconds, he thought that he was really in a firefight. Each of the minibattles lasted only a few minutes, but he had to change magazines, prioritize the targets and take cover when they returned fire.

"Not bad," Kissinger said as the screen displayed a big blinking Game Over logo. "You're not top gun around here yet, but keep that up and you'll get a gold star on your report card."

"You have a program like that for all of your weapons?" Gordon asked.

"Everything except artillery," the weaponsmith replied. "And I'm working on that one myself."

"That's amazing. You should let the Feds borrow that to replace the crappy simulators they use."

Kissinger shook his head and smiled. "No way, José. This is strictly a base exclusive."

"But where did you get it? I've never seen anything like it on the market."

"Our computer staff cooked this up in their spare time. We do a lot of our own development work around here. We have surveillance gear that not even the CIA can get their hands on, and anything any other government agency has, we have as well. You know that electronic security lock code cracker the U.S. Marshals were just given?"

Gordon nodded.

"That came from here."

"I'm impressed."

"We're not a big group," Kissinger said proudly, "but we do okay."

Gordon glanced at the simulator. "I believe it."

"Anyway, let's get your weapons and ammunition issued so you can go to work. We'll go through the rest of the drill later."

After picking up the Beretta and H&K MP-5 that would be his personal weapons, Gordon headed for the blacksuit living quarters to get settled in.

BUCK GREENE LOOKED OVER the duty rosters on the screen of his computer and noted where the new men had been placed. For the first two cycles, they would be probationary in that everything they did, or didn't do, would become a matter of record. Even though he was confident that he had picked the best of the candidates, sometimes a man simply didn't work out. It wasn't a measure of the man as much as it was the nature of the job.

A good blacksuit had to be able to endure a never-changing regimen that was completely unlike other security jobs. There weren't too many security positions that required that a guard pick peaches, repair fences or drive a tractor pulling a plow day after day. Since all of the probationary guards this time had rural backgrounds, though, he thought they would all make the transition with no problems.

He would, however, keep a close eye on them as he always did. The security of Stony Man Farm required no less.

CHAPTER SIX

Sheremetyevo International Airport,
Moscow, Russia

Hermann Schwarz stopped at the end of the stairs leading from the first-class exit of the SAS 747 that had flown the Able Team nonstop to Moscow from JFK. "Damn! I was hoping that I'd never have to come back to this place again."

"Welcome to Mother Russia," Rosario Blancanales said with a grin.

"Mother, my ass," Schwarz growled. "This place is a complete basket case. If it's any kind of mother, it's a crackhead, welfare mom peddling her ass for a quart of Colt .45 and a toke on a crack pipe."

"But that's why we've been sent here," Blancanales said. "We're supposed to help Mother Russia learn how to mend her ways and become a productive citizen of the world community."

"Fat chance."

"If you two are done," Carl Lyons cut in, "move out. I'm freezing my ass off out here."

For another moment, Schwarz scanned the terminal in front of him as if he were looking for hidden snipers. Instead, all he saw was an ugly concrete building with a handful of planes pulled up to it to discharge passengers. For an international airport, it would make a good pig sty. But only if the pigs were blind.

"Move it, Gadgets," Lyons prompted.

Schwarz reluctantly started across the tarmac for the door marked Customs in English, French and Russian.

"Wait for me," Jack Grimaldi yelled from the top of the stairs. With Able Team being transferred, the Farm's ace pilot and wheelman had invited himself to go along. Life got boring when the boys went out of the country and left him behind.

"Get it in gear, Jack," Lyons called back to him.

IT WAS ONLY three degrees warmer inside the passenger terminal, but any improvement was welcome, even if it was provided by aromatic body heat. Handing out free samples of underarm deodorant, however, would make it a more user-friendly place. Trying not to breathe too deeply, Schwarz vowed that he would never complain about JFK or O'Hare again.

Yakov Katzenelenbogen was waiting for them at the gate with a young Russian standing at his side. "This is Yuri Belakov of the SVR," Katz said, introducing the Russian. "He's been assigned to birddog us."

After the introductions had been made, the Russian gestured for Able Team to follow him. "I've greased the skids, as I think you say, so you won't have the customs police messing up your luggage."

"We appreciate that," Grimaldi replied, "but you didn't need to. My bags are already a mess."

THE MOSCOW SAFEHOUSE was in what had once been an upscale neighborhood. All of the houses in the area were in need of paint and a little cleanup, and this one was no exception. What made it different from its neighbors was that it was equipped with the best security system the Russian security agency could provide.

"Lovely place," Schwarz commented as he took in his tattered surroundings. "I wonder who the decorator is?"

"I think the minister is responsible for furnishing the safehouses," Belakov replied.

Schwarz's mouth popped open, but he couldn't think of a smart-ass comeback.

After greeting their old comrades-in-arms in the makeshift commo room, Lyons got down to business. "What's the drill?"

"Well, so far," Katz said, "we've been baby-sitting politicians, buying heroin and generally making ourselves useful."

"I thought you were supposed to kill someone here."

"We are, but we have to find out who to kill first."

"Just start wasting hoods," Lyons suggested. "Sooner or later, you'll off the right guy."

"We considered that," Encizo said. "The problem is that there are too many of them."

Lyons kept a straight face. "That's never been a problem before."

YURI BELAKOV LISTENED to the banter with both amusement and puzzlement. He had been with the American team for a week now, but he was still no closer to figuring them out than he had been on day one. He wasn't a complete stranger to Americans, having been assigned to work with groups of them several times over the past few years. But these men were like no other Americans he had ever met. And, as he had learned, they weren't even all Americans. One of the team leaders was British, the one-armed man was a French Jew and the third one, he didn't have a clue.

The big man with the black hair and ice-blue eyes was calling himself Mike Belasko, but Belakov was sure that wasn't his real name. For one thing, while his comrades usually referred to him as Striker, Katz occasionally called him Mack. The Striker moniker was obviously a unit nickname; commandos often went by colorful nicknames. The Mack might also be a nickname.

He had tried to access the SVR's database for information about these men and had drawn a complete blank. With his professional curiosity aroused and his pride in the Russian intelligence agency on the line, he had dug into the files of the old KGB. There, too, he'd hit a brick wall. What was strange about it was that while there were gigabytes of information about every U.S. organization from the CIA and the Secret Service to the Boy Scouts, there wasn't a single entry about these men. In fact the record was so clean that he suspected there had been a complete data wipe of any mention of them.

That suspicion was confirmed when he found reports referencing other reports that no longer existed. Most of the references were about American actions that had taken place in the battleground nations of the cold war, the drug wars and the war against terrorism. A mention would be made of a situation where the United States interests had been threatened, but the report of how it had been concluded was conspicuous by its absence.

The SVR's computer systems were designed so anything that was entered into the data banks stayed there forever. It was an old mindset that went back to the days of the Czarist Secret Police. Only one man controlled the erasure of data from the system and that was the Interior Minister himself. If something was missing, the minister had ordered it destroyed.

He was aware that there was a close relationship between the minister and the U.S. government. The Americans had loaned many kinds of experts to the ministry to help the new Russian government set up effective crime-fighting forces, solve economic problems and in other areas that the now-defunct

Communist Central Committee had handled in the past.

There were even rumors that a special American strike team had been invited into Russia to put down an earlier takeover attempt by a criminal gang. He had heard that these Americans had joined in on a Spetsnaz raid of a hidden command post used by those criminals. If those rumors were true, and he now believed that they were, he knew who those Yankees had been; he was working with them this time.

WHEN HE RETURNED from the Interior Minister's office, Yuri Belakov looked grim. "I have bad news," he told Katzenelenbogen. "I think you may have been compromised."

Katz froze. Ever since this mission had been announced, he had been telling himself that this wouldn't happen to them this time. But he should have known better. If there was an Olympics for treachery, the Russians would be the odds-on favorite for the gold medal.

"What happened?"

"I have this girlfriend," Belakov said, "and she is a dancer."

"An exotic dancer?" Schwarz asked.

The Russian frowned. "A sexy dancer, yes. But she is a good girl."

"Go ahead," Katz prompted him, but he'd lay odds on what was coming next. Along with treachery, the Russians were famous for attacking the weaknesses of the people they were after, particularly their families and loved ones.

"I stopped by my apartment on the way back here, and she was not there. The phone rang and a man tells me that she is captured. He says that if I want to have her back, I must meet with him. To prove that they are telling the truth, they let her say my name, then she screamed like they are hurting her."

Bolan's jaw was set as he listened to the Russian. Over his many years as the Executioner, he had run into this scenario many times. It seemed that the first thing any criminal thought of was to hurt the innocent, particularly women.

He caught Katz's eye and nodded. "We go."

Katz nodded his assent. "When is the meeting?"

"I have to meet them in two hours."

"How's your pain threshold?" Schwarz asked the Russian.

"Please," Belakov replied, "I do not know what you mean."

"Can you take a little pain while I implant a locator under your skin?"

"What is that?"

Schwarz opened his bag of goodies and pulled out a minitransmitter half the diameter of a dime in a clear plastic case. "This big. I put it under your skin and we can track you no matter where you go. You make the meeting alone and we'll track you to wherever they take you. We'll capture them and free your girlfriend."

"You can do that?"

"Piece of cake," Schwarz said. "It transmits to the Global Positioning System and is accurate to within three meters. We have a GPS locator, and it will pick up the signal no matter where you go."

Belakov nodded grimly. "I can take the pain."

"Let's do it."

GRIMALDI KEPT the Mercedes sedan well back from Belakov's Lada two-door when he left the safehouse. And, since the little Fiat 128 look-alike seemed to be running on three cylinders, it wasn't easy to keep the powerful Mercedes from running right up his tailpipe.

"I'm picking up his implant," Schwarz radioed back to Katz and Bolan in the follow-on car, another Mercedes.

"Don't lose him."

"Never happen."

"Here we are," Grimaldi said as pulled his Mercedes to the curb.

Peering through the telephoto lens of his camera, Lyons snapped several shots as Belakov got out of his Lada and walked up to the three men waiting by the end of the bridge. He held out his arms to be frisked, then allowed himself to be led away.

"Good boy," Lyons murmured when he saw that the Russian was following orders. As soon as Lyons saw Belakov and the three thugs get into the car, he snapped a final shot of the licence plate.

"It's a black Mercedes," he told Grimaldi.

The driver groaned. "I wish I had the Mercedes franchise in this town. Everyone drives one of the damned things."

"Including us," Lyons reminded him. "Which means that they won't spot us following them."

When the gangster's Mercedes headed out of the center of town, Grimaldi was forced to hold well back again. The suburbs were almost devoid of traffic, and they were obvious. "I'm afraid I'm going to have to let them go before they spot the tail."

"Wait till they hit the turnoff," Schwarz suggested, "and then drive past. I've still got him and can vector us in."

As if on command, the gangster's Mercedes turned right into what looked like a deserted factory area. Schwarz had a flashback to Prague when he and Blancanales had gone to a meet in a deserted factory on the outskirts of the town. This time, though, he wasn't going to be walking into a trap unarmed.

He keyed his com link. "Striker," he said, "they turned off to the right into what looks like an industrial complex. We drove past the turnoff and are parked on the side of the road a hundred yards down. Flash your lights when you spot us."

"Roger."

YURI BELAKOV BLINKED when his blindfold was removed. He had been taken to some kind of factory and was surrounded by at least eight men. From the looks of them, they had to be Mafia thugs. "Where's Karina?" he demanded. "I want to see her."

"You'll see her all right," the leader of the gang said with a sneer. "But don't be in such a hurry, Belakov. We have to talk first."

"I'll talk to you after I've seen her."

The gang leader nodded, and the man holding Belakov's right arm hammered his fist into the Russian agent's diaphragm.

Belakov doubled over with the blow and fought for his breath.

"You'll talk now or you'll join her sooner than you thought you would."

"Fuck your mother," Belakov gasped.

Another savage blow sent him to his knees.

"This can take as long as you want," the gang leader said. "But you will talk."

REACHING THE FACTORY, the Stony Man warriors split up. Bolan, Katzenelenbogen and Rafael Encizo took the front door of the factory building. According to the GPS, Belakov was roughly in the front half of the building. The problem was that the GPS was accurate only to within three yards.

David McCarter, Calvin James, Gary Manning and T. J. Hawkins worked their way around to the back of the building and found an entry point. When they went in, they would be the hammer for Bolan's anvil.

Jack Grimaldi and Able Team were holding back as a ready reaction team. Without knowing what kind of opposition was inside the building, they had to be ready to go wherever they were needed or to be the chase team for any rats that escaped the trap.

"Report," Bolan's voice said over the com link.

"We're in place," McCarter called back.

"We're ready," Lyons sent.

"We're going in now," Bolan announced.

Along with the full-sized sliding door on the end of the building, there was a side entry and it was unlocked. With Encizo and Katz backing him, Bolan eased open the door and slipped inside. Hugging the wall, he paused to let his eyes adjust to the lower light levels. From somewhere ahead, he could hear voices speaking Russian. Double-clicking his com link, he signaled the others that he was moving out.

With Bolan inside, McCarter and Encizo moved in behind him and took up positions on either side. With the front door barred, it was time for the Briton to make his entrance.

CHAPTER SEVEN

When Bolan sent the double-click signal over the com link, McCarter, James and Hawkins made their entry through a service door at the back of the building. Fanning out, they took cover momentarily to let their eyes adjust to the dim light.

"Belakov hasn't moved," Schwarz said over the com link. "He's still in the middle of the building, to the west."

McCarter single-clicked to acknowledge the message and signaled the commandos to move out. Making their way through the abandoned machinery and crates, they converged on the offices in front of them in an extended line. They could hear raised voices speaking Russian and what sounded like someone being beaten.

A shout of alarm from the right was cut off by a short burst of 9 mm slugs from Hawkins's subgun.

With the loss of surprise, the assault team rushed the office area.

At the first shot, Belakov was instantly forgotten. When the kidnappers left him, he dropped to the floor and rolled against the base of the wall. Out of the line of fire, he started to work on the rope binding his hands behind his back.

Outside, the kidnappers' leader shouted instructions over a roar of gunfire as his men fired almost blindly into the cluttered floor of the factory. They weren't marksmen, and they were panicked.

One by one, the gunmen went down to men who knew how to shoot to kill. Every move they made was countered by a hail of accurate fire. When their leader went down, the two surviving kidnappers broke and ran.

"Two coming your way, Striker!" McCarter sent over the com link.

"I've got them," Bolan replied as he stepped out of cover.

Even in the dim light, he had no trouble lining up the sights of his Desert Eagle on the fleeing Russians. The first man went down with a .44 Magnum slug exploding his heart. The second one tried to dodge in midstride, but the Executioner tracked him and put a round in his leg to take him down.

"We're clear back here," he called out over the com link.

"That was the last of them."

Encizo and Katz quickly moved out to secure the prisoner Bolan had tagged. With the bullet in his leg, the Russian wasn't in a frame of mind to resist. He was bandaged and had his hands bound behind his back before being led away.

WHEN THE LAST SHOT echoed away, Belakov struggled to his feet to look for his girlfriend. "Karina! Karina!"

"Cover Belakov," Bolan said over the com link. "There might be another one alive."

The SVR agent found her in the first place he looked, the factory's old main office. Her body was faceup on a blanket on the floor, her clothing torn away and her face bruised. The impossible angle of her head was the obvious cause of death; her neck had been broken.

Even so, he knelt beside her and laid his fingers on the side of her neck to check for a pulse. There was none, and her body was already cool. He paused over her briefly, his head down, before pulling her blouse and skirt back in place and folding the blanket over her.

"I'm sorry, man." James laid his hand on the Russian's shoulder.

The Russian shook himself and got to his feet. "Thank you," he said formally.

"We'll help you take her out."

Carefully carrying the woman's body, the Stony Man warriors and Belakov took her to Able Team's van. There was little to say at a time like this, and the trip back to the safehouse was made in silence.

EVEN WHEN THE PRISONER was in the safehouse, his blindfold was left on. Part of any good interrogation was disorientation, and blindness went a long way toward achieving that. The gag in his mouth and the shooter's earmuffs were part of it as well. Until Calvin James was ready to talk to the man, the gangster would be completely cut off from the outside world.

Belakov was in a blind rage and didn't even want to be in the same room with the man unless he had his hands around his throat.

"I know you want to get your hands on that guy," Katzenelenbogen said as he took the Russian aside, "but this is not the time for that. We need him intact, and we need you to translate for us. I don't think my Russian is good enough to handle the street slang."

"He must pay for what they did to Karina," the Russian vowed.

"He will," Katz said. "I promise you that. But the best way to avenge her death is to take the bastards out, all of them, and he's the key to doing that. If you'd like, when we're done, I'll give him to you to do with what you want. But we have to talk to him first. And I do not want this reported to your boss."

"But why?" Belakov frowned.

"The last time we did a job for the minister, there was a spy in his office and two of my men were captured. I know the minister swears that his staff is clean now, but I can't risk it, too much is at stake this time. Both for your country and for mine."

Belakov saw Katz's point and nodded.

"I'll get the bag," James said, "and we can get started on this guy."

Applying pain to entice a man to talk was the traditional method of interrogation. But, as with all traditions, there came a time when the old had to give way to the new, and that was the case here. The Stony Man team wasn't averse to using pain as a tool, but in all too many cases, it was inefficient and time-consuming. Chemical interrogation was much quicker as well as being much more reliable. Even in great pain, a man could lie, but he couldn't lie if his brain wasn't under his control.

Taking his medical kit from the bag, James filled one syringe with scopolamine and another with a home brew containing a little LSD, a lot of endorphins and a compound he had scored from a CIA lab contact. It was a foolproof mixture, and, unlike some of the earlier chemicals that had been tried, beyond a major hangover headache, it didn't have any serious side effects.

"Hold his arm," he told Belakov.

When the SVR agent had the prisoner immobilized, James found the vein and started the drugs into his system. The scopolamine immediately put the thug into a good copy of a drunken state. For years, scopolamine had been used by itself to question prisoners. In fact it had been used on the infamous Che Gueverra when he had been captured in Bolivia. His celebrated death had occurred only after he had been thoroughly questioned under the drug. The problem with Scope, as it was commonly called, was that a willful man could resist it in low levels, and using too much left the subject's brain scrambled. Gueverra had been drooling when he had been shot.

The new technique softened the subject with Scope, but LSD was added to break down his will and the endorphins to make it a pleasurable trip. People always talked more when they were happy.

It took a few minutes for the chemicals to take full effect. Peeling back one of the prisoner's eyelids, James examined the man's pupils. "He's done. Ask him his name."

Not only did the prisoner give his name, he started babbling so much that Belakov had trouble keeping the questioning on track. The interrogation took almost an hour and, when it was done, the reason for the woman's kidnapping was clear.

"They were after me." Belakov sounded shocked. "They were trying to turn me to find out what the SVR is doing."

He shook his head. "They had to do that because Karina had not been able to get anything out of me in bed. She was working for them all the time."

"I doubt that she had any choice," Katz said gently. "One of the first things the Mafia, any Mafia, does is prey on women. Once she had fallen into their hands, she had to do what they told her to try to save her life."

"It didn't work, did it?" The Russian's voice was hard.

"It rarely does."

"What do you want to do with him?" Belakov jerked his thumb at the prisoner who was still mumbling to himself under the influence of the drugs.

"I'd like to keep him on hand for a while," Katz said. "We may need to talk to him again."

"Until this is over," Belakov said, his jaw set. "Then he joins the others."

Katz had no problem with that.

"WE HAD SOMETHING HAPPEN today," Valery Fyodor reported to his boss that evening, "and I think we need to look into it very carefully."

"What happened?" Josef Leoninski asked.

"I've been working on getting a better informant in the SVR and I found a perfect target. One of their top men, a Yuri Belakov, was living with one of our girls, a dancer. She was not able to get anything out of him the usual way, so I set up a kidnapping on her and he fell for it."

Very early on, Leoninski had learned that one of the best ways to ensure a man's cooperation was to work through his woman and family. It was a rare man who could resist trying to protect his loved ones. "And?"

"And something went wrong. He surrendered in hopes of getting her back, but when my men took him away for questioning, I lost the whole team, eight of my best men."

"You lost eight men?"

Fyodor nodded. "Seven dead and one missing, and that's what I'm worried about."

"The girl?"

"The boys had been a little rough with her, and she died before my men picked up Belakov. But her body was missing too, so it's obvious that whoever the attackers were, they came to get her and Belakov back.''

Leoninski could only agree.

''The other thing I don't like,'' Fyodor continued, ''is that the cartridge cases they left behind all had blank headstamps.''

Blank headstamps were the mark of professionals who were backed by one government or the other. Criminals and freelancers usually didn't have the resources to have special ammunition manufactured for their use.

''Do you think it was those SVR pigs?'' Leoninski asked.

''No, they are using regular military-issue ammunition now. Plus, one of the weapons the attackers used was a .44-caliber pistol.''

''I'm not familiar with them.''

''No reason that you should be,'' Fyodor said. ''It's rarely used here in Russia, but often used in the United States.''

The Lion didn't have to have a picture drawn for him. First the hit on the candidate had been thwarted and now this. Someone was targeting his organization and that someone wasn't Russian.

As if reading Leoninski's mind, his second in command continued. ''There were stories about a group of American commandos who were sent over here to shut down Gregor Rostoff's operation, remember him? No one has any proof of their involvement, but the SVR suddenly went from losing at every turn to wiping out his organization, and I believe the rumors. I also believe that it is happening again to us.''

''But I don't understand. Why would the Yankees care about what happens over here?''

''I think they are afraid of what will happen if Zerinov becomes president and want to secure the election for one of their allies. You have to admit that the general has been shooting off his mouth to anyone who will listen about bringing back the Russian empire and restoring the military to its cold war level. The Americans are happy now that the cold war is over, and they do not want to have to go back to being afraid of us.''

Leoninski might have been a relative novice to the political arena, but he wasn't a man to ponder overlong when he was threatened.

''Stop everything we are doing,'' he said, ''and find out if any Americans have involved themselves here. If they have, find them and kill them.''

''Do you want me to let Zerinov know about this?''

''I'll do it,'' Leoninski replied. ''For all their big talk, they are amateurs when it comes to this sort of thing, and we can handle this ourselves. Doing it that way will give us something to hold over his head if he starts thinking that he is the top dog.

''I still need to find a way to get a man inside the SVR. That's the fastest way to find those Yankees.''

''I'll keep working on it,'' Fyodor vowed.

''And I'll go talk to our general.''

PAVEL ZERINOV LOOKED every inch the Red Army general he had been during the Afghan War. He had come up through the parachute regiments and had a reputation for the dash and daring that went with the airborne forces. Even in his early sixties, he was still paratroop-fit and ramrod-straight. He was the picture-perfect candidate to lead Mother Russia out of the catastrophe she had been put in by Boris Yeltsin and his greedy capitalist cronies. As the leader of the Progressive Party, he would put his beleaguered nation back in the seat of world power it had been toppled from. And, if he had to put his political enemies in their graves to accomplish that sacred mission, so be it. He had put more than one enemy underground in his day.

First though, he had to get one of his allies back on track. On a personal level, he had to admit that he liked Josef Leoninski. He recognized the man's power and ruthlessness, and saw those same traits in himself. Nonetheless, he wasn't comfortable with the fact that he'd been forced to ally himself with the criminal element in his country. It had been purely a marriage of necessity; hadn't someone said that politics makes strange bedfellows? This union would end in a fatal divorce once he had captured the presidency. Right now, though, he needed the Lion's underworld connections to do the necessary dirty work of the campaign.

His plan had been moving according to schedule until the recent abortive assassination attempt. For some reason, that incident had spooked Leoninski, and he had backed off until he could find out what had gone wrong. The Mafia boss had requested this meeting to express his fears and, while Zerinov hated that kind of thing, he had to get the crime lord back on board.

"The minister has called in his Yankee friends before," Leoninski concluded after reciting what he saw as evidence for outside meddling. "And I think he has done it again."

"But you have no real proof," the general pointed out. "Disastrous operations and blank-cartridge headstamps from foreign weapons are not evidence of Americans."

"I don't have any dead Yankees to put on display, no," Leoninski snapped. "But I have a dozen of my best men dead and my men don't die easily."

Zerinov held his opinion about the Lion's men. They were good at slapping women around when they didn't hustle their products, and killing street-corner drug pushers who didn't make their payments. But they weren't soldiers by anyone's definition.

"I will send an experienced team to help you investigate this."

"I have my own sources," Leoninski said, "and I am working on finding the Americans right now."

"The team I was thinking about is a specialized counterterrorist unit from the Spetsnaz Parachute Battalion. They have tracked down more terrorists than anyone in the world. They are the ones who secured the release of the Russian diplomat who had been kidnapped by that Hamas scum in Lebanon. If, as you suggest, these Americans exist, they will find them and eliminate them for you.''

Leoninski shrugged. At this point in time, he wasn't in a position to tell the general to stay out of his affairs. That would come after the election. ''I don't care who takes care of the Yankees as long as it's done.''

''I will send their officer over so you two can discuss how you can assist him.''

''Very well.''

CHAPTER EIGHT

Stony Man Farm, Virginia

Barbara Price glanced at the updated blacksuit duty roster, initialed it, put it in her outbox and moved on to the next item in the pile on her desk. Of all of the pieces that went into making the Farm work, the security force was the least of her problems. Most of that was thanks to Buck Greene. The Chief, as he was called, was an old pro and he ran his unit like a finely tuned race car. He picked good men to be blacksuits, trained them well and keep a sharp eye on their activities. Rarely, if ever, did anything happen with them that required her attention, and that was the way she liked it. Particularly at times like this.

The Russian mission wasn't going as quickly as she would have liked. She wasn't as impatient about it as the President or the Russian minister was, but she understood their frustration at the lack of progress. But, if the Russian intelligence service hadn't been able to get a handle on it, they could hardly expect Stony Man to jump in and start kicking ass from the get-go. These things took time.

Stony Man's earlier experience with the Russian Mafia had shown how deeply woven it was into all levels of Russian society, and it wasn't easy to unravel. The teams were going to have to work it from the edges like a tightly woven fabric until they could work a thread loose and follow it. Like it or not, it would take time and hopefully they would have enough time to take care of it before the election took place. But, at the rate that the political assassinations were happening, the election might be moot before they could find the lead they needed. At least they had stopped short one assassination. Hopefully that would slow things long enough for them to get that one vital lead.

It was so much easier when all the Stony Man commandos had to do was to paradrop into some remote location and kick ass to solve the problem. The military strike option was always quick and decisive. This situation simply didn't lend itself to that particular solution. That was why Stony Man might actually lose this one.

The President wasn't going to want to hear that, but he needed to be given a reality check every now and then. She hoped that he was also working on a plan to deal with a resurgent, militant Russia if Stony Man failed. If he wasn't, he was making a big mistake.

JIM GORDON'S first assignment as a blacksuit was to work the day shift, the boots-and-blue-jeans detail as it was called. These were the men in civilian clothing who did the day-to-day physical labor around the Farm, working the crops and orchard. Their weapons were never far from them while they worked, but the emphasis was on the work because it maintained the cover for what really went on.

According to his résumé, Gordon had spent the summers during his high school years working on his grandfather's farm in Oregon's Willamette Valley. He, of course, had actually spent his summers in Little Amerika, but he and his fellow "Americans" had been required to work summer jobs, many of them in agriculture. He'd had no way of knowing it, but that experience had been vital to his having made the first cut of the applicants.

The first task he was given was weeding the row crops in the ground. And, while the tools he was given were better than the ones he had used back in Mother Russia, the work was the same. Even though he was wearing gloves, he was nursing blisters by the end of the day. Being a federal marshal for ten years had made his hands soft.

When he came off shift that evening, he went to the mess hall for dinner. Like lunch had been, dinner was first-rate and there was a lot of it. Whoever was in charge of this place obviously believed in feeding the troops to keep them happy. After coffee and fresh-baked apple pie for dessert, he drifted over to the barracks with the other guards.

The night shift was getting ready to go on duty

when he walked in. These men were dressed in the night combat kit that gave the security force its nickname, and they were loaded with the tools of their trade. Everything from fighting knives to fragmentation grenades hung on their assault harnesses, and night-vision goggles hung on straps around their necks. If it came to a firefight, they looked like they would be ready for it. But, as he knew, it was the fight in the dog, not the dog in the fight that made the difference, and he had yet to see these men in action.

Being a new guy with the blacksuits was the same as being a new guy in any military organization. There was a certain amount of new-guy crap that had to be put up with and, stupid or not, he knew that he had to play the game. He was still on probation and, if he didn't fit in with the other guards, he'd quickly find himself looking for another job. Also, the sooner he could work his way into the confidence of these men, the sooner he could start gathering the information he needed to bring down this place.

He still didn't know how he was going to do it; he only knew that he would. And he didn't care if it cost him his life. From everything he had learned so far, these people had had a lot to do with causing the troubles that had finally overcome Mother Russia, and he was going to make them pay for that. He wouldn't feel that way if he had infiltrated a regular American military unit. It was the duty of uniformed soldiers to bring down their enemies, and it was an honorable profession.

Whoever the base's operatives were, rather than stand in uniform as men of honor, they had worked in the dark as spies and terrorists to kill his countrymen. And he would give them what the Russians had always given spies, death. The fact that he was a spy himself wasn't a contradiction to him. He saw himself as a KGB officer fighting for his country in civilian clothing, or in this case as a blacksuit, the uniform of the enemy.

The TV set in the barracks dayroom was tuned to CNN, and an American reporter in Moscow was reporting on yet another attempted political assassination in the campaign for the upcoming presidential election.

"There have been three candidates from the centrist party assassinated so far," the reporter said. "Russian authorities have not been able to find out who is behind these deaths, but fingers all point to General Pavel Zerinov of the ultranationalist Progressive Party. The fact that this attempt was thwarted may show that the government is finally getting a handle on the problem."

"Jesus!" one of the blacksuits polishing his boots said. "I really feel sorry for those poor people. They don't have a chance. If that Zerinov bastard gets in power, it's going to be the bad old days all over again, nukes and all."

He shook his head. "Man, we don't need to go through that shit again."

Gordon took the opening. "Is that what the action teams are doing over there, trying to take him out?"

The man shrugged. "Damned if I know. You know how it is around here. We should have a sign on the door—Home Of The Mushroom Detachment."

When Gordon frowned, the man laughed. "They call us mushrooms because they keep us in the dark and feed us bullshit. If we don't have a need to know, they don't tell us. It's as simple as that. As long as the bad guys don't show up at the gate, we don't ever get to know what's going down in the main house."

The man put his boots down. "Actually, for all the goings on over there, it's usually pretty quiet around here. The teams get to have all the fun. In all the time I've been here, I've never popped a cap on anyone."

"Sounds boring."

"In that sense it is." The man laughed. "If you wanted firefights, you should have joined the Marines or the Border Patrol. But they keep us busy enough around here that we don't have much time to get bored. Actually I get bored more on standby phase than I do around here. That's when you can really go bat-shit waiting around for something to happen."

Gordon liked what he was hearing. Nothing bred laxity in a situation like this than a static environment. From what he had seen so far, the blacksuits were more concerned about working the crops than they were about guarding the perimeter. But, if the perimeter was never challenged, that was to be expected. So far, this was looking pretty good.

AS PART OF his familiarization with his area of operation, Jim Gordon was next assigned to a crew that was cleaning the weeds out of the perimeter fence on the north side of the farm. It was the kind of make-work task that seemed to take up most of the time of the farmhand detail. There just wasn't enough legitimate farm work to keep them all busy during the day.

When he started working on the fence, he saw that like everything else about this place, it wasn't what it appeared to be at first glance. The split-rail fence posts looked like they were wood, but when he hit one with his sling-blade weed whacker, he found that it wasn't. Looking closer, he saw that it was molded out of some kind of plastic. It sure looked like wood, and it even felt like wood, but it was some kind of artificial compound.

This particular post was out of alignment, and he grabbed the top to try to bring it back into line with the others.

The blacksuit working with him chuckled. "You'll never get that straightened," he said. "There's a six-foot steel pole imbedded in concrete holding it exactly where it is. It's off true to give the fence that authentic look."

"But it's plastic."

"You're good," the blacksuit said, nodding approvingly. "It is. That lets us run current through the fence wires without having to have insulators showing and giving it away."

"You mean the fence's electrified?"

"Not to shock, but to run the sensors. Anything touching the wires alerts the guys in the security center. That's why we're cutting the weeds. If they touch the wire, they give false readings."

A little farther, he was kneeling at the base of one of the posts when he saw a camouflaged coax cable running back into the orchard behind him. On pure impulse, he picked up a sharp rock chip and started tearing at the sheathing of the cable. When he exposed the outer conductor, he cut at it a few times before stopping. Rather than cut the cable, he wanted it to look as if an animal had gnawed on it.

It was a small sabotage. The bare conductor should short out as soon as water reached it and take out a sensor or two. It would be easy enough to repair, but it would be a good test of the security center's vigilance and response. He wanted to see how long it took them to notice that something was wrong and how quickly it would take them to fix it.

A SOFT RAIN WAS falling when Gordon headed for the mess hall at the end of the workday. After another first-class meal, he went to the dayroom to watch television while he cleaned his equipment. It was mindless work and he hadn't even gotten his gear dirty yet, but equipment maintenance was one of the essentials of military life and it would look odd if he didn't do it.

He was putting a second coat of polish on his go-to-town boots when an alarm went off in the barracks room. Suddenly what had been a peaceful scene exploded into a frenzy as the guards dropped whatever they had in their hands and leaped to their feet to grab their weapons and equipment.

"What's going on?" he asked the man closest to him.

"Don't know." The blacksuit grabbed his H&K and headed for the door.

"What am I supposed to do?"

"Get suited up and wait here with the other new guys. We'll call you if we need you."

Gordon secured his weapon, then put on his night combat suit. After checking everything twice, he waited in the darkness by the door for further orders. He would have loved to go out and see how the blacksuits were reacting to this "emergency," but he had been ordered to stay put, and following orders was important for a probationary guard.

The men started coming back within half an hour. "What happened?" Gordon asked the first man to walk past him.

"Freaking tree rats," the guard spit. "A squirrel chewed on one of the coax cables and knocked out one of the video cameras."

"Does this happen often?"

"Too often."

EVEN WITH AN ONGOING mission, Barbara Price still had to take care of day-to-day chores that went with running the Farm. Brognola had once offered to create another position on the staff to take care of these details, but she hadn't wanted to do that. The Farm crew was big enough as it was, and she hadn't wanted to have to make room for another warm body in the house. Plus, when things were slow like they were right now, it was a relaxing way to spend an evening.

She was one paper away from clearing her desk when the phone rang. "Price," she answered.

"Barbara," Buck Greene said on the other end of the line, "we have a problem."

"What's that?"

"An entire bank of surveillance cameras has gone down."

She hit her keyboard, calling up the surveillance system. When the multiscreen view came up, she saw that an entire row was blank. "What happened?"

"It looks like one of the coax cables was chewed through by a squirrel or something."

"I thought those were protected with a chemical deterrent in the outer sheath?"

"So did I."

"Get on it immediately," she said.

"We already are," Greene replied. "And we're doing a sweep to make sure that it wasn't an intrusion."

She didn't think that was very likely, but it never hurt to check anyway. It also broke the monotony and kept the blacksuits on their toes. One of the biggest drawbacks to their doing their job so well was that there was so little for them to do most of the time.

"Keep me informed," she said.

"Will do."

Muttering about the damned squirrels, she polished off the last of her paperwork, checked her watch and left for the Computer Room. Brognola had a mission meeting scheduled, and she wanted to check on the latest reports from Moscow before she talked to him. The President was pressing him, and she wanted to make sure that she was doing everything she could to get the Man off his back. As frantic as things got at the Farm, she wouldn't take Brognola's job for any amount of money.

JIM GORDON HAD LEARNED a lot by watching the blacksuit reaction to his sabotage. Even though most of the security force had a laid-back attitude, they had reacted with startling swiftness to what they saw as a threat. Under the cover of a peaceful, rural setting, this place wasn't as serene and bucolic as it looked. It was guarded like Fort Knox, and the blacksuits were deadly serious about their job.

It was a good thing that he had tried this little exercise before he tried to do something more serious. It had made him see that he was going to have to find a foolproof way to take the organization out. And he now saw that a series of pinprick events wasn't going to do it. To take this place down, he was going to have to do something serious, and he might not be able to do it alone.

But, by the time he finished his first tour of duty, he should know what it would take. And while he was on his R and R time, he'd contact the Russian Mafia if he thought he needed more manpower.

CHAPTER NINE

Moscow, Russia

Ex-Red Army Major Vasily Lebedev looked uncomfortable in the gaudy, but plush surroundings of Leoninski's headquarters. He looked exactly like what he was, a veteran paratroop officer wearing shabby, ill-fitting civilian clothing. One pair of the Mafia boss's shoes alone cost more than Lebedev's entire wardrobe. The dozen men with the former major were a little better dressed, but no more comfortable being out of uniform. But, with the Russian army fallen on hard times, it wasn't uncommon to see such men working menial jobs in Moscow. In fact it wasn't unknown to see the wives of serving officers working as maids for wealthy businessmen to supplement their husbands' meager incomes. Some of the younger wives even worked the tourist hotels making more in one night than their husbands did in a month.

Lebedev and his men, however, hadn't fallen that low. After their counterterrorist unit had been broken up, they had stayed together, living in the same fleabag apartment and sharing what little they had in between the jobs Lebedev found for them. Their work now was in what was called "executive security." They were bodyguards for the capitalists and were available for wet work when it was necessary.

Business practices in the new Russia weren't what they were in the Western world. Hostile takeovers were usually accomplished with AK-47s rather than lawyers in expensive suits. Buying a businessman's holdings from his heirs was considered a good move in the Moscow market. Lebedev's price for his services was high, but he always came through with the goods.

Lebedev didn't like Leoninski's thugs anymore than he had liked the Afghan bandits, the Dushmen, he had hunted and killed during the war. But he lived by the soldier's code and he would follow the general's orders to the death if it came to that. When this whole thing was over, however, he was going to take great pleasure killing this bunch of pimping, thieving, drug-dealing scum, starting with this so-called Lion.

"What do you want my men to do to help you?" Leoninski asked the paratroop officer.

Lebedev kept a straight face and didn't say that they could cut their own throats for all he cared. "Right now, nothing," he said. "As soon as we have located these mysterious Yankees, I may need to use some of your men. Right now, though, my veterans work best alone."

The crime boss saw the insult implicit in the major's insolent stance as well as his words. But he knew that he couldn't afford to have his people take this tin soldier out and beat him to death. He was one of Zerinov's pets, so he would put up with him for now. But, if he didn't deliver on the Americans as he promised, his time would come sooner rather than later. The Lion hadn't gotten where he was by ever forgetting an insult.

"How are you going to go about doing this?"

Lebedev smiled faintly. "The same way I did when I hunted the Dushmen in Afghanistan—track them down. If they exist, no matter who they are, they will leave tracks and my men are good trackers. Once they have been found, they will be killed. It is as simple as that."

"Get to it, then," Leoninski said. "I cannot do what the general wants until they have been eliminated."

"It will be done then," the paratrooper said simply.

"Good."

"THE MINISTER SENDS his congratulations on your handling the kidnapping operation," Major Yuri Belakov reported back to Katzenelenbogen after his morning meeting at the Interior Ministry. The SVR officer still showed the effects of the kidnapping and the loss of his girlfriend, but he was doing his job like a good soldier. For extra security, he was handling all of the contacts with his boss himself so that no one would spot the Americans at the ministry building.

"He's concerned about the missing armored brigade, though. Word about it has gotten out, and it's causing panic."

"I can understand that," David McCarter said. "A loose tank battalion is bad enough, but an entire brigade is something really to get concerned about. Particularly if you don't trust the rest of the army. They could become the core of a widespread military revolt."

"He's also picked up a rumor that affects you people directly."

"What's that?"

"There was a Spetsnaz Parachute Battalion during the Afghan War that specialized in counterterrorist duties. They were disbanded as part of the reduction in forces that took place after the fall."

"And?" McCarter didn't have to be a mind reader to see where this was going.

"And one of the better assault teams, the Wolverines, stayed intact after they were disbanded."

"And now they work for General Pavel Zerinov, the would-be savior of Mother Russia," McCarter concluded.

"How did you know?"

"It's only logical," he replied. "And we've heard that story a couple of times before. The general might have signed on the Mafia to help with his campaign, but the only men he really trusts are his old Red Army comrades-in-arms. And now you're going to tell us that they've been given the mission of exterminating us.''

When Belakov hesitated, McCarter continued. ''How many of them are there, and who's leading them?''

''There are a dozen Wolverines, and they are led by an ex-Major Vasily Lebedev.''

''Who is a brave, highly decorated officer who leads his men in person like he did during the war.'' McCarter smiled. ''We know the type.''

''Can you deal with him?''

''It's going to be quite different than going up against Mafia scumbags,'' McCarter admitted, ''but I think we should be able to handle them. I'll let you know more after we learn more about them.''

''That's not going to be easy,'' Belakov warned. ''The records for many of the army's special units were destroyed when the new government took over.''

''That, too, is expected,'' McCarter stated. ''But never to fear. We have our own sources. We didn't let you guys run around for seventy years without keeping a real close eye on what you were doing. Remember the cold war?''

''I was just a young officer back then,'' Belakov said, smiling thinly. ''And I was stuck in a desk job.''

''The way this thing is going, maybe you should have stayed there.''

''Not a chance.'' Belakov's jaw was set. ''As I think you say, I have a dog in this fight now.''

"That you do, lad."

Now THAT Belakov had returned, Katzenelenbogen called a team meeting. So far, they had been taking potluck, reacting to events as they happened. But now that Able Team was on board, it was time to plan a conclusion to this operation.

"With Belakov's new 'heads up' on these Wolverines," he told the commandos, "we need to stop and take another look at what we're doing. Fortunately, with Carl and his boys here now, we'll have a little more flexibility, but we need to change our modus operandi."

He turned to Belakov. "The first thing is that you can tell the minister we're out of the VIP-protection business, effective right now."

He raised a hand to forestall any complaints. "Tell him that we just can't afford to waste the personnel. Not if he wants us to find that missing tank brigade as well as deal with these Wolverines. Either mission would be a full-time job for us."

The Russian nodded his understanding.

"Next," he said, looking at Encizo, "as soon as you can arrange a meeting with your drug contacts, Rosario and Carl are going to take over the buy operation with Calvin. Rosario will pose as the principal sent over to take the deal into its next phase."

Encizo nodded, glad to be off the hook for that one. Give him a firefight anytime over a drug buy. He'd had a difficult time not wiping out the scum he'd been forced to deal with.

"And speaking of drugs," Katz said to Belakov, "what does your agency know about this Lion Leoninski guy our prisoner mentioned?"

"I'm not familiar with the name," the SVR agent admitted. "But I'm not a Mafia specialist." He grinned. "I've been tasked to the America Desk, assigned to keeping track of you people."

Katz grinned back. "You've been wasting your time, Yuri. We're much too slippery for you guys. In case you haven't noticed, every McDonald's in Russia is the base for an American spy team. Our agents behind the counter keep track of every bite you Russians take and every gallon of the 'special' sauce that goes on Big Macs. We know more about you Russians now than we ever did."

Belakov dropped the grin. "That's why we have the America desk," he said. "We're trying to protect the Russian borscht and sausage industries."

"Good luck."

"What are we going to do about those Wolverines?" McCarter asked. "We have too much on our plates as it is to have to mess with them as well as try to deal with all the rest of this crap."

"Well," Katz said, "the way I see it, we have two options. We can continue on our original track and wait for them to come to us, or we can go into a preemptive strike mode and take them out first."

He looked at McCarter. "I already know your vote."

"And mine," Bolan stated.

"But what do I tell the minister?" Belakov

looked worried. "All he can talk about is finding that tank brigade to keep it from affecting the election, and we have to keep the candidates safe."

"Both of those things are only part of the greater question," Katz explained. "And that question is, who is behind all of this? If someone has decided to send a hit team after us, then we're doing our job well enough to worry him. Now, since we didn't sign on for a suicide job, we have to protect ourselves. We won't be able to do anything for your minister if we're dead."

Belakov could only agree with that. And he almost felt sorry for the Wolverines. The job these commandos had done on the kidnappers was firmly etched in his mind. He had never seen anything like that even in the American action movies he loved.

"What do you need from me?" he asked.

"Since your agency's files on the Wolverines have been dumped, I'm not sure. We'll use you as a resource guy and run our plans past you in case we've missed something only a Russian would notice."

"When the time comes," the agent said, "I want to be included in the assault team. I owe them."

When Bolan nodded, Katz said, "We can always use another gun."

"Thank you."

Stony Man Farm, Virginia

HAVING SOMETHING USEFUL to do put Aaron Kurtzman in a much better mood. Particularly something that required as much digging as finding out about the Wolverines did. Since he didn't feel like messing around with reprogramming recon satellites, he had given the task of finding the missing Russian tanks to Hunt Wethers and Akira Tokaido. He was up for a manhunt conducted the old-fashioned way with a cybersearch. He had a lot of information that had been compiled during Russia's disastrous war in Afghanistan, but it had been several years since he had worked with it.

Using Major Vasily Lebedev's name as a key word, it took half an hour before the first notation came up. Someone had found a citation for the award of the Hero of the Soviet Union medal merely saying that he had defended the motherland from bandits and counterrevolutionary forces in Afghanistan. There was no mention of his unit, nor its designation or members. A second notation came up regarding a classified report on the suppression of Afghan guerrilla groups. Again, there were no details. Searching for key word "Wolverine" came up with a complete blank.

The problem he was having was that the work of the Russian army's counterterrorist teams were as highly classified as that of the old KGB's hit teams had been. The second half of the problem was that they'd never had the good sources in the Red Army that they'd had in the KGB. As a general rule, professional soldiers were less willing to betray their country than spies were. There were, however, exceptions to that rule.

Calling up his source menu, Kurtzman scrolled through it until he found the name he couldn't quite remember, ex-colonel of the Russian special forces Nikita Kalkin. As a Spetsnaz commander, Kalkin had run successful insurgency and counterterrorist operations in several nations. When the Communists fell, he had seen the writing on the wall and defected to the United States while the information he had was still worth selling.

After months of cooperating with American intelligence agencies, he had been given a generous pension and was living comfortably in Florida where he played chess at a professional level and was popular in his retirement community. Niki, as he liked to be called, was doing a lot better here than he would have done at home and had no regrets. He also was cleared to be an SOG asset.

"Aaron!" Kalkin bellowed into the telephone. "Have you decided to match your infernal machine against me again?"

Kurtzman laughed. "Not yet. I'm still working on the new program."

"To what do I owe the pleasure of your call, then?"

"I need some information, Niki, at your usual rates, of course."

Now the Russian was all business. "Who?"

"A Major Vasily Lebedev and a parachute unit he led called the Wolverines."

"He is a nasty piece of work, that man, and his troops are even worse. I recommend that you take extreme caution with him, Aaron. He is truly dangerous. It will be best to kill him as soon as you see him.''

''We intend to. But first I have to find him.''

''There is a veteran's club on Pogorny Street you might want to look into. He has a business interest in it. Most of the members are old farts from the Great Patriotic War, but it is a front for bad boys from that nasty business in Afghanistan.''

''What do you mean?''

''It is what you Americans would call a mercenary clearinghouse. If you want someone killed, you go to Pogorny Street and hire a killer. If you want to hire an entire unit, you can get that there, too. If you want to buy weapons, you go there, or even if you want women. Although,'' Kalkin said, chuckling, ''I must say that the women I saw there were not really first-class. They were soldiers' whores.''

''So you think I'll be able to find Lebedev there?''

''Maybe not him, but they will know how to contact him there. And Aaron...''

''Yes?''

''Don't send some CIA college boy looking for him. He will not last the day out. They will eat him for lunch.''

''Don't worry, I'll be careful.''

''Call me when you and your machine are ready to be defeated again.''

''I will.''

Kurtzman chuckled when he thought about the

picture Niki Kalkin had of who he was. The Russian émigré was sure that he was a field operative for the CIA, not a computer hack stuck in a wheelchair. Nonetheless, his information was their first real lead.

Calling up a detailed map of Moscow, he located Pogorny Street. As he had expected, it was in a section of town that mostly consisted of workers' apartment blocks. He didn't have to see a photo to know what it looked like. The identical, chunky, gray-concrete apartment blocks rising in treeless, ordered rows had been built by Stalin, and had all the grace of the dictator's reign. It had been a grim period of Russian history, and the buildings reflected their times. In post-Communist Russia, they were now a symbol of all that had been wrong and were home to the lowest levels of Moscow society.

The club would be a good starting point for the teams. But, from what Niki had told him, they would have to be careful. The Russians had always had good irregular warfare units. All the way back to Napoleon's invasion of 1812, Russian partisan forces had always inflicted horrendous losses on their enemies. The war in Afghanistan had created the finest irregular units the Russians had ever fielded. While their armored units had gotten bogged down, their special forces had enjoyed success after success against the Mujahideen rebels. The failure of the venture hadn't been the fault of the units like the Wolverines. They would be very dangerous opponents. But Bolan and the Phoenix Force commandos weren't combat virgins when it came to going up against pros.

They gave a new definition to military professionalism, and it would be tested again on this mission.

Making hard copies of all of the information he had been able to discover, he ran them through the fax machine and they were on their way to Moscow at the speed of light. Thank God for laser communications.

CHAPTER TEN

Stony Man Farm, Virginia

Probationary blacksuit Jim Gordon's next duty assignment was as mechanic for the day. He wasn't expected to do any real mechanical repair work, but instead to help ready the farm machinery for the day's work and man the refueling station.

As with most refueling stations in this age of mandatory federal safety regulations, the Farm had several No Smoking signs posted around the gas tanks and the pumps. Were the local farmers to see the signs, they might smile, but not the blacksuits; they expected them to be there. It didn't make the guards more cautious, but only a complete idiot would light up a cigarette around gasoline, and morons didn't make it into the Stony Man guard force.

Only two tractors were working that day, so Gordon didn't have a lot to do. After getting the tractors on their way, he tidied up around the machinery shed and tried to look busy. When one of the tractors came in a few hours later, he jumped up to ready the mogas hose. When the driver shut down his rig and undid the gas-tank cap, Gordon handed him the nozzle and walked back to the pump controls.

"Okay," the driver called out when the nozzle was in place in the tank opening.

Gordon hit the pump switch and watched the digital counter trip off the gallons flowing into the tank. As he watched the gas vapors shimmering above the nozzle, he had an idea.

"Okay," the tractor driver called out when the tank was full.

Gordon cut the power to the pump, but left his hand in the switch. When the driver took the nozzle out of the fuel tank, he held it over the hot exhaust pipe while he put the fuel-tank cap back on. Seeing his opportunity, Gordon tripped the fuel pump switch. The pint-sized gout of gas burst from the nozzle, hit the hot exhaust pipe and exploded in flame.

The driver jumped back, but the flames caught the sleeve of his jacket on fire. Dropping the hose, he fell to the ground to try to put out the fire.

Gordon leaped to his aid, slapping his gloved hands against the flames and putting them out before they burned through the cloth.

"Thanks, man." The driver stared at the charred sleeve. "I don't know what happened. There must have been some gas left in the hose."

Gordon looked concerned. "We're going to have to tell the other guys to watch that damned thing until we can get a new nozzle."

"Damned straight."

Climbing back onto his tractor, the driver headed back to finish his work. Gordon entered the number of gallons he had pumped in the daily fuel log and settled back to wait for the end of his shift. As he had learned so long ago, a victory was built on a series of small events, and he had racked up two scores already.

JIM GORDON WAS COUNTING the minutes to the end of the working day when he saw a woman walking toward him. As far as he knew, there was only one woman working at the farm, someone named Barbara Price, one of the head honchos. This woman, however, didn't look anything like a federal lifer to him. She looked like she had just stepped out of the *Sports Illustrated* swimsuit issue. Not that he could see her body through the faded jeans and men's Western shirt she was wearing. But there was something about her walk and long blond hair drawn back into a ponytail that made her look like a model for a Western outfitter. Also, she was much younger than he had thought she would be.

"Afternoon, ma'am," he said, nodding as she walked by.

"Good afternoon," she replied, her blue eyes glancing over to take him in.

"You're one of the new blacksuits I believe." She stopped and extended her hand. "I'm Barbara Price, the mission controller around here."

"Jim Gordon," he said as he took her hand. "Glad to meet you, ma'am."

She smiled. "Just call me Barbara. We aren't very big on 'sirs' and 'ma'ams' around here."

He grinned. "I've noticed."

"How are you finding things so far?"

"Well...." He paused. "I have to admit that it's not quite what I'd expected. This is sure not like any other federal facility I've ever seen."

She laughed openly and the musical sound aroused him. It had been entirely too long since he had been with a woman.

"I think that's the common reaction," she said. "This is too peaceful a setting to find a place like this. According to all of the movies and TV shows, we should be buried several hundred feet under a mountain somewhere with armored vehicles patrolling an electrified chain-link fence complete with minefield and lights."

"That's the usual top secret federal operation," he agreed.

"We have the mines, fence and lights, all right," she stated. "It's just that the fence is rather rustic, the mines are all command-detonated and the lights are all IR."

"But you're completely out in the open here."

"It does present some particular security problems," she admitted, "but it's the only way we could get out from under official notice. If we were stuck in the basement of Langley or even under a mountain, everyone would know that we were there. This way, we simply don't exist."

"But what do the neighbors think we're doing here?"

"Half of them think that we're some kind of secret government experimental agricultural station, and the other half think that we're running a rich man's hobby farm. They all know, though, that we're good neighbors and we don't bother anyone. They also know that if they have an emergency, we'll help them out any way we can. If someone breaks a leg at harvest time, we'll help them get their crop in, that sort of farm-life thing."

"Does it work?" he asked.

"It has so far," she replied. "We haven't had any trouble with the locals yet."

She glanced at her watch. "I've got to run, but it's nice to meet you, Jim, and I'm sure I'll see you around."

As he watched her walk away, Gordon temporarily regretted the life he was leading. If he were a real American, he could make a play for her and take his chances as a man. As an agent of an enemy organization that no longer existed, anything like that was out of the question. It almost made him wish that his father had chosen a different career for him.

Meeting her had also put a more practical idea in his mind. If things went wrong and he needed a safe conduct out, she would do nicely as a hostage. He was certain that no one here would be in a big hurry to risk her life. The Feds could get deadly serious,

but not when one of their own was in the line of
fire.

When he saw her walk into the building that
housed Kissinger's weapons shop, he had an idea.
Taking his Beretta M-92 from its on-duty hiding
place by the fuel-pump controls, he ejected the magazine. Depressing the first round against the follower
spring, he placed one of the feed lips against the
wall and pushed, bending it slightly. Now it
wouldn't feed the ammunition properly and needed
to be replaced.

"YOU REALIZE, of course," Hunt Wethers said, tow-
ering over Aaron Kurtzman's wheelchair, "that you
have given Akira and I quite an impossible task."

Kurtzman grinned to himself. Wethers had come
to the Farm from academia, and some of the schol-
arly mannerisms were hard to shake. When he got
frustrated, they all came out. "I'd imagine," he said,
"that an entire armored brigade should be easy
enough to find, Hunt."

"Maybe in a desert," Wethers shot back. "But,
in an environment such as Russia where there is
more than one such unit, it's not that simple."

"Just look for the base that has too many of the
damned things parked on the hard sand."

"That thought had occurred to me as well,"
Wethers admitted. "The problem is that we don't
have good order of battle information on the new
Russian army. It's almost like once the old Red
Army went out of business, someone decided to stop

keeping close track of Russian military forces. We don't think we're ever going to have to fight them now, so we don't need to know where they are every minute of the day and what they're doing."

To a methodical man like Wethers, that kind of thinking was tantamount to not wearing one's seat belt and going for a high-speed cruise on a freeway crowded with drunken drivers.

"I've accessed the CIA, the DIA and the NRO, and the latest order of battle for Russian armor units they have is well over a year old. It's useless for our purposes."

Kurtzman thought for a moment. If Wethers was right, and there was no reason to doubt that he wasn't, they needed outside help. They could work up their own OOB information, but it would take too long and would be a waste of human resources. Since the Russians wanted those damned tanks tracked down, they could at least provide the troop unit list of the ones that weren't missing.

"I'll have Hal ask the minister to send us a current armored unit OOB."

"That will save us a lot of time trying to work one up here."

"Until that arrives, though, keep looking for tanks where you wouldn't expect them to normally be— abandoned airfields, parks, hidden in the woods, that sort of thing. And we don't know if they'll all be together in a brigade formation either. They might have been sent out in smaller units to make it easier to hide them."

INSTEAD OF GOING directly to the mess hall at the end of his shift, Jim Gordon headed for the armory. He hadn't seen Barbara Price come out yet, and she might still be on the range. Any woman who practiced her marksmanship would be someone to be reckoned with if he wanted to make her an essential part of his emergency-exit plans. Cowboy Kissinger had been a talkative type at their first meeting, and maybe he could get a better feeling for her from the armorer.

When he walked into the weapons shop, Barbara Price was handing a Beretta 92 pistol back to Kissinger. "Thanks for the workout, John. I know I need to come in here more often, but I just never seem to find the time."

"Anytime, Barbara," he said. "If all you can get are late-night hours, let me know and I'll run the simulators for you after-hours."

"Thanks, I appreciate that."

"Anytime."

Both men tracked her with their eyes as she walked out.

"Does she shoot as good as she looks?" Gordon asked.

"Better," Kissinger said curtly. "What can I do for you?"

Sensing the armorer's hostility, Gordon instantly backed off. Apparently showing too much interest in Ms. Price wasn't cutting it with this guy. "I've got a bent magazine, and I'd like to exchange it."

Reaching behind him, Kissinger took a new Beretta magazine from a bin and handed it to him.

"Thanks."

"Don't mention it."

GORDON WAS WELL into the blacksuit off-duty routine now. It was actually rather simple, and he'd been able to come up to speed quickly. The evenings in the blacksuits' dayroom were starting to become comfortable for him—watch a little TV or read a book, clean some of his gear and go to bed. It was mindless, but it was the essence of military life. The other guards had started to ease off giving him the new-guy treatment. The fact that he was losing consistently in the nightly poker games was a large part of that. He didn't lose too much, which would get him tagged as a "fish," but he never seemed to win, either.

Since he had struck out with Kissinger, he'd try his luck interrogating his fellow poker players. "What's the story on Barbara Price?" he asked the man sitting next to him in between deals. "She introduced herself to me today, and she's quite a looker."

The man broke into a big grin and turned to the pool table at the end of the room. "Johnson!" he called out. "You owe me fifty bucks. Barbara's struck again."

When Gordon looked puzzled, the guard grinned. "It's a pool we run every time one of you newbies comes on board. I had fifty bucks that you'd trip on her today.''

''What do you mean?''

''It's okay, man,'' the card player reassured him. ''We do it every time we get a new guy in. You're not the first guy who's fallen at her feet. She has that effect on damned near everyone who meets her. I know she's got to be one of the most beautiful women I've ever seen.''

''But what's she doing here?'' Gordon looked confused.

''Shit, man, she runs this place,'' the guard said. ''This is her show.''

''I mean how did a woman like that get into this line of business? I've been in federal service for over ten years now, and I've never seen anyone who looks like her taking Uncle Sam's paychecks.''

''It's a long story and none of us really know it, but apparently she was handpicked for the job. And, believe me, don't let the looks and blond hair fool you. She's no cupcake. Occasionally she goes to the range with us just to keep her eye in, and you don't want to go up against her in a firefight. She's as quick and as cold-blooded as a snake.''

He shook his head. ''I've never seen a woman use weapons the way she does. I don't know who taught her, but he taught her well. It was probably Striker. They seem close.''

Gordon didn't want to ask who Striker was. He had already asked his quota of questions for the day and didn't want to seem to be too interested in things that weren't part of his job. As a spy, he had to blend in without giving anyone a reason to question him. Someone with a name like Striker, however, had to be an important part of this operation, and he would keep a sharp ear out for other comments about him.

Now that he had been the butt of a traditional blacksuit joke, Gordon felt more like one of them. All units have their initiation rites, and he had just gone through one of them. More of this good-natured joshing would probably come when he got to the stand-down phase of the cycle, but for now, he had passed the test.

Arranging the five cards he'd been dealt, he saw that it was going to be difficult for him to lose again with this hand. This would be one of the times that he didn't. But he'd be sure to give it away. He smiled widely and impatiently tapped his fingers on the table.

"I'm in for five."

CHAPTER ELEVEN

Moscow, Russia

When Gary Manning handed Yakov Katzenelenbogen the faxes with the information Aaron Kurtzman had been able to gather about the Wolverines, the Israeli smiled. The Bear had come through again. That the Wolverines were considered to be bad news wasn't surprising. Mediocre military units didn't last long after they were disbanded. Only men who had worked well together and had been good at what they did had the spark to survive something as dramatic as the breakup of the Red Army.

He would have liked to have had an order of battle lineup on the Russian commandos complete with their rap sheets and mug shots, but that was asking a bit much. Even from the Stony Man Farm crew.

"Ironman," he said, "I think we're in business on those Wolverines. I need you and Pol to get suited up in your drug-dealer's kit. I'm sending you guys and Rafe to check out their reported hangout."

"You want me to take a grenade launcher?"

Katz smiled. "This is just a recon, so I think your bodyguard hardware should do."

Lyons looked disappointed.

LIKE A RIPPLE flashing across a still pond, a ring of silence spread through the Pogorny Street Veterans' Club when Rosario Blancanales walked in flanked on either side by Rafael Encizo and Carl Lyons. All three were dressed in fur caps and expensive cashmere overcoats in the height of Muscovite fashion. In their roles as a drug lord's bodyguards, Lyons and Encizo had their coats open showing their MP-5 subguns hanging on shoulder slings.

It wasn't every day that well-dressed foreigners dared to venture into a place like the Pogorny Street Veterans' Club, particularly openly armed foreigners. The Russian people didn't have a constitutional right to bear arms and, while gunfire was heard almost as often in nighttime Moscow as it was in L.A., it was worth major jail time to be caught with a piece. For a man to carry one openly meant that he had connections in high places.

Looking to both the left and the right, but smiling all the time, the trio made its way past the tables to the battered oak bar. "Do you speak English?" Blancanales asked the bartender.

"A little," the man answered.

"Good." Blancanales smiled broadly as he laid a large denomination Russian bill on the bar. "A drink for everyone here, and there's more where that came from if someone can answer a couple of questions for me.''

When the bartender obviously was having difficulty digesting all of that, a younger man stood and walked over to them. ''I may be able to help you with the language,'' he offered.

''Good,'' Blancanales replied. ''I am afraid that my Russian is limited to *da* and *nyet*.''

''Allow me,'' the Russian said, as he passed on the offer of free booze from the Americans. As soon as the bartender heard the translation, he started to put bottles on the bar.

''Thank you,'' Blancanales said.

''What are these questions you have?'' the Russian asked.

''I am looking to hire some men.''

''What kind of men?''

''Experienced men who can protect a valuable shipment. I was told that there is a group called the Badgers, or the Wolverines, something like—''

''Wolverines,'' the young man interrupted.

''Wolverines,'' Blancanales acknowledged. ''Anyway, I was told that they hang out here and that they do good work.''

''Who told you that, mister?''

Blancanales smiled widely and put on the charm. ''You hear these things when you talk to people about trucking items across the border that you don't want anyone to find out about.''

''The Wolverines aren't smugglers,'' the young man said indignantly.

"But I didn't say anything about smuggling," Blancanales replied smoothly. "I spoke only of the need to hire men who aren't afraid and who can be trusted. I apologize if you thought I was asking to hire smugglers."

He looked around the room. "I am sure that there are no smugglers here."

When that was translated, he got a chuckle from the drinkers. Smuggling, both for the black market and legitimate outlets, made up a great part of Russia's struggling economy.

"Now," Blancanales continued, "I'd like to leave an address where I can be contacted in case these Wolverines do show up. Just tell them I'd like to talk to them about a job."

The young Russian took the card Blancanales held out. "I cannot promise that I will see them," he said.

Blancanales shrugged. "There are other men in Moscow, but I'd like to try them first."

"If they come, I will give this to them."

"Thank you," Blancanales said as he put another bill on the bar. "Have a drink yourself."

"THAT PLACE LOOKS like a combination of an American legion hall and a VA hospital," Lyons reported to Katz. "Except that most of the men are a decade or so younger. Some of them aren't fit for duty, but there were quite a few who looked like they could still get down and dirty. If, that is, they could sober up long enough to see."

"Drunks or not," Encizo said, "there's still some dangerous men in there. Someone took their army away, and they're not happy about it. They're good recruiting material for the Russian Mafia like my Bay of Pigs Brigade brothers were after we got out of the Isle of Pines prison. Not all of us went into the CIA and Special Forces. Unfortunately the cartels and the Mafia got quite a few of us."

"Do you want us to follow up on them?" Blancanales asked.

"No." Katz shook his head. "That was really just a recon. The next thing I want you to do is get back in contact with the sellers and arrange for the big buy."

"How big?"

"Make it two mil," Katz replied. "I can have Hal send the currency by courier, and we'll have it here tomorrow. That's a lot of money around this place, and it should be enough to make them greedy."

"Greedy scumbags become easy targets."

"That's exactly what I had in mind."

As KATZ HAD PREDICTED, the two-million-dollar proposal was eagerly snapped up by their Mafia contacts. In fact Blancanales had to ask them to hold up the deal until the money could be brought in from the States.

After another convoluted trip through the outskirts of Moscow in a black Mercedes sedan, Blancanales, Lyons and Encizo arrived at another abandoned factory. When they got out of the car, a small truck escorted by two more sedans pulled around the corner of the building.

The van carrying the rest of Phoenix Force followed Blancanales's locator beacon to the factory. Stopping short of their destination, the commandos got out and vectored themselves the rest of the way in on foot.

Unlike the earlier buy, this transaction went much faster and didn't involve vodka. The Russians opened the truck to reveal the neatly packaged five-kilo bricks of heroin and offered a sample to Blancanales. After tasting it with his tongue, Blancanales opened his briefcase to show the money. "Here it is," he said.

David McCarter could hear Blancanales clearly over the open concealed mike of his com link. When he heard the words "Here it is" over his earphone, he clicked in his com link. "Take them down."

Three Phoenix Force warriors and Yuri Belakov stepped in the open, their weapons at the ready. "Put the guns down and back away from them!" the Russian shouted. "Keep your hands where we can see them!"

For a long second there was complete silence. The only thing that was certain about what was going to go down was that the Russians would fight. If they failed to protect Leoninski's goods, they knew they would die and it wouldn't be as easy as falling in battle. The Lion liked to play with his kills. Though the Mafia hoods had been caught flat-footed, they went for their guns.

The first Russian went down before he could even bring his weapon into play.

Reacting to the "ambush," Blancanales, Lyons and Encizo pulled their MP-5s and returned fire. But none of the Phoenix Force attackers went down to their subguns because their magazines had been loaded with reduced-charge ammunition. These weren't blank rounds because the adapters needed to make the weapons function with blanks would have been too obvious. These special cartridges had enough gunpowder to make the weapons cycle, but their projectiles were made of a compressed plastic powder that disintegrated a few feet out of the muzzle. That way they could put up a realistic fight, but wouldn't risk hitting one of their teammates in the process.

Right out of the chute, the battle was one-sided. The Stony Man commandos scored in the first exchange of fire and kept right on scoring. Nothing the Mafia gunmen could do seemed to make any difference. One by one they went down.

"We can't stop them," Blancanales yelled. "They're wearing body armor."

Putting out a blaze of covering fire from their impotent subguns, the three "Mexican drug dealers" started backing up. The two Russian gunmen closest to them followed their lead, seeking the protection of their guns.

Taking his Beretta 93-R in a two-handed grip, Bolan carefully aimed at one of the Russian gunmen fleeing with Blancanales. A single, aimed shot took his leg out from under him. Another single shot nicked the other man's upper arm.

Bolan slowly lowered the pistol. Now there would be no doubt that a real firefight had taken place.

Lyons and James picked up the more seriously wounded Russian and carried him out of the line of fire. Once they were around the corner of the building, they ran for their car and scrambled into it, shoving the two wounded men in the back. Tires squealing, Lyons sent the big sedan racing for the main highway.

"The area's secured, Striker," Katz reported. "And we have the money."

"Let's get out of here."

Since the Russians no longer needed their other Mercedes sedans, the team took one of them and led the little convoy off the factory grounds. Manning drove the truck with the two million dollars' worth of Afghan heroin in the back while James rode shotgun in the cab with him. Schwarz and Lyons drove the team van and took the drag position.

They had no fears of anyone from the ambush site following them, but Leoninski might have had another team watching a transaction that large. A man like him had to be professionally paranoid.

AFTER DITCHING the Mercedes by a Metro subway station, the team van led the way back to the safehouse. The truck was quickly driven into the large garage on the compound and the doors closed behind it.

"What are we going to do with all this shit?" Lyons opened the rear doors of the truck to see their haul.

"We'll destroy it eventually," Katz replied, "but we have to hang on to it for now. We can't risk having Leoninski find out about it being burned. He'll really smell a rat then. You don't burn up two million dollars' worth of dope unless you're a cop."

"Good point."

Inside the safehouse, Gadgets Schwarz watched the tracker monitor as it followed the locator Blancanales was wearing. As long as the tiny bug kept sending its signal, it would give them the exact location of Leoninski's headquarters.

"I've got it," he said, pointing to the map. "It's this building here."

"Now all we need is Rosario's report on the layout inside," Katz said.

"Is it really going to be that easy?" Belakov asked.

"No," Katz stated, shaking his head, "it's never that easy. But now at least we'll have a better idea of what we'll be up against if we have to go in there."

"The minister will be pleased."

"Only after the fact, though," Katz said. "I'd rather you not mention any of this to him right as yet. We can't afford to have this leaked either."

Belakov reluctantly nodded. For him to be effective in his role, he had to defer to the Americans. He just hoped that the minister would understand.

WHEN ROSARIO BLANCANALES was finally allowed in to see Josef Leoninski, he swept into the crime boss's office with his rage barely controlled. Lyons and James flanked him on either side, and they weren't smiling either. Since they had been relieved of their hardware in the outer office, though, there was nothing they could do about it. The guns in the hands of Leoninski's guards made rash actions seriously inadvisable.

"I just lost two million dollars, Leoninski," Blancanales stated without preamble, "and I want it back now."

"I lost two million dollars' worth of heroin," Leoninski snapped back, "and I want it back too."

"Your men were responsible for security at the drop," Blancanales pointed out. "And from what I saw, they couldn't guard a sick whore in a hospital bed. If that's the best you can do, you should go back to selling your dope on street corners and let the professionals handle the major transactions."

"No one talks to me that way in my own office," the gang leader thundered.

Blancanales leaned forward. "Let me tell you how things are, Leoninski. My principals are aware of your organization's activities in my country. Most of which, I might add, are very amateurish operations. Do you know that just last week, one of your biggest networks was completely destroyed by the FBI?"

When Leoninski didn't immediately reply, Blancanales smiled thinly. "I didn't think so.

"When I go home and report what has happened here," he continued, "I can tell you what the response is going to be. My bosses are going to order a war on your remaining operations in the States. We will shut them down completely and will never allow them to start up again. The only way to prevent that is if I get my money back or the product I bought immediately. And I expect to be paid in U.S. dollars, not your worthless rubles."

"Before anything is done," Leoninski said firmly, "I have to investigate this incident. If I find that you have not played any part in this, you will get your money back."

"Don't take too long." Blancanales turned to go. "When you're ready to give me my money, you'll find me in the Metro Grand."

"I know where you are staying," Leoninski said.

"But," Blancanales said as he faced the man again, "I don't expect to be there long. My bosses will probably call me back as soon as they hear what has happened."

"WHAT ARE WE GOING to do?" Valery Fyodor asked.

Leoninski found himself in a bit of a bind over this situation. He had lost two million U.S. dollars' worth of heroin himself and was facing having to pay the Mexicans two million more to make good on their losses. He made a great deal of money from his enterprises, but he didn't have that kind of money to throw around. Right now, he particularly didn't have it. He had been fronting a great deal of the funds the general needed to conduct his campaign.

He realized that while the Mexican might make good on his threat to have his people cause trouble for his American operations, the problem of leaving him alive in Moscow was a certainty. There was an easy way to deal with this problem, however, that didn't involve him spending his money. Zerinov had given him Lebedev's commandos, and he might as well make use of them.

"We won't do anything," he told his second in command. "Not when others can do it for us."

Picking up the phone, he dialed Lebedev's number. Telling the major that he suspected the Mexican was linked to the American unit would ensure that his Wolverines would be sent in to take care of him.

CHAPTER TWELVE

Stony Man Farm, Virginia

Hal Brognola read through the latest stack of reports from the teams in Moscow. Katzenelenbogen and Bolan were doing their usual good job, and they were starting to make real progress. But it was a slow process, as these things so often were. He understood where Katz was coming from, but it wasn't raising Brognola's personal stock in the Oval Office. The President wanted action, and he wanted it now. Apparently the Russian minister's expectations weren't being met quickly enough.

He sympathized with the man, but, as the old saying went, "When you're up to your ass in alligators, the first thing you have to remember to do is drain the swamp." That was one of the world's greatest truisms and one of the hardest to remember, particularly if you were a politician. They had a habit of thinking that once a thing had been said, it somehow magically became so.

The minister wanted the infestation destroying his country's hard-earned freedoms cleaned out immediately. But the Stony Man teams were going for the king cockroach, not the lesser bugs. Once he was dead, the others would go back into the woodwork. In the meantime, though, Brognola knew how hard it was to sit and watch your country go to hell in a hand basket.

The heroin-buy gambit had been a typical Katz operation, which was to say brilliant, and it had been flawlessly executed. It had gotten the Stony Man warriors in to see the big man himself, and now they knew exactly what they were up against. It had also shown them that it would take more firepower than they had to take him out there.

Short of using artillery or a fighter bomber, the Lion wasn't going to be taken in his own den. He would have to be drawn out into the open where he would be an easy target for a man with a rifle. The question now was how to entice him away from his fortress. He had put Kurtzman's team to work on that problem as well and, if they came up with any bright ideas, they would pass them on. Until then, like it or not, the minister was just going to have to wait it out along with the rest of them.

The hardest part of any operation was never the fighting; it was always the waiting.

JIM GORDON'S NEXT CHANCE for sabotage came by sheer accident. He was using a small tractor equipped with a backhoe to dig a trench to bury an electrical cable. He didn't know what the cable was going to be used for, but he didn't have a need to know. All he knew was that the ditch he needed to dig had been laid out with engineering tape and he was to follow it.

He had been at his task for half an hour when he felt the backhoe blade catch on something under the ground. Thinking that it was a root, he increased the pressure until the blade cut through the obstruction. A shower of electrical sparks erupted from the trench and a shock knocked him from the tractor seat.

Several of the other blacksuits saw him fall and ran to his aid. Another man raced for an electrical panel inside the armory to cut off the current. An angered Cowboy Kissinger stormed out a second later.

"Shit!" Kissinger spit. "That's the power line to the air defense radar."

"Damn!" Gordon said. "I'm sorry, man. I didn't know that thing was buried there. I was just following the engineer tape like I was told to."

Kissinger just shook his head. Every blacksuit knew that a power cable ran through there, but no one had bothered to tell the new guy. "Who in the hell laid this thing out that way?" he asked.

"Sorry, Cowboy," one of the shift leaders said. "That's what was on the drawing you gave me."

Muttering to himself, Kissinger went to get his cable repair tools.

Since there was no way that Gordon could have known about the cable, there was no way that cutting it could be his fault. Nonetheless, he felt uneasy.

This was the third time that he had been in the vicinity of something going wrong. He hadn't planned this accident, but the worst thing an agent could do was to stand out in any way. He would have to be careful that he wasn't around the next time something went wrong.

Backing the tractor past the severed cable, he went back to digging his ditch.

BUCK GREENE LOOKED OVER the reports on the probationary guards he had just hired. Two of them were on Farm shift, and the other two on standby. In many ways, the two on standby were having a much rougher time making the transition to blacksuit life. Standby was a lot like being in jail. It was a nice jail, to be sure, but it was a jail nonetheless. At least the men on duty at the Farm had something useful to do with their time.

Both of the new guys on Farm shift, Jim Gordon and Rick Denison, seemed to be doing well for their first tour. Gordon was getting better reports, but that was probably because he had already done ten years in federal service and knew the drill cold. Denison had been a Marine embassy guard, but he was having a bit of a time getting rid of the jarhead mentality. Greene had once been a Marine himself and knew that he'd be able to bring the man around.

The only troubling thing about the two new guys was that Gordon had been involved in three minor incidents in the short time since he had come on board. He had worked on the perimeter fence detail right before the chewed cable had shorted out, he had been on the gas pump the day there had been that small gas fire and now he had dug up the power cable to the air defense radar with a backhoe.

Each incident had a rational explanation that didn't involve purposeful wrongdoing, but Greene liked to think of himself as a real bloody-minded bugger, as McCarter would say, a professional paranoid. He wasn't paid to take anything at face value. As with most of the other blacksuits, he wasn't married. His life was Stony Man Farm, and he wouldn't let anything happen to his home and family. Not while he was still breathing.

On paper, Gordon was working out well. He was pulling his own weight, and the other men liked him well enough. He had no bad habits, he didn't gripe nonstop and he took part in the nightly poker games. He noted, though, that he always seemed to lose at the table. Not too much, but he lost constantly. That could mean that he was a piss-poor card player, but it could also be a sign of something else.

Greene wasn't ready to put any of his suspicions on paper, yet. But since he was paid to be professionally suspicious, he wouldn't brush them aside either. Jim Gordon didn't know it, but he was about to become the most watched man on Stony Man Farm.

The Farm was no place for anyone who craved privacy. In fact the average federal prisoner had more privacy than the Stony Man crew. Damned near every movement they made was monitored.

The only two locations that weren't under constant video surveillance was Barbara Price's bedroom and the women's latrines. Everything else was watched every minute of the day. And, with the federal government picking up the tab, the tapes weren't destroyed at the end of the week or even the month. They were reviewed quarterly, and the tapes deemed not worth saving were erased and reused. Those that were to be archived were transferred onto CD-ROMs and were available through only a few keystrokes.

When he got a little time, he'd scroll though the tapes covering those three incidents and see if he could spot anything that he shouldn't be seeing. Right now, though, he had to work on the rosters for the shift change. He would, however, leave the newbies off the night shift for a little longer until he could run the tapes.

AT THE END OF THE DAY, Jim Gordon ate his dinner and went into the dayroom, but he didn't feel like playing poker. Grabbing his boots and shoe polish, he took a chair in front of the TV set.

The last segment on the evening's CSPAN broadcast almost brought Gordon straight out of his chair. The man being interviewed was a retired CIA operative who had written a book on Soviet cold war espionage operations targeted against the United States. Among the material he had used to research his book were a group of long classified documents he had been able to get through the *Freedom of Information Act.*

"The most important piece I got released, David," the CIA man said, "is a summary of the Little Amerika operation the Soviets ran against us for so many years."

Hearing those once-top-secret words spoken on television jerked Gordon upright.

"That was the training program they put their people through to teach them American English and acquaint them with American society, wasn't it?"

"That's right, David." The CIA man launched into an abbreviated background of the program. He then went into how difficult it had been to get the information he needed even with the *Freedom of Information Act.*

"The fight was worth it, though," the CIA man concluded. "The most important piece of information I recovered is something that has only just come to light. A Russian defector recently brought us a list of the cover names used by the Little Amerika agents who were sent over here. It's quite an extensive list covering the last twelve years, and the names number in the hundreds."

"Won't the FBI be checking those names to see if we still have Soviet agents operating in our country?"

"One would think so," the CIA man said. "But when I inquired about that, I couldn't get a confirmation or a denial from them. The FBI is being very guarded about the list."

"Interesting." The host turned full face to the camera. "My guest has been retired CIA officer Roger Luciano and his book *Little Amerika and Other Tales of the Cold War* is due out next month. This is David Houseman saying good night from CSPAN's Week in Review. I'll see you next week."

Feeling like every eye in the place was on him, Gordon calmly put his Beretta back together, walked to his wall locker and put the pistol back in its holster on his assault harness. He picked up the paperback on the shelf of his locker and headed for his bunk.

Reading was a popular way to pass time in the blacksuit barracks, but the selection of books in the floating library left a lot to be desired. Most of his fellow guards seemed to be addicted to military-action thrillers and murder mysteries. Lying down, he snapped on the reading light.

Over the years he had been in the United States, he had become a big fan of the tell-all books about the cold war that started coming out as soon as the Soviet Union collapsed. Now that the threat was seen to be over, men who should have known better were rushing to publish their accounts of what had "actually" happened during those years. Some of the books were little more than self-aggrandizing novels, but some of them were serious accounts of long-held secrets, as serious as death, and very revealing.

Until he read the most recent accounts of the Cuban Missile Crisis, he hadn't known how serious that incident had been. Neither had the American people known, which had made the books bestsellers. The fact that U.S. intelligence hadn't been aware of the Russian tactical nuclear weapons that had already been operational on the island amused him. Only now was the American public learning how close they had come to nuclear annihilation.

The accounts of the CIA operatives who had supported the Mujahideen in Afghanistan during that debacle also interested him. Several of the young Russians who had lost their lives in that struggle had been classmates who hadn't made the final cut for the Foreign Service arm of the KGB. To learn what a great part the CIA had played in defeating the Red Army infuriated him.

If this CIA agent-turned-writer was telling the truth, he was in serious jeopardy. A list of the Little Amerika cover names for the agents who had been dispatched in the last twelve years of the program would contain the name James T. Gordon, and that Jim Gordon was him.

One time, he had gone on the Internet and had searched for his name and had come up with almost a hundred James Gordons. He had even found a dozen James T. Gordons. Even the FBI should be able to check out the names on that list and come up with him sooner or later. While he knew that it would take them longer rather than sooner to find him, he knew that they finally would.

Having been a federal marshal, Gordon didn't

have a high opinion of the FBI's ability to pour water from a boot with the instructions printed on the bottom of the heel. The bureau was so top-heavy with self-serving bureaucrats that it was a wonder they were able to do anything at all. The only time they got off their apexes and did something useful was after a disaster like the Trade Center bombing or the Oklahoma City tragedy. In his opinion, the rest of the time they were a highly paid federal clown show. Waco, the Ruby Ridge incident and the Atlanta Olympic Village bombing investigation clearly illustrated that point.

Even so, he also knew that the FBI headquarters had an entire floor populated with computer nerds who had nothing better to do than run lists through their data banks. He had no idea how long it would take them to run that list, but he didn't think it would take very long. What would take forever, though, would be getting the information down to the field offices to check out each of the names. The field agents would then have to schedule that task in between their other important investigative work, like keeping the local doughnut shops in business and trying to infiltrate the region's militia groups.

He had to decide whether to cut and run now, or to wait out his tour and disappear during his R and R phase. The safest course of action would be to clear out now. But he was determined to take this organization down, and he didn't have enough information to do that yet. Though it would mean accepting a greater risk, he decided that he would stay in place until his normal rotation came. But he would start working on his escape and evasion plan tomorrow morning. If it came down to needing it, he wouldn't have time to make it up as he went along.

The number-one item on that list was figuring how to get his hands on Barbara Price if he had to leave in a hurry. With her as a hostage, no one would be too anxious to pop caps on him and risk hitting her.

The blacksuit defense plans included detailed diagrams of the buildings on the property, and he would have to memorize the layout of the main house. Since that was where she lived and worked, that was where he'd be most likely to find her day or night. He was scheduled to work the close-in team in the morning, and he'd get his first good look at the layout.

Once he'd done that, he'd have a better idea of what he was facing and could take it from there.

CHAPTER THIRTEEN

Moscow, Russia

Ex-Spetsnaz Major Vasily Lebedev intended to go about fulfilling his new mission as he had always done, by starting with a careful recon. The problem this time was that he didn't know where these elusive Yankees were or if they were really in Russia. It wasn't his place to argue with the general, but it could be that he and his men were being sent on a fool's errand. Either way, he didn't care as long as he was being paid. He actually would enjoy going up against Americans again, though. His Wolverines had tracked down a few American mercenaries who had been working for the rebels during the Afghan War, and they had died like all the rest.

A couple of the Americans he had encountered had been worthy opponents, CIA agents who were supplying the rebels. But the others had been like children caught up in something they hadn't expected. They had been idealistic, anti-Communists who had dreams of being the next Lawrence of Arabia, but the Afghans weren't Arabs and the harsh terrain of Afghanistan made the Arabian deserts look positively hospitable. The biggest difference was that the Red Army hadn't been the third-rate Turkish forces Lawrence had fought.

Political considerations had prevented him from parading the Yankees' bodies through the streets of Kabul for the Western TV cameras. Instead, he had simply hunted them down, killed them and buried them where they fell. When he caught up with this new bunch of Yankees, they would get the same treatment, a quick death and an unmarked grave. First, though, he had to find them, and that was the challenge. He had no doubt of the outcome, though. If they were in Russia, his men would hunt them down. The Wolverines never gave up.

First, he would start by dogging Leoninski's criminal thugs. If the Americans were onto them, they might lead his men to the target. While the Yankees were busy chasing them, they might not be paying too much attention to whoever was following them. That was a common enough tactic, and he had used it many times in Afghanistan where the rebel factions had fought each other as often as they had fought the Russians.

He had also been given an expense account over and above his usual mercenary fee. That gave him the means to hire other men to keep an eye on the places his own men couldn't watch. He would hire only veterans, though, good Red Army men. There were more than enough of them with free time on their hands, and they were always up to make a few extra rubles. He would make a rare appearance at his Veterans' Club on Pogorny Street to do his recruiting.

A call from Lion Leoninski put that on hold, however. When he hung up the phone, he didn't know what to think. But he had to admit that the crime lord's suspicions were worth looking into. Even if these Mexican drug dealers weren't Yankee commandos, they were foreign scum and Russia would be better off without them. Checking his roster, he chose two of his better men and gave them their orders.

MOSCOW'S FAMED Metro Grand Hotel was a showplace of Slavic elegance, the very best that a struggling Russian democracy could provide. The building itself was a masterpiece of architectural grandeur. Gold leaf and mirror-polished marble blended with rare woods and expensive Oriental carpets to create a fairy-tale palace. It took the term ''home away from home'' to new heights.

Only the absolute best was good enough for the guests of the Metro Grand. The food was unlike anything that could be found anywhere else in Moscow. The same could be said of the liquor in the hotel's many bars and cabarets, and the entertainment was world renowned. It was the unofficial entertainment, however, that drew Western businessmen to the hotel in droves, regardless of the expense. The Metro Grand simply had the best-looking women in Europe working the bars and guest rooms.

Unlike in American hotels, the Metro Grand's staff made no effort to prevent the working girls from plying their trade on the premises. In fact the management encouraged hustling as long as it got its cut of the girls' earnings. To maintain the reputation of providing only the best for their guests, the management carefully selected the girls and had them medically inspected like so much prime beef. This supervision, however, wasn't conducted on the hotel's premises. That job had been subcontracted to Leoninski's organization. The Lion had a lot of experience in that area, and his girls knew better than to cross him.

The Mafia boss also took a cut of the girls' wages, but any woman lucky enough to get a job with him was ensured of making more money than any three independent streetwalkers combined, and the list of willing applicants was long. The Lion not only made a great deal of money from this flesh trade, the working girls were also one of his most important sources of information. Most men like to brag to their bed partners, and Western businessmen were no exception, particularly Americans. Using what the girls heard and saw, Leoninski was able to stay well ahead of his competition as well as sell what his network picked up.

This time, however, his spies hadn't given him much. The Mexican drug dealers were staying in the Metro Grand, but they weren't sampling the hotel's delights. It wasn't for lack of trying, though. The girls were trying hard to score with them. He had offered a nice bonus to the first girl who brought him the information he wanted, and he knew they were hustling their shapely assets. But, for some reason, it wasn't working this time.

This bothered the Mafia boss. To his mind, all men had weaknesses, but these men were acting like they were monks. And not only were they resisting the exotic, Slavic charms of the girls, they weren't drinking much, either. In a country where alcoholism was rampant, that alone was enough to draw attention to them. But not to drink or fornicate was unnatural behavior for a man. It spoke of military-style discipline, and that raised his suspicions.

Leoninski had studied the American Mafia and the Colombia cartels carefully, but he didn't have much first-line information on the Mexican drug gangs. They were Hispanics, though, and he would have expected them to be hot after the women, and the fact that they weren't only reinforced his suspicions. The thought that they might be American agents started to surface in his mind. Leoninski had long-since learned to trust his instincts and to act on them.

A studied response was fine and good, but a gut feeling came from information buried in his subconscious. His brain had been working overtime since the Mexicans had shown up, and the shoot-out at the drop site was the final piece of the puzzle he had needed to make up his mind about them.

He wasn't going to get drawn into another ambush and, since the general had given him the services of the Wolverines, he didn't have to. Since they weren't making much progress on locating the Yankee commando team he had sent them against, they should have time to take care of this other matter for him.

The thought had crossed his mind that it wasn't impossible that the two groups were working together. He was aware that many Americans were of Mexican descent, and it wasn't beyond possibility that the Mexicans weren't drug dealers at all, but enemy agents. Either way, though, he had made his decision and, if it did turn out that they were legitimate drug buyers, he could always say that a rival gang had been responsible for their deaths.

THE TWO WOLVERINES automatically took the stairs from the lobby of the Metro Grand, heading for the third floor. Being caught in an elevator in enemy territory wasn't the kind of move they were likely to make. In their profession, they wouldn't live long if they made too many amateurish moves. Plus, the two men were in such superb physical shape they could have sprinted up the stairs, taking two steps at a time. Lebedev didn't let his people run to flab.

The first Wolverine cleared the third-floor hallway before signaling for his comrade to join him. Their overcoats were open as they walked down the corridor, their hands on the butts of the silenced Czech Skorpion machine pistols hanging on shoulder straps. Their orders were to capture at least one of the Yankees if possible, but the others were expendable. Since neither one of them had any great love for Americans, it was no big deal. It would also be no big deal if all of the Yankees died. They weren't going to take risks to effect a capture.

"IT'S GOING DOWN." Gadgets Schwarz sounded almost gleeful. "I've got two goons coming down the hall with their coats open, and they look like they're ready to rock and roll."

"Are they alone?" Carl Lyons asked.

"So far."

One of Schwarz's first jobs after stepping foot on Russian soil had been to wire the "drug dealer's" hotel room with subminiature video cameras and other security devices. An enclosed room wasn't a trap unless the occupants didn't know that it was. With the proper preparation, a room could become a fortress, and a trap for any attacker. It was a game the Able Team warriors had played many times before.

Lyons grinned at the news. "Let's do it."

The ex-LAPD cop took his position behind the protection of the bed in the master bedroom of the suite, a silenced Beretta 93-R pistol in his hand.

Schwarz had a silenced MP-5 SD to do the heavy work if things got out of hand, but the plan didn't call for him to use it.

Rosario Blancanales had the dangerous job this time. He was the "tagger," and his weapon was a dart gun designed for animal control officers. With the proper load in the dart, it would work on a self-styled Wolverine as well.

Watching the monitor above the bedroom door, the trio waited.

THE WOLVERINES PAUSED outside the door to room 307. Reaching into his pocket, the lead man produced a pass key and silently opened the lock. There was no point in booting the door when Leoninski had been kind enough to provide them the key.

On a silent count of three, they slammed open the door and raced into the sitting room. Seeing the room empty, they headed for the master bedroom, their weapons at the ready.

Blancanales took his shot as the lead Wolverine dashed into the bedroom and was rewarded by seeing the dart take him in the neck. His work done, he dropped to the floor to give his teammates a free field of fire.

The second Russian got off a quick burst, the bullets chewing the bedding, before Lyons put him down with two quick shots to the head.

"NICE SHOT," Schwarz said when he saw the end of the dart sticking out of the first Wolverine's neck. "Looks like you got him right in the carotid."

"Pull it out, so he doesn't OD on it," Blancanales said.

"The other one's dead," Lyons announced with no surprise. Head shots rarely resulted in anything else. "Get that guy on his feet and let's get out of here."

The suite had been cleaned out already, so as soon as they closed the door behind them, all traces of their presence would be gone. Except, of course, for the body on the floor. They left it to send Major Lebedev a message. The Wolverines weren't the only predators in the jungle, and sometimes the lesser animals needed to be reminded of that fact.

Lyons and Blancanales supported the unconscious Russian commando between them as they headed for the service elevator at the end of the hall. If anyone saw them with their prisoner, they would think that he was just another passed-out drunk being helped to his room.

Schwarz walked far enough behind them that he might have been on his own rather than being part of the party. If they were interrupted, he'd provide covering fire while they got their prisoner to safety.

INTERROGATING the captured Wolverine didn't go as well as Calvin James would have liked. Even with the drug cocktail, all he got out of him was a mumbled name that not even Belakov could understand.

"We're going to have to let him sleep off the tranquilizer before this is going to work," he told Katzenelenbogen.

"Toss him in with the other guy."

The Mafia prisoner from the tragic kidnapping raid had been housed in the basement cell of the safehouse. Holding cells were popular in Soviet architecture, and this building had once been used by the KGB.

"What are we going to do with him anyway?" Encizo asked.

"He stays for now," Katz said. "When this has been wrapped up, I promised him to Yuri."

Encizo understood.

THE ATTACK at the Metro Grand represented a dramatic escalation, and it was time for the Stony Man team to reassess the situation and look at their options.

"Okay," Katz said, opening the team meeting, "we drew first blood on these Wolverine guys, but we all know it's not going to stop with that."

He turned to Belakov. "You were right about them being targeted against us. Do you think your sources can help us track them down? I'd like to hit them again as soon as we can to keep them off balance."

"We can try," the SVR agent replied. "But I can tell you right now that the minister is going to want more movement on locating the tank brigade in return. He sees the threat that the Wolverines present, but he thinks the tanks are even more of a problem."

"Not for us they aren't," Lyons said. "We haven't been shot at by tanks."

"Not yet."

"Also," Katz continued, "the Metro hit indicates that we've run our string out with the drug-buy scam. The Lion's obviously on to us, so we can drop that gig.''

"Thank God," Lyons said. "Now we can burn that shit we captured."

"Not quite yet. After all, as Calvin would say, 'two mil's a lot of bread in this "hood".' I think that if Leoninski were to hear that his product was being transported to a burn site, he might want to try to get it back."

McCarter chuckled. "You're a bloody-minded bugger, mate."

"Aren't I just?"

Belakov was looking a bit confused. This tactical planning session was going in more directions than a grenade explosion. "And you think he'll call the Wolverines to do it?"

"The chances are good that he will, yes."

"But how will he learn about it?"

"That's the fun part," the Israeli said. "Our cover has been blown, so it's time that we make our official appearance. You are going to take James, Lyons and Blancanales in to talk to the minister."

He looked over at Lyons. "I want you three to go on stage because Leoninski has already met you and your cover's blown. That'll leave the rest of us in the shadows for now.

"Anyway, Yuri," Katz continued, "while you're briefing the minister on our progress so far, you'll ask his permission for us to burn the heroin we captured. Make sure that our operation is trumpeted as a roaring success against the Mafia, the first blow in a planned series of actions intended to rid Russia of this scourge.''

Belakov blinked. The whole mission had been planned around the American commandos remaining completely anonymous. The fear was that the rival parties would see them as Americans meddling in Russian internal affairs.

''I'm not sure that the minister is going to agree to doing that,'' he said. ''You know our concern about word of American intervention in our internal affairs getting out. He's afraid that it will do more harm than good.''

''The only candidate who's going to play that card already knows that we're here,'' Katz pointed out. ''The general knows who we are and what we're doing here. He might make it public, true. But your minister can easily counter that by making the general's connection with the Mafia public knowledge, so I wouldn't worry too much about it. And, now that we're going to be in the open, so to speak, I'd like to borrow a couple of RPG launchers and a dozen rockets or so.''

Now Belakov was really confused. ''What for?''

Katz grinned widely. ''I want to send Leoninski a personal message. A few antitank rockets in the right place will go a long way to getting his attention.''

The SVR agent blinked hard. These Americans didn't take half measures.

CHAPTER FOURTEEN

Moscow, Russia

As he surveyed the room in the Metro Grand Hotel where the body of his man had been found, Vasily Lebedev no longer had any doubt that an American hit team was operating in Russia. The earmarks of professionals were all over the scene. The fact that the second Wolverine was missing wasn't half as troubling as why he was. Lebedev had sent two of his best men to take care of what should have been a routine job, men who should have been able to handle it blindfolded. That they hadn't been able to do it spoke volumes.

Part of him was glad that this had gone down this way. He wasn't happy that he had lost the men, his men were his family and he would mourn them. But he would avenge them first; that was the Wolverine way. Every time one of his men had fallen in Afghanistan, he had made the Mujahideen pay dearly. The Afghan village closest to each ambush site where a Wolverine had died had been razed and the inhabitants left impaled as a warning to others.

He couldn't go to the United States and devastate Washington, D.C., in retaliation, but he would see that every one of the Yankee commandos were in their graves before this was finished. Blood called for blood.

This incident had also shown him that Leoninski wasn't quite the overbearing buffoon he had appeared to be. As a professional soldier, Lebedev tended to see criminals as scum who were hardly worth the bullet in the head they all deserved. But he had to admit that this particular scumbag was a cut above the usual criminal. At least he had decent sources of information. He would remember to pay more attention to the crime lord in the future.

The only part of this affair that brought him joy was that he finally had worthy opponents and a good reason to take them down. He would have done it anyway because the general had ordered him to do it. But, this way, he had an added incentive to make the kills—vengeance. It was the spice that made the blood of an enemy taste so sweet. He knew, though, that they wouldn't be easy kills to make. What had happened here proved that only too well. But that made it more exciting. Killing men who were no better than animals held no joy for him. A kill was only satisfying when he had to work for it even when the work wouldn't be easy.

The hotel room had been completely cleaned of evidence as only professionals would do. Not a trace of them had been left behind. The room had been paid for with cash, not a credit card that could be traced. They had made no phone calls from the room, nor had they sent any faxes. There was no way to trace where they had gone or what they had done during their stay at the Metro Grand. But he was confident that they wouldn't remain hidden very long.

The rest of his Wolverines were already on the streets trying to develop a lead. The general also had an informant inside the Ministry of the Interior trying to locate the Americans' hideout. Once he had that information, his men would do what they did so well. Until then, he had a job to do. With the Wolverines two men short now, he knew where to go to find their replacements.

WHEN LEBEDEV LEFT the hotel for the Pogorny Street Veterans' Club, Josef Leoninski was in General Pavel Zerinov's Moscow office. When the body had been discovered, the hotel staff had called him immediately. Rather than go to the hotel, though, he had gone directly to the general.

"I told you those damned Yankees were here," Leoninski growled, fighting to keep his temper under control. He didn't know why it was so difficult to get through to this man. "Now do you believe me?"

For once Zerinov dropped the superior attitude and was listening to Leoninski as if he were almost an equal in this endeavor. The fact that Lebedev's Wolverines had lost two men, combined with the report from his man in the ministry, could not be ignored. An American commando team was on the loose in Moscow.

"I am sorry I doubted you. There is no longer any question about what you say. The Americans have involved themselves in our affairs, but I can assure you that they will be taken care of immediately."

"By your Wolverines?" Leoninski sneered. "They've already had their chance at the Metro, and they failed. I might as well have called in a platoon of Young Pioneers to handle the job."

The general stiffened momentarily. To have his men spoken of that way by a street criminal would normally be a capital offense. He reined himself in, though, and relaxed. He had to keep in mind that he was a politician first now and a general last. When he took over the presidency, however, those positions would be reversed and he'd take care of this piece of human garbage then.

"They will be punished," Zerinov stated flatly. "You have my word on that."

"I cannot afford to wait for your action," Leoninski said. "So I'm sure you will not object if my men go after them as well."

"Not at all, Josef. It doesn't really matter who kills them, just as long as they die."

To Yuri Belakov's amazement, the minister readily agreed to Katz's plan. That afternoon, Rosario Blancanales and Calvin James went to the ministry for a meeting with him. While they weren't carrying their ID cards around their necks, the word quickly got out that they were two of the Americans who were assisting with the minister's ongoing operations against the Mafia drug lords.

After going over the plan and getting the minister's approval, most of the actual meeting was small talk, but it had the desired effect. Everyone in the building learned about their score of the heroin shipment, and rumors about what they were going to do with it hit Moscow's streets almost before James and Blancanales themselves did.

When the team returned to the safehouse, Katz took their report, then filled them in on what had happened while they had been gone. "We're not going to be able to get anything out of the guy you tagged at the hotel," he warned Blancanales.

"What happened?"

"It looks like our captive Wolverine killed the Mafia guy, then opened his own wrists. It was done silently and we didn't hear a thing. We'll leave the bodies in Gorky Park tonight," Katz said, "so the cops will find them in the morning."

"Are you going to send any messages with them?" James asked.

"I think they'll be message enough."

ANYONE SEEING THE CONVOY slowly moving along the dirt road west of Moscow the following afternoon would have thought that nuclear material or gold bullion was being transported. A pair of BRDM armored scout cars armed with 37 mm machine cannons in their turrets led the procession, followed by a two-ton troop carrier. A black Mercedes sedan trailed the truck, and was itself followed by a large white van. Another troop carrier followed the van and another BRDM brought up the rear.

The only thing that was out of place was that the convoy was headed for the city's largest dump site, not a bank or a nuclear repository. The contents of the truck, though, while only an agricultural product, were almost as valuable as gold and as potentially explosive as a nuclear bomb.

The convoy guards were handpicked internal security troops from the Ministry of the Interior, and their orders were to protect the shipment to the death. Only the leader of the detachment had any idea that the truck's contents weren't what they had been advertised to be. He really didn't care one way or the other as long as he got a chance to target the Mafia scum who were threatening the security of Mother Russia. He didn't know who had put this operation together, but he hoped that they were given a medal for it.

As Katz had suggested, the capture of two million dollars' worth of Afghan heroin had been trumpeted in the media as being a great blow to the Russian Mafia. After consultation with Hal Brognola, the Interior Minister announced that the seizure had been accomplished through information that had been developed by American law-enforcement agencies. Since the American FBI and DEA had worked with the new Russian government before, this was accepted without much comment.

The plan to destroy the heroin wasn't released to the press, but the ministry made sure that the word got out after James's and Blancanales's visit to his office. Within hours, it was being openly discussed by every gangster, cop and SVR agent in town. Bets were being placed as to who would actually end up with the heroin shipment, the Mafia or the burn pit. The bookmakers' odds were running that the Mafia would recover the load.

Even Yuri Belakov put a few rubles in the pot, but he was betting against the odds. If Katz's plan worked, he'd become a wealthy man. If, that was, he lived to collect his bet. Katz's plan depended on the bait being taken. If it wasn't, he'd be on the firing line again.

THE HEAVILY GUARDED heroin convoy was still two miles from the dump when it came under attack. As had been done to convoys in Afghanistan, the first and last vehicles were attacked first to block the road. Once it was halted, the convoy came under heavy fire.

"I almost feel sorry for those guys," Schwarz said as he watched the smoke rise over the site of the battle raging a mile away. The roaring cough of the scout car's 37 mm auto cannons could be heard over the rattle of small-arms fire. Someone was getting their butts kicked, and he didn't think it was the good guys.

Just then he heard a sharp explosion, and a fireball roiled over one of the armored vehicles. Someone had cut loose with an RPG rocket launcher. It was a heavy-duty piece of hardware that could cause some serious damage to the minister's troops.

"You won't feel so sorry for them if they break through and find out that truck isn't carrying the goods." Lyons followed the battle through his field glasses. "If they get it in their heads to search all of the trucks going into the dump, we might have a battle on our hands ourselves."

"I thought that's why we're driving this damned truck," Schwarz said. "No one's going to want to paw through the contents of a Russian garbage truck."

While the convoy had taken the side road that led to the sanitary fill, Schwarz's battered garbage truck was in-line with all the rest of Moscow's reeking trash haulers moving at a snail's pace to the main entrance of the burn pit. His truck had been taken off one of the city's regular pickup routes. It was no less battered and no more clean than any of the others in the slow-moving line waiting to tip their loads and go out to collect more. It was, however, the only garbage truck in Russia with two million dollars' worth of heroin buried under the trash it carried.

"Don't bet on that," McCarter called out over the com link. "We've got a couple of cars coming up behind us in a big hurry."

The vehicle following Schwarz's garbage truck was a big van not unlike many of the other miscellaneous trucks waiting to off-load at the burn site. In this case, however, the van was being driven by Jack Grimaldi, and it was carrying the Phoenix Force commandos in the back. Katz was betting that his ruse would work, but he wasn't betting the farm. If Leoninski's thugs figured this out, he and the Stony Man team would try to hold them off long enough for Blancanales and Lyons to set the garbage truck's load on fire with thermite grenades.

One way or the other, the heroin shipment was going to be destroyed.

"Get ready with the door," McCarter said as he watched the two cars approach. "It looks like they're onto us."

"Got it," Encizo said.

T. J. Hawkins stood ready with an over-and-under M-16-M-203 combo in his hands. Calvin James stood beside him with his H&K.

"Now," McCarter yelled to Encizo.

When the door whipped open, Hawkins and James stepped forward to deal with the threat.

"Hold it," McCarter cautioned. "I think they're just trying to pass us."

Leaving the rear door open, James and Hawkins stepped back.

"How much farther is it, Gadgets?" Grimaldi asked over the com link.

"Just a couple hundred yards more," Schwarz radioed. "I can't push them out of the way."

"At least nudge the bastards with your bumper,"

Grimaldi suggested. "We've got to get inside the fence."

BY THE TIME the attackers of the convoy were beaten off, Schwarz's truck was inside the fenced area of the dump and was the next in line to drop its load. The Phoenix Force's van had stopped right inside the gate, and the commandos were preventing anyone else from coming in until they were finished burning their contraband.

As soon as Schwarz had his truck positioned on the ramp, Lyons hit the hydraulic ramp control to tip the bed. Under the mass of common street garbage inside, the bundles of heroin started dropping into the fire.

When the sanitary workers saw what was being burned, they shouted in alarm. They had all heard the rumors and rushed forward to try to salvage the bundles.

"Get back!" Lyons sent a burst of 9 mm lead from his subgun into the burning refuse.

Belakov brandished his submachine gun in one hand and his SVR ID badge in the other as he shouted at the workers in Russian. "Stand back! This is State security business. If you interfere, you will be shot."

Faced with the weapons, the Russian workers were forced to back off. Some of them had tears in their eyes as they watched two million dollars' worth of heroin go up in smoke. The burning took some time, and the Stony Man warriors made sure that they stayed downwind during the process to avoid a contact high from that stuff.

With the burn site shut down while the heroin was being destroyed, the drivers of the trucks waiting to dump their loads started to get angry at the delay. Again Belakov flashed his badge to back up the weapons of Phoenix Force, but the drivers were made of a little sterner stuff than the garbage-pit men. They were ready to face-off against the commandos until the surviving scout car from the decoy convoy rolled up. Since none of the garbage-truck drivers wanted to deal with a 37 mm auto cannon, they immediately calmed down.

When the last plastic-wrapped bundle of heroin had been burned, Schwarz pulled his garbage truck off to the side and left it. Belakov would make arrangements to have it delivered back to the sanitation department later.

When Able Team joined Phoenix Force in the back of the van for the ride back to Moscow, McCarter slapped Schwarz on the back. "That's a new one to put on your résumé, Gadgets," he said. "Garbage-truck driver."

"Russian garbage-truck driver," Schwarz said. "The distinction is important."

CHAPTER FIFTEEN

Stony Man Farm, Virginia

"A big part of the problem," Hunt Wethers reported to Aaron Kurtzman, "is that the old Soviets didn't take very good care of their part of Mother Earth. If they'd been better caretakers, this task would have been much easier. It's almost like they did it on purpose."

Kurtzman had to resist the urge to ask Wethers what in the hell he was talking about. He knew him well enough, however, to know that he was building up to something and that this seemingly meaningless preamble would come out as usable information at the end.

"It's like they really didn't care what they were doing to their environment. It's unbelievable. It seemed their philosophy was 'anything goes.'"

That shouldn't have been big news to Wethers or anyone else who could read a newspaper. The Soviets had left a real mess behind in their frantic quest to outproduce the West and establish world domination. The most severely polluted water and land on earth was all within the boundaries of the old Soviet Union. Thousands of square miles were so radioactive that they almost glowed in the dark. Lakes and rivers were so contaminated that drinking their water was a death sentence. What that had to do with a missing tank brigade Kurtzman had no idea, but it was fascinating background information.

"And...?" he prompted, trying to nudge Wethers forward.

"And the sensor readouts keep giving us large magnetic masses that, on closer inspection, turn out to be mine tailings, particularly in the Urals, or abandoned heavy equipment. You can't believe the amount of land that is covered with them. They've made no reclamation efforts at—"

"Bottom line, Hunt." Kurtzman broke into his lecture on the mining industry and land-reclamation practices.

"Oh, yes. We have a strong MAD reading in what is supposed to be a national forest. But it's close to an old iron mine, so I'm not sure. We also have some IR traces, but the trees are so thick, it could be something else. Then, of course, there's the—"

"Hunt!"

"We picked up diesel pollution from multiple sources and the combustion byproducts indicate low-sulfur fuel, so we don't think it's from oil heaters."

"It's tank engines?"

"We think so."

Kurtzman remembered reading Field Marshal Guderian's accounts of the war on the Eastern Front and how the Russians would run their tank engines throughout the night to keep them from freezing, ready to move out instantly. Since the Germans were always low on fuel, they were sometimes caught with their tanks immobile until they could be started and warmed up.

"Can we work that site more?"

"Not with the satellites I have right now," Wethers said. "I need the Deep Look bird, and it's watching that China launch site right now."

"There's no penetrating radar capability on hand?"

"Not for three more days."

With Hal Brognola breathing down their backs on behalf of the Man, who was preoccupied with the Russian minister's concerns, three days wasn't going to cut it.

"Give me hard copy on what you have—the readouts, the topo maps, the photos and the analysis of the pollutants—and I'll show it to Hal. If he think's it's good, Katz can break a couple of the guys loose to go take a closer look."

"They'd better hurry. If it is the brigade, I think they're getting ready to move."

If Kurtzman could have jumped he would have. "Dammit, Hunt, you should have said that first."

"But I'm not sure that it's the right target. It could be a logging or mining camp."

Kurtzman reached out for the intercom button to

Brognola's office. "Get me the hard copy now," he told Wethers. "I want to run it past Hal."

"It'll just take a minute."

WETHERS'S CONCLUSIONS were good enough for Hal Brognola. It sometimes took the former professor awhile to come to a conclusion, but when he did, it was rarely off target.

"Good work," he said. "I'll get this to the White House right away.

"And," he added, turning to Kurtzman, "send this to Katz ASAP."

"It's on the way."

Brognola stopped off to see Barbara Price before leaving for Washington. He was planning to spend a day or two clearing his desk at his Justice Department office before returning to the Farm. A mission with this level of political interest was always sensitive, but it wasn't helping to have him hanging around looking over everyone's shoulders.

He found Price in her office taking care of her other full-time job, running the Farm. She looked up as he walked in. "You have that 'go to Washington' look again. What's up?"

"Hunt thinks he's found the missing tanks, and I'm going to deliver it to the Man so he'll get off our backs."

"While you're there, you might want to ask him what he thinks the team is going to do about it now that we've found them. Less than a dozen guys taking on a brigade of armor with H&Ks isn't my idea of a plausible scenario for success. I know our guys are good, but there are limits to what even they can do. I suggest that the minister roll a couple of armored divisions to deal with the problem.''

Brognola took the guest chair next to her desk. There was a part of this program that he hadn't told her about yet. The President had ordered him to release the information only when he said it was time. But the time for this bit of bad news had come.

''Well,'' he said, ''It seems—''

''Hal,'' she broke in, ''you promised that you were never going to piecemeal information to me again. If you've been holding something back from me, I swear I'm going to kick your sorry ass.''

''Barbara—''

''Don't 'Barbara' me, dammit. We can't do business that way, and you know it. We have to have everything up front before we go in. Katz and I can't plan for something we don't know about, and you know that, Hal.''

''This came to light after the guys flew into Moscow,'' he explained.

''And it just slipped your mind.''

''Actually it did.''

''Hal, if I have to go to Washington to get this sorted out I will. You know that. And if I think that the President's playing games with us, I can lock this whole place down and nothing will get done.''

''It didn't come from the President,'' Brognola said. ''It came from Moscow as an FYI for us. The minister said that he's not sure that he can send army units against the renegade brigade. He's afraid that if he tries, it might spark a military coup.''

"Beautiful.'' She closed her eyes and started to massage her temples.

"It seems that the tank generals are waiting to see what happens with Zerinov's candidacy. If he loses the election, they'll move on his supporters and put them down. If he wins, they don't want to be out of a job.''

"But if they don't move now, that brigade will ensure that Zerinov wins.''

"That's about it,'' Brognola admitted.

She leaned back in her chair. "Can you tell me why we're even over there, Hal? Why is the Man so willing to get our teams involved?''

"We have to try to help the Russians,'' he said simply. "If we can pull this off and save their democracy, we'll all be better off. If we can't, and the cold war starts up again, at least we can say that we tried. There's no guarantee, but I think we owe it to ourselves to at least try.''

"I hate it when you're so logical.''

He smiled thinly. "Sorry.''

"You should be. And,'' she said, glancing at the monitor showing the chopper pad outside, "your ride is here. You don't want to keep the Man waiting.''

THE INFORMATION Stony Man Farm forwarded about the tank brigade's location put Katzenelenbogen's Moscow operation on hold. Like it or not, the armor had the higher priority.

"I hate to stop when we're on a roll," he told Bolan and McCarter, "but I think we need to act on this one immediately."

"We can turn it over to the Russians," McCarter said. "They can send their own army to take care of the bastards. You're talking about a bloody tank brigade, remember."

"Normally I'd agree with you," Katz replied. "But that might not be possible this time. I also got a heads-up on the side from Barbara about a little problem neither the minister nor Belakov have bothered to mention to us."

"What's the catch this time?" Bolan asked Katz.

"It appears that all of the army's armored division commanders have gone on holiday, waiting the outcome of the election. They're afraid that if they try to move against Zerinov and he wins anyway, they'll be put up against the wall and shot."

"I think we need our SVR representative sitting in on this conversation," Bolan said. "He needs to know about this too."

"What makes you think Belakov doesn't know already?" McCarter asked.

"I don't think he does," Bolan replied. "I think he's trying to play the game with us and his minister stonewalled him on this one."

"Not bloody likely."

"Let's try him and see."

When Yuri Belakov walked into the makeshift

war room, he instantly saw that something had gone wrong. McCarter looked like he wanted to go for his throat, and Katz wasn't smiling. Only the one called Striker looked as he always did, watchful and ready.

"What is it?"

"Take a seat," Bolan said. "The problem is that we just received a communication in a roundabout manner telling us that your minister doesn't trust his armored unit commanders to carry out their orders."

"It is true that some of them seem to be favoring Zerinov in the election," Belakov replied, "but I know nothing about their refusing to obey the lawful orders of the government. Why do you ask?"

"We have also probably located the missing armored brigade," Katz said, "but our people in Washington tell us that your minister has warned our President that he doesn't trust the army to investigate it properly, much less to move against it."

It was clear to see that Belakov was stunned. For a long moment, the young Russian didn't know what to say.

"Gentlemen, I know nothing of this. If you will excuse me, I will call the minister right now and ask for clarification."

"Stay seated," McCarter told him.

"If this information is true," Bolan explained, "it means that our mission here is pretty much over. If the tanks are where we think they are, there's nothing we can do about them. No eleven men on earth can take on a Russian tank brigade and live. It's as simple as that. We were asked to find the missing tanks, and we have done that. If the Russian army won't move against them if ordered to, there's nothing else we can do here.''

"But you have been making such good progress against Leoninski and his men."

"Which means nothing if the tanks roll before election day. Zerinov will be elected and Russia will be his, Mafia or no Mafia."

Belakov saw the truth in that and realized that he, too, had been betrayed. "Gentlemen, I do not know what to say. All I know is that you men are the last chance we Russians have to salvage something from the ruins we have worked so hard to create. There are times that I am ashamed to be a Russian, but I have told myself that I've to keep trying to bring my people into the light. But, after so many years of darkness, it is not an easy task."

He got to his feet. "It has been a pleasure to work with you and I shall never forget what you have tried to do for my people. On behalf of those few of us who want to do right, I thank you for your efforts and wish you all Godspeed back to your own country."

Belakov bowed his head. "Gentleman, if you'll excuse me."

"Sit, Yuri," McCarter said gently. "We're not done here yet."

"But, if what you say it true, what can you do? You don't have tanks to fight with."

"First off," Katz replied, "we can take a look at

the information we were sent, talk about it and see if there is any way we can deal with the problem. Tanks are all fine and good, but I've seen more than one of the bloody things burned to a crisp by a pissed-off infantryman. You Russians have always put too much emphasis on armor.''

Belakov was stunned.

''Sit,'' Bolan said. ''Please.''

The Russian sat.

''Now,'' Katz said, ''let's see if we can come up with a way to stop those damned tanks from rolling.''

CHAPTER SIXTEEN

Moscow, Russia

It was early afternoon before Katzenelenbogen was ready to hold a full-team meeting. In those hours, however, a plan had been worked out that might yet save the Russians' election from being ground under the steel treads of the renegade armor unit. It was risky, but it had a chance of working. No one wanted to calculate the odds on that chance, though; the numbers would be too small.

The first thing he did was to lay out the military topo map Hunt Wethers had faxed them so the commandos could get a feel for what they would be going into. Map recon it was called, and it was always the first step of operational planning.

"The photos tell me that the map is accurate," Katz said. "So you shouldn't have any surprises when you get there and look at the ground."

During the cold war, making accurate maps had been a passion with the NRO, the National Reconnaissance Office, the supersecret organization that was responsible for America's spy satellites. Waging war successfully depended as much upon maps as it did on ammunition and men.

"What moron would put a tank brigade in a location that only has one exit?" T. J. Hawkins was incredulous when he saw the location of their target. "Even a brand-new second lieutenant fresh out of ROTC knows better than to do something that stupid."

According to the map, the brigade was parked on a flat-topped, forested hill with a rocky cliff on one side and a white-water river on the other. The only access to the hill was across a bridge spanning the chasm.

"Normally I'd agree with you," Katz said. "But you have to remember that this guy is trying to hide his tanks from curious eyes, and this location gives him absolute control of access to the area. All he has to do is guard the bridge and no one gets in."

Hawkins shook his head. "Man, I'd think of doing something else, anything else. We take that bridge down and we've got him cold unless he's figured out a way to make tanks fly."

"Don't forget his VLBs," McCarter pointed out. "A Russian armored brigade has organic Vehicular Launched Bridging equipment, and we have to assume he took them with him. If we don't take out enough of that bridge, he can throw a VLB span across the gap and move anyway."

"I guess we just have to blow up the whole damned thing then, don't we?" Hawkins grinned. Blowing up things was one of his passions.

"Easier said than done." Gary Manning looked up from the recon photos. Maps were fine to plan the overall movement, but photos were the only way one could really see what they were going to have to deal with.

"That's not your usual Eastern European under-engineered bridge," he explained. "This span was designed to handle heavy mining equipment. From what I can see from the photos, we're going to have our work cut out for us, and we're going to need a lot of specialized demo."

"Give me a list," Katz said. "I'll have it on the next plane out of Andrews."

"Is there anything we can supply for this job?" Belakov asked.

"Do you have access to Semtex blocks?" Manning asked. "It's an RDX made in Czechoslovakia. I mean the old Czechoslovakia."

Belakov thought for a moment. "That's what terrorists use to blow up planes, isn't it?"

"Too bloody right," McCarter responded. "Your old government used to give it away by the truckload to any Arab with his hand out. And the bloody Irish as well."

"I'll see what I can do," Belakov said, passing on McCarter's remark. The old KGB's support of antiWestern terrorism was still a sore spot. The new government was doing its best to open the files on Soviet contacts with terrorists, but too many of them had been purged when the KGB went out of existence.

"Find out quickly," Katz said. "If you don't have it, I'll need to put in an order ASAP."

Belakov got up from his chair. "How much do you need?"

Manning ran a few numbers on his pocket calculator. "I'd say at least two hundred pounds," he replied. "And we can use a mile of det cord and several hundred feet of linear shaped charge. We also need standard blasting caps and electric detonators."

"Det cord and the detonators I can get," Belakov said. "But I've never heard of linear shaped charge."

"What we really need," Calvin James said as he studied the map, "is an ADM."

"A small nuclear device," Manning explained.

Belakov recoiled. "But, we cannot—"

"We know that," Katz soothed. "Calvin was just saying that it would be easier to do it that way instead of having to pack in all of that demo."

"We'll also need a couple of vehicles," Manning said. "A one-ton truck and something faster if we have to get out of there in a hurry."

"They will be no problem," Belakov replied. "And I will be sure to get a—what do you call it—four-wheel drive?"

"How are we going to split our forces?" McCarter asked.

"The bridge team will be Striker, McCarter, Manning, Hawkins and Encizo," Katz replied. "That should be enough to go in and take care of the demolition and still be small enough not to be spotted.''

"Calvin," he said, turning to James. "I'd like you to stay back here to help me run the CP and give Able Team a hand with their chores. We have to maintain a presence here to cover the bridge mission. The last thing we need is to disappear suddenly and have someone wonder where we went.''

"Can I go to the bridge, too?" Belakov asked.

Katz glanced at Bolan, who nodded.

"Sure," he said. "We might need you if we run into a language problem.''

Belakov was proud that the team thought him trustworthy enough to be included in the action. Beyond being another gun hand, he wasn't sure how he could help them, but he'd do his best or die trying.

"What do you want us to do while Phoenix is blowing up the bridge?" Carl Lyons asked.

"There's still Leoninski to be taken care of," Katz said. "Even if we can keep that tank brigade off the streets, the Mafia can still buy a lot of votes on election day, so we need to keep the pressure on him.''

"What about the general?"

"If possible," Bolan said, "we want to leave him alive for the new government to take care of. I know he's a threat, but if we start killing legitimate candidates, we're no different than they are.''

"I can live with that," Lyons stated. "If, that is,

he keeps his ass out of the line of fire. If he pops a single cap at us, he's dead meat.''

"Fair enough.''

BY THE TIME Yuri Belakov returned with the demolition materials and the vehicles, Katz had received the update on the movement of the tanks Hunt Wethers had spotted and decided to dispatch the team now rather than wait for the specialized explosives to be flown in from the States. Belakov had come through with more than enough Russian-army-issue demolition material to take down that bridge and a couple more like it. They would go with what they had.

Along with another van, Belakov had secured an American-made Hummer. This was a civilian model of the rugged, versatile vehicle instead of the U.S. Army's M-998 version, but it could still climb mountains like a goat.

The demo and fighting gear were quickly loaded into the two vehicles and, with Belakov navigating, the Stony Man team headed south out of Moscow.

NOW THAT THE BRIDGE team was on its way, Katzenelenbogen could focus on the Mafia crime lord and his Wolverine allies. Even if they were able to immobilize the tanks, the battle wouldn't be won yet. The Mafia could still put enough pressure on the voters in the major cities to swing the election.

"Okay,'' Katz said as he assembled Calvin James, Jack Grimaldi and Able Team for a skull session. "Since we've lost Belakov's services as our resident Russian-language expert, I'll try to step in and cover that angle as we go into phase two."

"What do you have in mind?" Lyons asked.

"Well, I was thinking about cutting into the ranks of those so-called Wolverines again. They're the real danger to us. We take care of them, and Leoninski's thugs will be a piece of cake."

"Aren't you forgetting that we don't have a home phone number for those dudes?" James commented.

"I know. And that does present a bit of a problem. But I was thinking about setting out a target that they won't be able to pass up."

"What's that?"

"You and Blancanales," Katz replied.

"In your dreams, Katz," James snorted. "If you haven't noticed, man, I kind of stand out in a crowd around here. You have to go a long ways to find another brother in Moscow. And, when you do, he's wearing some kind of African getup. I've got to be the only American homeboy for a thousand miles around here."

"Precisely," Katz said. "That's why I want to use you two for the bait. You for the obvious reasons and Blancanales because he's been seen before in his Mexican cartel role. If one of the Mafia thugs see you two, the word will be passed on immediately."

"We're a little thin on backup right now," James pointed out.

"That, too, plays in our favor. We'll have fewer

bodies hanging around to be spotted by the opposition.''

James shook his head. "Man, I don't know if I like the sound of that."

"What were you thinking of doing?" Lyons asked.

"Well, I don't have a definite plan yet. I was hoping that you'd be able to help me come up with something."

"How about sitting tight until the guys get back?" James suggested.

"That's too much like playing reactive. I was thinking of going proactive in a big way."

"With just the five of us?"

"Six," Katz said. "I'll be available too."

The addition of one man to the mix might not have seemed like much with the odds the way they were, but Yakov Katzenelenbogen wasn't just any man. His operational experience started when he had been barely a teenager, and he had more combat time than anyone in the Stony Man organization except for the Executioner himself.

"And—" a smile slowly crossed the Israeli's face "—to kick off this new operation, I think we need to draw attention to ourselves."

James shook his head. Sometimes Katz's ideas bordered on the downright dangerous. "Why don't we just march across Red Square carrying signs saying 'Here we are! Come and get us,' Katz? Then we can hand out business cards with a map to this place printed on the back. That should get us a few customers.''

''That's not a bad idea,'' the Israeli said, grinning, ''but I was thinking of something a little more explosive.''

''Did someone mention explosives?'' Schwarz asked. ''I hate seeing Mack and the others have all the fun without me.''

THE ATTACK on Leoninski's Mafia headquarters was a repeat performance for Able Team. This time, though, they had Jack Grimaldi as their wheelman for this drive-by attack. Gadgets Schwarz and Rosario Blancanales would be the RPG gunners while Carl Lyons would be the lookout and take care of the security chores.

Leoninski's building had once been a Communist Party officers' club. It was a gaudy stone edifice built in what could only be described as Soviet neo-colonial style, which was to say that it was bulky and ugly. It did, however, have large second-floor windows that were perfect for launching RPG rockets.

The two goons standing on either side of the entrance were wearing long overcoats open in the front. The commandos didn't need X-ray vision to know that they were wearing folding-stock automatic weapons under their coats.

''Give them the first shot,'' Lyons said, ''and I'll take care of the leftovers.''

''Got it,'' Schwarz said as he thumbed back the hammer on the loaded RPG.

Grimaldi pulled the van up to the curb on the opposite side of the street and left the engine running. Reaching back, he unlatched the sliding side door. ''Ready?'' he asked.

When Schwarz nodded, he slid open the door that faced the building. At the same time, Lyons opened the door on the other side of the van so the backblast from the RPGs wouldn't blow it open.

At that short range, Schwarz didn't need to use the sights, it was just point and shoot.

One of the guards spotted the RPG launcher and shouted as Schwarz dropped the hammer. With a whoosh, the rocket streaked across the street, missing both guards before striking the massive door and detonating.

When the smoke and dust settled, Lyons spotted one of the guards struggling to clear his weapon from under his coat, and he stitched the man up the side with a long burst. The man collapsed to the ground.

No sooner had Schwarz launched his round than Blancanales took his place and aimed his launcher at the second-story windows. His aim was a bit off, and the rocket hit the frame instead of the glass. The detonation took out the window as well as a large chunk of the stonework, so the shot wasn't wasted.

When he stepped back, Schwarz was loaded again and he sent his second shot into the stonework right above the ruined front doors. The blast collapsed the facade blocking the door. The building probably had a back door, but no one would be using the front entrance to cause them any trouble this day.

Blancanales's second rocket went into the upper floor again, sailing through the opening the first round had blasted in the wall. It had to have hit a partition inside the room because an instant later, a gout of smoke and flame shot out of the blasted window.

Schwarz had a third round loaded and sent it rocketing through an undamaged second-floor window. The detonation blew out the rest of the glass and sent it showering onto the sidewalk below.

Lyons spotted a muzzle poking out of a shattered window and sent a burst after it. "That's it!" he shouted to Grimaldi. "Get us out of here!"

Grimaldi slammed the gearshift into first, dropped the clutch and pulled away from the curb. The van wasn't a Mercedes, and it seemed to take forever before he had to shift up to second. The next time they tried something like that, he'd insist on having a better set of getaway wheels. Scattered shots followed them as they rounded the next corner, but they took no hits.

"Whoeeee!" Schwarz yelled and pumped his clenched fist. There was something so satisfying about blasting the hell out of a building with anti-tank rockets.

"We have a tail," Grimaldi called out after glancing in his side mirror. "Black Mercedes sedan coming on fast."

"I've got him," Schwarz said, as he picked up his over-and-under M-16/M-203 combo. Opening one side of the van's rear doors, he spread his feet in a wide stance to steady his aim. The passenger in the Mercedes was firing an AK out the window, but Schwarz ignored the hail of rounds, took careful aim with the grenade launcher and triggered it.

The 40 mm high explosive grenade punched through the windshield right in front of the driver's face and detonated. With a dead man at the wheel, the heavy sedan went out of control and plowed into a concrete power pole.

"We're clear now," he called up to Grimaldi.

"Take a left," Lyons said, "then do a right, another right and that will get us back on that main street."

CHAPTER SEVENTEEN

Stony Man Farm, Virginia

Now that the missing tank brigade had been located, the Computer Room crew was back to sitting on their thumbs. Hunt Wethers and Akira Tokaido were still providing satellite overwatch on the tanks hidden in the forest, but it would be awhile before Bolan and Phoenix Force could get in position to blow the bridge. They were in downtime again, the worst part of a mission, and the hours dragged.

To keep his mind occupied, Aaron Kurtzman was scrolling through the latest batch of intelligence reports that had come in. These documents were routinely inputted to the data banks, but he liked to read them when they came in so he could file them in the back of his mind as well. Data banks and cyberanalysis were fine and good, but nothing beat a well-connected set of neural synapses when it came to picking out that one piece of information that would fit in with a thousand other snippets and complete a picture.

Regardless of how much he depended on his cyber-sleuthing to solve the problems they were given, Kurtzman still liked to keep his mind active. And the best way to do that was to feed it new information as often as possible.

Even though the Soviet Union had been gone for some time now, it was amazing how much new material kept coming through on the defunct "Evil Empire" of communism. Some of it was recently declassified material that had never been committed to any computer file, but they were still getting in new information from defectors almost every week. It was a little-known fact that the United States was still offering asylum to old KGB operatives and other Soviet-government functionaries who had fought the cold war against the free world. But, to be eligible for asylum in America and a small federal pension, an ex-Communist needed to have new information for sale, not just rehashed stuff that everyone knew. The rule of thumb was that if it had been on CNN, it was old news.

Much of the information that was bartered for a safe haven in the U.S. was only good for future historians who would dissect the moldering corpse of international Marxism for years yet to come. It was good material, true, but not really germane to the problems of the here and now. Some of the information, however, was pure dynamite. Though communism had died, it hadn't been buried. Like a rotting corpse, it had spread its virulent disease throughout the world. It would be another decade or two before all of the Communist-inspired madness was ended.

One of the sources in this batch of reports had been a KGB officer who had worked the Foreign Intelligence branch and had been in charge of terrorist support and training. Since Soviet-trained terrorists were still a threat to the West, any new information on them was desired.

As Kurtzman scrolled down the debriefing report, he noted several new bits of information and mentally filed them away. None of them were earthshaking, but some day one of them might be the missing piece someone desperately needed. The best part of this particular debriefing, however, was when the ex-KGB officer started talking about the final days of the Little Amerika program.

This clever infiltration program had long been known to American Intelligence agencies and steps had been taken to guard against it. For the most part, the Little Amerika graduates had been only marginally successful. The best results had come from the women who had been able to secure jobs as secretaries or mistresses for high-ranking officials. In those positions, they had been able to put their highly trained sexual skills to good use for their cause. Even so, the old "honey pot" ploy was a well-known tactic, and several female KGB agents had been uncovered over the years the program had been in operation.

Even with the Soviet Union out of business, the Little Amerika program hadn't been put in the dead file. While the women agents had had their hour, even more dangerous were the male agents who had gone into "deep sleep" status. These men, all of them quite young, had infiltrated into American society and had taken up normal lives. They were to wait until they received orders before taking any action against the United States. When the Communists fell from power, a few of these men went back to Mother Russia to rejoin their families. Exactly how many wasn't known. More important, however, were those who had stayed under cover, and again, it wasn't known how many of them there were.

The interesting thing about this source's report was that he had been able to secret away a list of Little Amerika graduates and their cover identities. It wasn't a comprehensive list—the program had been operating for decades—but it did cover the majority of the placements from the last twelve years of its existence.

It had always been assumed that the deep-cover Russian agents who had been stranded in the United States had just given up the fight to continue living their comfortable lives in Middle America. Considering the difference in the standards of living between the two countries, that was the only thing that made sense. However, as Kurtzman well knew, common sense wasn't common when political ideology was involved. Some of these men could still be planning to take action against their old enemies.

Now, though, these people could be tracked down and brought in for debriefing before the authorities decided what to do with them. It would be an involved process, but he was confident that it would be done. It would be insane not to.

He had no intention of memorizing the list of names the source provided, the computer would do that for him. But his curiosity compelled him to run through the A, B and C names on the list before putting it aside to look at the next file. It was an analysis of the military potential of the Albanian armed forces, and that was far more relevant right now. The Balkans would be a hot spot for the next decade, and it looked like the Albanians would be heard from before it was finally over.

PROBATIONARY BLACKSUIT Jim Gordon was well into planning for his escape should that become necessary. His "close-in" duty had given him a good look at the main farmhouse, and he had to admit that he was impressed. After his experience with the rustic perimeter fence, he hadn't been taken in by what he was seeing, but with only what he had been able to detect. And, for every security measure he had been able to pick up, he was sure there was at least one more that he had missed. He had learned that the organization didn't do things halfway.

For one thing, the house was armored. He had no way of knowing how good the armor was, but he expected it to be at least proof against rifle-caliber fire if not light autoweapon shells up to 20 mm. Even the glass wasn't what it seemed to be; it was bulletproof Lexan and thick enough to stop a .50-caliber round.

The weak point, and there was always a weak point, were the electronic locks that controlled the farmhouse's two doors. The doors looked like wood, but they were steel with multiple lock bolts like a bank vault. It would take a tank to break them down, but the locks themselves were vulnerable. He knew that the electronic code was changed once a week. But the code was given to the close-in team so they could respond to any emergency inside the house. A code that was handed out like airline peanuts wasn't a security measure.

He had also decided that he would need a diversion to help cover his escape. As he knew from his years with the marshal's service, a hostage wasn't always a guarantee of safety. Many times he had seen firsthand, or read in an after-action report, of a sniper killing a hostage-taker. From what he had seen of his fellow guards, there had to be a sniper or two in their ranks, and he knew they wouldn't hesitate to shoot him or anyone else.

The best diversion was something that made a lot of noise or that would threaten to destroy the place—preferably both at the same time—and that usually meant an explosion. Considering the amount of ordnance on hand, finding something to blow up shouldn't be much of a problem. He would continue to keep his eye out as he rotated through all of the guard posts and duties.

CHIEF OF SECURITY Buck Greene had finally found time to go over the surveillance tapes of the three accidents that had occurred since the two new men had come on board. One of them, the backhoe accident, completely cleared Jim Gordon of any wrongdoing. One of the fixed-position surveillance cameras had recorded the whole thing. The engineer-tape guideline Gordon had been following had been misplaced.

The perimeter coax cable incident couldn't be proved one way or the other. The camera covering the area had been set on automatic sweep, and the area hadn't been in view when Gordon had cleared the weeds out of the fence. The tape showed him right before he came to the cable and after he had passed it, and nothing was wrong with what he had been doing in those segments.

The fuel-pump fire incident, however, was still puzzling to him.

Again, the camera covering the fuel transfer point had caught the whole incident, but the angle wasn't good. The tape clearly showed that Gordon's right hand had been on the pump controls when that brief spurt of gas had shot out of the nozzle and burst into flame. The problem was the blacksuit's shoulder was covering most of his hand from the camera's eye.

Even enhancing the shot didn't make the picture any clearer. The only thing it made clearer was that there looked to have been a slight motion of the tendons controlling the first two fingers of that hand.

That could be interpreted to show that he had tripped the pump purposefully.

On the plus side, though, he could plainly see that Gordon had instantly gone to the tractor driver's aid when his jacket caught on fire. His quick action had probably saved the man from a serious burn. Gordon had also filed an accident report as was required, suggesting that a faulty cutoff valve in the nozzle was the culprit.

The chief leaned back in his chair and lit his midday cigarette. It was an hour too early for it, but it helped him think. At the end of his smoke, he decided that he needed to take this to Barbara Price. After making a copy of the tape segments, including the enhancement of the fuel-pump incident, he rang her office.

"Barb, it's Buck Greene. You got a minute?"

THE SECURITY CHIEF sat quietly while Barbara Price ran through the short tape several times. "What do you think?" he asked when she snapped off the video player.

"It's a tough call," she said. She remembered meeting this Jim Gordon one afternoon on the way to the firing range, and he had seemed to be a regular guy. He had been a little overly polite, but she had put that down to his being new to the job.

"Other than this, how's he doing?"

"He's doing quite well actually," Greene admitted. "The men seem to like him and he does his work without griping or slacking. The only thing

I've noticed is that even though he always loses at poker, he still plays all the time.''

"Does he lose big?"

"No, just a buck or two, but he loses consistently and doesn't seem to learn anything from it.''

"Don't do anything for now," she decided, "but keep him under close personal surveillance. If he's clean, he has nothing to hide. If he's bad…''

"If he's bad," Greene finished for her, "he has to be terminated.''

She nodded.

The chief shook his head. "You know, I never thought I'd see something like this happen around here. I know it's happened at other organizations, but I've always been so careful with the background checks and the psych profiles on our people. Sure, we've had a couple of ringers run in on us over the years, but I've always been able to pick them up long before they were offered a position here. I really screwed the pooch on this one.''

Price smiled to herself. Greene was always so careful about his language around her, and his use of that colorful phrase showed his state of mind.

"Do you want me to tell the shift leaders to keep an eye on him too?" he asked.

"No," she said. "Leave them out of it for now. If this guy's bad, he's well trained and he's sure to notice if too many people are watching him.''

Greene nodded.

"I do, though," she said, "want you to tape those poker games so you can have Aaron take a look at them. If this guy's not playing to what he draws, we have him.''

"That's a real good idea." Green brightened. "A guy who loses at cards when he doesn't have to is worse than a guy who cheats.''

"It is a form of cheating," she reminded him. "And if he's cheating to lose, something's wrong, dead wrong.''

"You got that right.''

"Keep me informed.''

"Yes, ma'am.''

BACK IN HIS OFFICE, Buck Greene started going through Jim Gordon's file in detail. Everything from his U.S. Marshal annual physicals to his high-school yearbook. His eyes fell on his physical application form to be a blacksuit. Stony Man used the standard military physical exam form, and one of the blocks was titled Identifying Scars and Marks. This was a relic from before the days of DNA testing, and the scars were listed in case the subject turned up dead and couldn't otherwise be identified.

Listed on Gordon's form were the usual hand and leg scars that most adult American males carried, particularly those who had been in active federal service for any length of time. Most of the scars were small, but on the back of his right leg was a three-inch scar running from his ankle up to the calf. It had been prominent enough that it had been listed first. A cut that big would have required medical attention of some kind and several stitches to close.

Following his hunch, he called Aaron Kurtzman. "Bear, it's Buck. Look, I need a little favor from you and your mainframe. I need you to look up the entire medical history of one of my new blacksuits for me."

"How far back?" Kurtzman asked.

"All the way back to his birth," Greene replied. "It's James T. Gordon, born March 14, 1964, in Eugene, Oregon. SSN 394-54-8921. I need this now, Aaron, right now."

"I'll see what I can find out for you."

KURTZMAN SMILED as he hung up the phone. He really liked Buck Greene, but like a lot of people, the man didn't have too strong a grasp of the realities of cyberspace. The medical records of all the Americans who had ever lived weren't entered in some humongous database in a secret facility hidden somewhere under the Rocky Mountains. In fact the ACLU was screaming about the routine entering of medical records into hospital computers as it was. It would be a long time before anyone would be able to log on and go to anyone's medical records with a click of a mouse.

That didn't mean, however, that he wouldn't be able to help the security chief with this information. One of his established cyberpersonas was that of Dr. George Kurtzman, medical adviser to the White House. He could also pose as Dr. John Wainwright of CDC Atlanta if he needed to. Brief calls from either of those men should get him what Greene said he needed.

Why the chief wanted this information he didn't know. Apparently at this point in time, he didn't have a need to know. But, as he well knew, that status could change at any moment. It was hard to keep secrets from the Bear.

CHAPTER EIGHTEEN

Moscow, Russia

Back at the safehouse, Yakov Katzenelenbogen cut short the self-congratulations at their having pulled off the attack on Leoninski's headquarters without a hitch. "Gentlemen," he said seriously, "I'd like to suggest that we pack up and get out of here immediately."

"Where're we going?" Schwarz asked.

"Anywhere but here. I think we've about worn out our welcome. If Leoninski marshals his troops, this place will be difficult to defend with just five people."

No one disagreed with Katz's assessment.

"And Gadgets, when we pull out, I want you to leave a few calling cards behind."

"What kind of job do you want?" Schwarz asked. Belakov had provided more demolition material than was needed for the destruction of the bridge, and there was more than enough left over to take down the whole building. "I can slow them down or really make their lives miserable."

"Leave the house standing," Katz said, "but I want them hurt badly."

GENERAL ZERINOV'S MAN inside the Ministry of the Interior wasn't highly placed in the organization. He was merely a lowly clerk in the communications center. He was also a man with a thoroughly investigated background. When the minister had discovered that his young wife had been on the Mafia's payroll, he'd had everyone in the entire organization investigated back to birth.

The clerk had passed this new examination of his background because he was completely clean. He was a poster boy for the new democratic Russian citizen. There wasn't a trace of Mafia connection, drug use or illegal activities in his entire family. One of his younger uncles, however, had been killed in Afghanistan while serving in a unit of General Pavel Zerinov's division. The connection was so tenuous that none of the investigators had picked up on it. Hundreds of men had died under Zerinov's command, and they had thousands of relatives all over Russia.

As he had been instructed to do, the clerk had been keeping his eyes and ears open for information about the Americans reportedly working for the minister. The brief appearance of the three of them at the ministry had given him an opportunity to pass on that they did, in fact, exist, along with their physical descriptions.

But that was all he had been able to do until now.

With the new emphasis on security at the ministry, asking the wrong questions could get him sent to the basement for interrogation. The new democracy hadn't been able to erase all of the legacy of communism yet, and the basement cells were a part of the old KGB that he didn't want to experience.

When Yuri Belakov's request for support was received, the minister's assistant who had been handling these matters for the Americans had been rushed with another task and had given the job of procuring the necessary vehicles to the communications clerk. All that was required of the man was to call one of the SVR motor pools and have them deliver the vehicles to a Moscow address. The clerk was more than happy to take care of that for him.

GENERAL PAVEL ZERINOV was in full combat mode now. The two attacks in two days had finally shown him that the Americans were a force to be reckoned with. His political campaign was showing signs of faltering, and the antigangster policies of his main opponent were playing against him. He wasn't about to throw in the towel, though. He had been in danger before and had always been able to fight his way free. It was time to go back on the offensive, and that meant taking care of those meddling Yankees once and for all. He had called a meeting to hammer out a plan of action.

At the appointed time, Leoninski and his second in command swept into the general's office as if they owned the place. Zerinov was aware that if he couldn't pull this off, they might very well own it because he would be dead. Until then, though, the bastard could at least act like a subordinate should and show a little courtesy.

When Major Vasily Lebedev marched in, he clicked to a halt the prescribed three paces in front of the table and stiffened at attention. Although he was in civilian clothes, his right hand came up in a crisp military salute. "General," he said.

"Major," Zerinov said, returning the salute. "Please take a seat."

Now that the heads of his action divisions were present it was time to lay out a campaign that would end in victory, both for him personally and for the party he led.

HALFWAY THROUGH the meeting, the general's aide, an ex-Red Army officer, like all of his staff, walked smartly into the room. "Excuse me, General," he said, "but I have a message I think you need to see immediately."

The general's face broke out in a smile as he read it. "Comrades," he said, "I believe I have just been given the solution to our problem. My man at the ministry has just supplied me with the address of the safehouse the Americans are staying at."

"Can we trust this man of yours?" Leoninski asked.

"He is a comrade," Zerinov snapped.

"Major," the general said, turning to Lebedev,

"I want your Wolverines to hit this location tonight."

"It will be done, General." Lebedev stood. "And, if I may be excused, I will see to it now."

THE EIGHT MEN who approached the house just before midnight were mere shadows on the darkened street. Moscow had once been known for excellent street lighting, but, as with so many other things of the new urban infrastructure, there was no money for lighting maintenance. The fact that all the streetlights on that block were dark wasn't alarming.

Gathering at one corner of the wall around the compound, the Wolverines boosted their point man to the top of the wall. He lay there, his night-vision goggles searching the darkened compound in front of him.

"Action front," Schwarz announced as he watched the monitors inside the van. Along with the booby traps, he had left behind a number of surveillance cameras. Even with the van parked at a curb two blocks away, he was getting a good look at the assault on the safehouse.

"I have visual on eight intruders right outside the southwest corner of the wall," he said. "They're in night camou suits, and they're packing. I think the Wolverines have come to call."

"Too bad we're out at the moment," James said.

"One of them's on top of the wall. They're taking the bait."

When the Wolverine point man didn't see any

sentries on the grounds, he clicked his radio to signal the all clear and continued to scan for signs of life while his comrades came over the wall. When all eight Russian commandos were inside the compound, they spread out as per the attack plan. One man moved around to the front of the house, one went to cover the back door and the others broke down into two three-man assault teams to cover the sides of the house.

Knowing that they were going up against professionals, they moved cautiously. Attacking a structure at night was always risky, but they knew the drill. On the west side of the house, no light shone through the floor-length windows of the study, and the draperies were open giving the attackers a clear view of the inside of the darkened room.

Motioning for his comrades to wait where they were, the lead man moved up carefully, checking the outside of the house for alarm devices. When that was clear, he examined the windowframe for security devices or alarms. Finding a wire on the right side of the window, he followed it down to a magnetic contact pad. Opening the window would break the circuit and sound the alarm.

Taking out a glass cutter, he affixed the suction cup to the glass and inscribed a large circle. Tapping the glass, he freed the piece, then carefully withdrew it. After laying it aside, he went through the hole he had made and crouched inside the room to scan for more devices. The filters on his night-vision goggles would let him see black light, IR and blue laser.

A laser beam cut across the room from corner to corner at waist height, covering both of the room's doors. That was expected, and it wasn't difficult to bypass. Dropping the laser filter, he went to IR to see if he could spot the faint hot-air plume from the heat of an active motion detector. When he didn't see one, he gave the all clear and the assault team on the other side of the house started its entry.

As soon as all six Wolverines were inside, they started silently clearing the rooms on the bottom floor.

"I'VE GOT SIX of them inside," Schwarz announced as he looked up from his video monitor, "and they're starting to go through the rooms."

Looking over his shoulder, Katzenelenbogen watched the black-clad Russian commandos the microcam was picking up. With a video recorder that small, the picture wasn't good, and the fish-eye lens distorted it even more. But he could clearly see that the intruders were armed. "Take them out as soon as they're in range."

"Got it."

Rigging the safehouse with booby traps hadn't been easy. Schwarz hadn't had enough gadgets in his travel kit to cover every room with his trademark devices, so he decided on a single kill-zone approach. After placing the decoys he expected to be found, he had concentrated his efforts on the hallway that led to the stairs up to the second floor. After the Wolverines had searched the ground floor and didn't find their targets, they were sure to want to examine the upper floor as well.

The end of the hall closest to the stairs was rigged as a remote-ambush kill zone. Two tall, ornate dish cabinets had been moved to stand against each wall. The china had been left in the glass-covered upper portion of the cabinets, but the enclosed compartments on the bottom had been emptied so Schwarz could make use of them.

Thirty half-kilo blocks of plastique had been stacked in each of the compartments. Lacking anything better to use as a backing plate, he had stacked books behind the explosives to completely fill the rest of the space. Since he didn't have a stock of nails or ball bearings to use for shrapnel, he raided the silverware drawers in the kitchen and used the eating utensils as fragmentation pieces. They wouldn't fly as straight, but they would do the trick.

When this was over, the minister's safehouse would be in need of a little renovation, but no one had ever said that freedom came cheap.

"They're heading for the stairs in teams," Schwarz said. "I'll only be able to get the first team, three of them."

"Go for it!"

Punching the bottom on his remote detonator, the monitor instantly went blank. Before the image faded, though, he caught a glimpse of the blast enveloping the first group of Russian commandos.

The darkened windows of the ground floor blew out with the overpressure, scattering glass over the grounds. The blast echoed off the neighboring walls like a thunderclap.

"That's all folks," Schwarz said.

"Good work," Katz stated. "Now let's get out of here in case they have backup standing by."

Grimaldi cranked the van and eased it away from the curb. Blancanales had secured them rooms in a small hotel, and they would stay there until Bolan and Phoenix Force returned.

SOME 280 MILES south-east of Moscow, the Potemkin National Forest clung to a series of jagged peaks. Once an iron-mining region, the forest had recently been designated as a national wildlife refuge. With everything else the Russians had to contend with during their country's growing pains, ecological concerns weren't a priority. But, with UN wildlife preservation funds available, it seemed to be a good move to make. Particularly since the region wasn't suitable for large-scale farming

Now herds of deer and wild pigs again roamed the dense woods, but among the grazing animals were the hulking steel shapes of T-72 tanks. Parked underneath the forest canopy was almost a complete brigade of the armored vehicles, three hundred of them, along with the other vehicles and equipment that were needed to support them.

Recently promoted Major General Viktor Malkin, late of the 3rd Guards Tank Regiment, had been given command of the armored force. For the moment, his tanks and their crews had nothing to do.

In fact they were prohibited from doing anything more than starting their engines on schedule to ensure that they would start when they were needed.

As an experienced tanker and a veteran of the Afghanistan War, Malkin knew the dangers of letting a force such as his sit idle for too long. It was bad enough for the tanks, but it was even harder for the troops.

Like many Russian army officers, Malkin wasn't political, or at least he hadn't started out that way. When the old Soviet Union fell, he had taken it in stride as a soldier who followed orders. But, when he saw what had happened to his beloved regiment under the new government, he'd had no choice but to get involved with his nation's political future. To him, his men were his family, as his father's and grandfather's men had been theirs. This was a sacred trust that went beyond mere politics. His honor as an officer required that he take care of his men as best he could, and that best had not been very good lately. Pavel Zerinov had promised on his honor that he would make it possible to give his men their due once his Progressive Party came to power under his presidency.

This was a desperate gamble, and he knew that he might even have to order his men to fire on other Russian units before it was all over. But he could see no other solution to the crisis. The Russian army was very near collapse and electing another drunken fool to the presidency would only bring worse chaos. He held dear his honor as a soldier, but there were times when even a soldier had to take sides. His grandfather had done it during the glorious revolution, his father had done it during the "Great Patriotic War Against Fascism" and it was his time now.

The worst thing about his decision was the waiting, but it had to be done. As in any battle, to expose his brigade too soon would be disastrous, both for them and for the general. They had to wait, hidden, until Zerinov sent the word for them to move. Then the tanks would roll and their guns would secure the future of Mother Russia. Until then, he had to keep his men under control and the tanks ready to play their role in this critical juncture in history.

He had to admit that whoever had chosen this assembly area had known what he was doing. The forest was dense and easily hid the tanks from aerial observation. Since the trees had grown up around an iron-mining operation that had been abandoned for almost a hundred years, even space radar would have a difficult time telling his vehicles from the junk that littered the area. Best of all was the fact that there was only one way into the site.

Normally having a restricted access route set a tanker's teeth on edge. Armored warfare depended on mobility, and a static tank was useless. But the bridge over the gorge that cut off the forest made it easy to maintain the security of the tank park. A pair of T-72s and a platoon of men could hold the bridge against three times their number long enough for reinforcements to come to their aid. It would take a division to dig him out of the woods, and Zerinov had promised that none of his armored brethren would move against him.

When the call came, he could have his tanks in Moscow in under six hours, having secured the smaller towns like Tula en route. It would take longer for the units to get to Novgorod in the east and Volgograd in the south, but they, too, would be in place within eighteen hours of the order to move out. With the large cities under control, everything else would fall in place.

His brigade was ready for action now, but he couldn't guarantee how much longer he would be able to keep it in fighting shape. The troops were always the weakest part of any military organization, and his men weren't made of the same steel that the tanks were. Even with plenty of good food and the prospect of going down in history as heroes, the forced inactivity was beginning to show on them. If General Zerinov didn't send him the call soon, he couldn't guarantee the results.

CHAPTER NINETEEN

Stony Man Farm, Virginia

Jim Gordon had finally found a way to create the diversion he would need if he had to leave the area in a hurry. One of the barns had a room beneath the main floor that housed the emergency diesel power generators. A sizeable diesel fuel tank shared the power room, and it was big enough to do tremendous damage if it were to detonate.

He could get the same result by rigging the Mogas tanks at the fuel station, but they were out in the open and it would be difficult to work on them unobserved. Also, too many people used the gas pumps. With one man on duty there every day and the others bringing in farm equipment for refueling, anything he tried to hide there was sure to be found. He should be able to work in the underground generator room without being seen, and there was more than enough room to hide an explosive device.

Diesel fuel wasn't as volatile as Mogas, but it would burn, and under the right circumstances, it could be made to detonate. A single thermite grenade would burn through the steel tank and set the diesel on fire. If it was set up properly, a secondary plastique charge would cause the burning fuel to detonate.

The secondary would have to be big enough to cause an overpressure in the room, but the room wasn't large. He might be able to get the effect he wanted with only two of the new assault grenades the blacksuits were carrying. The problem was going to be getting the thermite he needed to start the process.

Unlike a Hollywood spy, Gordon didn't carry an arsenal around with him in his hip pocket. The average American didn't have a spy kit at his disposal, and he didn't either. In fact he had come into the country completely unarmed and without contacts to supply him. Only when he was activated would he be issued the tools of his real trade that he would need to complete his mission.

But his extensive training had taught him to use every explosive device known to man and to make his own field-expedient demolitions if it was necessary. It would be much easier, however, if he could find something to use from the blacksuit issue. Being caught mixing a batch of home-brew plastique in the latrine sink would be a little difficult to explain.

In the barracks ammunition ready racks, he had seen flash-bang grenades and frags ready for self-issue if they were needed. He would have to check to see if thermite grenades were stored there as well.

If not, there were still ways to use the diesel tank as a diversion. If nothing else, it would start a good fire, and with the exception of the main house, the buildings were all of wooden construction. A roaring fire would go a long way to cover his escape.

A DAY AFTER ASKING for Jim Gordon's medical records, Buck Greene walked into the Computer Room with a videotape in his hand. "If I remember correctly," he told Aaron Kurtzman, "you used to be some kind of a hotshot poker player."

Kurtzman smiled widely. "Damn straight. You have some money you want to lose? Look, it'll be a whole lot easier on you if you just hand it over and skip the frustration of trying to play with me. I hate to see a grown man cry."

Greene shook his head. "You know I don't play cards anymore, Aaron, and particularly not with a cheating bastard like you. I just need you to take a look at another man's game for me."

Kurtzman was intrigued. If the chief was coming to him, it had to be something serious. "Let's have a look."

Reaching out, Greene put the cassette in the video player and punched it on. The monitor flashed on to show a view of four blacksuits sitting around the barracks' poker table. The man with his back to the camera was unknowingly showing his cards to the unblinking glass eye.

"That's one of the new guys," Kurtzman said in recognition. "Jim Gordon, isn't it?"

"It is," Greene replied.

Kurtzman caught the note in the chief's voice and the pieces fell into place. "What's he done?"

"That's what I don't know, Aaron. Not yet."

"What do you think he's done?" Kurtzman asked as he watched the monitor. The camera was set high and enough to one side that he had a good view of Gordon's hand as he held his cards.

Greene took a deep breath. He should have known better than to try to keep a secret from Kurtzman. "He could be a ringer."

"If he is, this'll show him out."

Kurtzman watched the spirited play for a full ten minutes before speaking and when he did, it was what Greene had feared he would hear.

"He's a bad one, all right, Buck. On the last three hands, he's discarded cards that would have let him win. Watch." He backed up the tape, then hit Play again. "Here he was dealt a low straight. He discards the ace and the four, and that makes the hand worthless."

He forwarded the tape again. "Here he gets three of a kind and dumps two of them. He's cheating all right, cheating to lose."

"So he can lull his barracks buddies into accepting him as an okay guy," Greene said. "What a bastard."

"You have to admit that you're not going to be too hard on a guy who's keeping your wallet fat."

"Have you found his medical records yet?"

"Some of them," Kurtzman said. "You have to

remember that they aren't all in some computer somewhere. I've had to call doctors and hospitals and pretend I'm one of the White House medical staff to even get what I've got. Even so, they've all asked for medical release forms, so I've had to fax them ones I made up using Gordon's signature from the file copy of his background check.''

"I don't care what you have to do," Greene growled. "Just get them. I need them.''

"If you tell me what you're looking for," Kurtzman said, "it might help speed things up.''

"He's got a big scar on his right leg, and I want to know when he got cut.''

"You want to know if it was stitched up here in the States or in Mother Russia?''

"That's about it," Greene said. "He's too damned good to be from anywhere else. He was a U.S. Marshal for ten years before he came here, and they would have picked up anything obvious in his background. If they cleared him, you know he looked good.''

"Could he have been turned?''

Greene shook his head. "I don't think so. Turncoats are fanatics, and he doesn't have any of the earmarks of having an idealistic bent. At least not modern idealism.''

Kurtzman knew what he meant. The current crop of ecofreaks, Luddites and antigovernment people all shared a fanatical mentality that was difficult to hide. While their goals were radically different, the mentality was all the same. The classical Marxists like Kim Philby of MI-6 and the Rosenbergs, however, were a different animal. They could hide their true goals while working to destroy the free world. Even after researchers working in the old KGB files had definitively proved that the Rosenbergs had been Soviet agents when they had handed over American atomic secrets, their innocence was still in debate. If Greene was right, they were dealing with a cool-minded, well-trained professional.

"Have you talked to Barbara about this?"

"Once," he said as he punched the videotape out of the player. "But I think I need to talk to her again now that we've found this."

Kurtzman released the brakes on his chair. "I'll come with you."

BARBARA PRICE WAS a bit surprised to see both Buck Greene and Aaron Kurtzman at the door of her office. Being double teamed like this was a rare event. Usually a conference call took care of group meetings. "To what do I owe the pleasure of this visit, gentlemen?"

"Do you have a minute?" Greene asked quietly.

"Sure."

Greene stepped aside to allow Kurtzman to wheel his chair in. "Can I close the door?" he asked.

"Of course." In an environment where individual secrets simply didn't exist, a closed door was a rarity. Stony Man could only operate if everyone within the organization knew everything that was going on at all times.

Greene shut the door and took a seat in the chair by the end of her desk. "I'm afraid I've confirmed that we have a serious security problem."

"Jim Gordon?" she asked.

"Aaron agrees with me," he said. "We have a bad blacksuit."

She had expected to hear anything but that from him. Buck Greene ran such a tight ship that they had never had any problems with the security force. The world might be coming apart around their ears with Armageddon marching up the valley, but she knew that she could count on the blacksuits being out there doing their jobs.

"What happened?"

"I'm not sure," Greene stated. "All I know is that I'm convinced now that Gordon's an enemy agent."

She reached for the phone. "Let me get Hal in on this."

Greene reached out to stop her. "I'd like to leave him out of this for now."

"I agree, Barbara," Kurtzman spoke up. "We need to keep this to ourselves for a while longer."

She sat back in her chair. "Okay, boys, I'll bite. What's the deal?"

Greene took a deep breath and launched into how he had come across the poker-game scam. "And," he concluded, "as soon as Aaron can get the rest of the bastard's medical records, we'll know for sure."

"Let me see if I remember this correctly," she said. "You suspect that Gordon may be involved in three minor 'accidents' recently. You have a sur-veillance tape that may show that he purposefully activated the gas pump, but it's not conclusive. Now you have learned that he cheats at cards so he'll lose and he may or may not have an undocumented in-jury. Is that it?''

"I know it doesn't sound like much," Greene said, "but I don't like it."

Price knew that there was nothing here that would stand in a court of law, but Stony Man was a law unto itself. The rules of evidence didn't apply at the Farm. Also, there was the gut factor. If Greene said that Gordon didn't feel right to him, she would go with that.

"Okay, how do you want to handle it?"

"Well," Greene said, "if you don't mind, I'd like to continue watching him for a while. I want to fig-ure out if he's planning an attack on us or if he's just on a recon."

"Why don't you want Hal involved yet?"

"I'm afraid that he'll want me to drag this guy in and start working on him."

"What's wrong with that? A good interrogation should be able to answer those questions for you."

"The problem is that I don't know if he has some kind of contact to the outside. If he does, his dis-appearance might trigger another action I don't know anything about and won't be able to prepare for."

That was a valid concern. Gordon might have put

a dead-man cutout in place. It was a common enough practice.

Price turned to Kurtzman. So far, he had said very little beyond confirming that Gordon cheated at cards. "Aaron?"

"I'm with Buck on this," he said. "I don't think Gordon's an immediate threat, and I'd like to find out what the hell he's doing here. We've never had something like this happen to us before, and we need to learn everything we can so we'll be able to guard against it happening again."

"Okay," she said. "For now, you watch him and I'll keep Hal out of it. But I want a daily report, and if it looks like it's getting out of control, take him out of action. Save him for interrogation, though. We need to know what his mission is and who he's working for."

"No problem," the chief replied.

"And Aaron," she said, "keep trying to get those medical records. And, while you're at it, get his dental records too."

"Damn, I forgot about that."

She smiled. "You have to watch forgetting things like that, Aaron. I don't want to have to replace you with a computer."

Her playful threat tripped something in his mind and he remembered the list of Little Amerika cover names he had recently received, but hadn't had a chance to go over yet. "Let me borrow your keyboard for a moment."

Price got up and pulled her chair out of the way

so he could get his wheelchair in. His hands flashed over the keys, retrieving the file. When it flashed up, he keyed for the *G*. The fifth name down was James T. Gordon.

"I'll be a son of a bitch," Greene spit. "There he is."

"To play devil's advocate," she said, "we don't know that that's our Gordon."

"We also don't know that it's not," Greene replied. "And I don't want to take any chances with him. I want to drag his ass in here now and start working on him."

"Let's just keep watching him for now like we agreed," Price said. "But don't let him slip away from here."

"He's not going anywhere except hell," Greene growled. "I can promise you that."

"We want him alive," she cautioned. "He's no good to us dead."

"That's going to be up to him."

"I mean it, Buck. When the time comes, I want the bastard taken alive."

Greene took a deep breath. "Yes, ma'am."

BACK IN THE COMPUTER ROOM, Kurtzman and Greene worked out a plan to pipe the surveillance tapes into the Computer Room live rather than store them for the weekly review.

"I can program the computer to recognize him," Kurtzman said. "That way, it'll tag any tapes he

appears in, and we won't have to go through everything that comes in.''

"You just do what you have to so we can keep
an eye on the bastard."

"And Buck..."

"Yes?"

"You might want to stay in the background while
we have him under surveillance. If he sees the expression on your face, he'll know that he's stepped
in it big time."

Greene smiled thinly. "You've got a point."

CHAPTER TWENTY

Potemkin National Forest, Russia

The distance from Moscow to the Potemkin National Forest was a little under three hundred miles, but Russian roads weren't American freeways. The Stony Man team's vehicles had been lucky to average forty miles an hour.

"How the hell do you people get around in this country?" David McCarter asked Yuri Belakov when they hit another stretch of badly rutted highway. "The only other place I've seen roads this bad was in Albania."

"We use the trains to get around in Russia," the SVR agent answered with a smile. "Russian trains are very fast and efficient."

"Like your subways?" McCarter couldn't resist the dig. The Moscow Metro had once been the pride of Russia, but now the system had become more like the subways in too many American inner cities. They were dirty, overcrowded and dangerous, in addition to being prone to breakdowns.

"Better. The conductors are all young women with giant breasts, and the vodka's free."

Bolan smiled at Belakov's retort. The Russian was learning that the only way to get along with McCarter was to give back as good as he got.

"I still think we should have taken a chopper."

"If there had been a way to do it and keep Zerinov from knowing about it, we would have," the Russian explained again. "But I would have had to go to the army to get one, and there was too great a risk of word getting back to him."

"We still should have flown," McCarter grumbled.

SIXTY-THREE MILES out of Tula, Manning turned the Hummer off the main road and started up a dirt road into the foothills. This was a thickly forested, mountainous region, and it had been miles since they had seen the last house or farm. An entire tank army could be hidden here, and no one would ever be the wiser.

A few miles short of their objective, Manning pulled the Hummer to the side of the road and motioned for the van to pull in behind him. Carrying their weapons, the commandos got out to stretch their legs and survey their surroundings. According to the map, they were a little over four miles from their target area and the aerial photos showed it to be thick forest all the way in.

"That faint rumbling sound," Belakov said, "what is it?"

"Tank engines," McCarter said. "They have to run them every few hours to keep the batteries charged and the oil warm. Tanks don't like to get cold."

"So we've found them," Belakov said.

"We have." McCarter nodded. "And now we have to go see if we're going to be able to stop the bastards."

"And if we cannot?" the Russian asked.

The ex-SAS commando shrugged. "Pray that we can get out with our asses still attached."

Stony Man Farm, Virginia

NOW THAT THE TEAM was at its jump-off position, the Stony Man Computer Room staff swung back into action. Hunt Wethers and Akira Tokaido were still controlling the satellites, and Kurtzman was monitoring everything that came in from their sensors. Now, though, they were getting better pictures than they had before. Wethers had been able to get a Deep Look bird on station and was getting radar pictures of what was happening under the dense foliage. The radar images weren't as good as photography would have been, but they were good enough to tell the difference between a battle tank and a smaller support vehicle.

Hal Brognola was also standing by so he could call the Oval Office the instant that bridge came down. He didn't particularly like the solution Katzenelenbogen had come up with to deal with the renegade tank brigade. It would put the team at great risk, and there was no guarantee of success. Bolan and Phoenix Force were a strike squad and were able to do what they did by moving fast and shooting straight. As Barbara Price had so vividly pointed out, taking on an armored brigade wasn't a task for a handful of men, no matter how good they were.

But Katz was the man on the spot, so it had been his decision to make. Had it been his choice, Brognola would have passed and would have tried again to pressure the minister into ordering in the Russian army to take care of the tanks. He had tried to suggest that approach before without success. The minister had pointed out that if word of the brigade's discovery got back to Zerinov, he would roll the tanks immediately and Russia was sure to fall to a military coup or a civil war.

For the life of him, Brognola didn't understand why the Russians seemed to enjoy killing one another so much. But history had proved time and again that they would just as soon kill their own countrymen as a foreigner. Even during World War II, Russian troops killed far more of their own citizens than the Germans had ever done.

While he was trying to be optimistic, he wasn't sure that this was going to have a happy ending. Even with the tanks out of the way, Russia was still critically unstable and could erupt at any moment. When a people were determined to commit suicide, there was little that could be done about it. The country that used to be known as Yugoslavia was a recent case in point.

"We may have a problem," Hunt Wethers called out from his work station.

"What is it?" Kurtzman and Brognola asked simultaneously.

"I think the tanks are getting ready to move out," Wethers answered calmly. "Some of them have come out from under the trees. The fuel trucks are topping them up, and they're not going back into their hiding places. They're not forming into march columns yet, but it looks like the troops are loading their personal gear into the external cargo racks. It could be the preparation for a move out."

"Get that to Striker immediately," Brognola ordered.

"It's on the way," Kurtzman answered.

As Kurtzman reached for the mike to the satcom radio, Brognola went to inform the President that they had confirmation of the brigade's location. He would try one more time to convince him to put the hammer on the minister. He knew that it would be another exercise in futility, but he had to give it one more shot before the team went into the mouth of the lion.

THE COMMANDOS DIDN'T need Stony Man's warning to know that the Russians were getting ready to do something with all that armor. The low rumble of tank engines echoed off the mountainsides like a distant storm. The confirmation, though, gave them a greater sense of urgency. Rather than take a day to recon the situation, they would go in immediately and try to set the charges on the bridge that night.

After pulling their vehicles deeper into the woods to hide, they quickly loaded their weapons and supplies. T. J. Hawkins took the point position as the team made its way through the dense undergrowth. Along with his weapons and ammunition, he had a fifty-pound pack full of explosives on his back, so it was slow going. His night-vision goggles showed him the terrain in shades of glowing green and gray, and he was being careful on the approach. But interestingly enough, he had encountered no sensors or antipersonnel devices. Apparently the Russians were confident that no one knew where they were hiding. Confidence was fine, but too much of it could lead to making mistakes.

It took several long hours for the commandos to reach the edge of the gorge that cut off the brigade's mountain hideout from the rest of the crags. By the time they arrived, the tank engines had fallen silent, but they had listened to their deep coughing roar all the way in.

"It would be quiet now," McCarter whispered. Sound carried far in cool night air.

The bridge was as the photos had shown. Riveted steel girders made up the four pylons that suspended it over the chasm. It had a single-lane roadbed, but it was strong enough to carry the weight of armored vehicles. Sandbagged positions flanked the western abutment, and four sentries were on duty.

Were it not for the opposition, it would be only an hour's work to take it down.

After a quick recon, Bolan ordered the two teams into action. Manning and McCarter shouldered the bags of explosives, and Belakov went with them as far as the edge of the cliff. His job was to guard them from above, while they worked.

On an outcropping overlooking the end of the bridge, Encizo and Hawkins moved into position so they could watch the guards through their night-vision binoculars. If the demo team was discovered, their job would be to create a diversion long enough for the others to climb back out of the gorge. Since the Russians they were expected to hold off were driving tanks, they had brought two RPG-7 rocket launchers with them, and two dozen rounds.

Considering the sharply sloped, thick forward armor of the T-72s, though, RPGs were a little light for that kind of work. But the team didn't have the personnel necessary to have brought heavier wire-guided, antitank missiles along with all the demo they needed for the bridge. If the gods of war were good to them, they'd be in and out before the Russians knew they were there. Anything else would be a disaster.

Bolan found a spot on the other side of the bridge where he could support the other teams.

ONCE THE DIVERSION TEAM was in place, Gary Manning and David McCarter left Belakov and started their descent. The sides of the gorge were covered

with enough brush to provide them with conceal-
ment as they climbed down without hindering them
too much. Fortunately there was little water in the
chasm that time of year, so they wouldn't have to
deal with trying to set the charges in cold water.

When they reached the first pylon, Manning
quickly examined the steel girders and found them
to be what he had expected. Sometimes it was difficult to look at an aerial photo and be able to tell
what you would be working with. This time he had
lucked out. McCarter clicked his com link to let the
others know that they were starting the job.

The demolition plan was simple. They would
drop the first two bridge pylons on the west end into
the gorge, sending half of the roadway down with
it. That would create a gap too long to be covered
by the brigade's Vehicular Launched Bridges. The
crewmen would be able to walk out anytime they
wanted to by going down into the gorge, but their
tanks would have to remain where they were until
the bridge could be rebuilt.

The first group of charges went on the bottoms of
the girders that made up the first pylon. After being
emplaced, each charge in that group was connected
to the next with a length of det cord. It was slow
work in the dark, but it couldn't be rushed. This
wasn't a job they could return to and make right if
it didn't work the first time.

When all of the charges on the bottom of the
girder had been set, Manning hitched his demo bag
around to ride in the center of his back and started

to climb the girder to reach the point where the side braces were connected to the pylon. This was the dangerous part of the job. In spite of wearing rubber-soled boots, he had to be careful not to make any noise. Even a slight metallic clink was sure to make one of the guards look down over the side.

While Manning worked halfway up the bridge pylon, McCarter stood guard from down below. If the Russians spotted the demo man, he would keep them busy until the Canadian could get back to the ground.

There was little for the diversion team to do while Manning was rigging the bridge except watch the Russian sentries and the camp, but it wasn't boring. Every new noise from the tank park and every sentry who went to relieve himself sent their fingers to their triggers. It was a long wait.

THE SKY WAS LIGHTENING by the time Manning started up the second pylon to lay the last group of charges. When it was light enough, McCarter flipped up his night-vision goggles to let his eyes adjust to the dim light. He was just in time to see a Russian sentry walk over to his side of the bridge, lean over the edge and peer into the dim chasm.

"Freeze," he whispered to Manning over the com link.

McCarter had managed to crouch behind a rock without being seen, but the light was enough for the sentry to spot one of the backpacks they had used to carry the explosives down into the gorge. He called out to his partner, and the other man came running.

When the second man leaned well over the side to try to peer underneath the superstructure, McCarter had no choice. "Contact," he radioed as he took his shot.

The diversion team opened fire an instant later, taking down the other two sentries.

"Get a hustle on it down there!" Bolan radioed down to the demo team.

"We're working as fast as we can!" Manning sent back.

All he had left to do was to affix the last remote detonator. Flipping the switch to receive, he dropped his empty demo bag, hooked his feet in the flanges of the girder and, braking with his gloved hands, started to slide down to the ground. "Go, Go!" he shouted to McCarter.

The sentries on the other end of the bridge were firing into the rocks, and the coughing roar of a dozen diesel engines firing up sounded loud over the rattle of small-arms fire.

"They're bringing up the tanks!" Bolan radioed.

"We're on the way," McCarter sent back the instant Manning's boots touched the ground.

Keeping to the cover of the brush, the two men scrambled up the side of the chasm as the battle raged above them. If they wanted to go back to Moscow in one piece, they had to get clear before they could set off the charges.

The Canadian had done a masterful job of rigging

the bridge. The mark of a demolition expert was his ability to let gravity do most of the work for him. Explosives were nice, but they worked much better when they were used in conjunction with the inexorable tug of Mother Earth. That was how tall buildings could be put down with only a few hundred pounds of explosives packed in the right places.

Semtex was a superfast cutting explosive, and the lower charges had been placed to slice through the steel girders, severing them from their anchors in the bedrock. Firing a microsecond later, the secondary charges would cut the side supports of the pylons and gravity would bring half of the bridge down.

Hawkins was at the top of the chasm to give a hand to the two climbers. Manning was panting with the effort of the climb as he took the remote detonator from his side pocket. The first tank was charging across the bridge, raking the rocks with its co-ax machine gun and there was no time to rest. "Fire in the hole one," he said, giving the traditional blaster's warning as he hit the switch.

The blast of the exploding charges at the bottom of the girders slammed off the cliffs, overpowering the echo of tank engines. Smoke puffed at the base of the pylons, and chunks of the concrete bridge footings shot out like jagged cannon balls.

"Fire in the hole two," Manning called out as he hit the detonator switch again to fire the explosives in the pylons. The silence was deafening. He checked to make sure that the battery LED was green and the selector was in the number-two position before hitting the firing button again. Again there was no explosion.

"The fucking detonators won't fire the secondaries," he shouted over the com link.

CHAPTER TWENTY-ONE

Potemkin National Forest, Russia

The first T-72 had almost reached the western end of the bridge when the first charges blew. Cracks appeared in the concrete roadbed under its treads and the bridge sagged a foot or so, but it didn't collapse.

The tank driver revved his diesel engine and raced the last few yards to solid ground. Once he was safe on the bridge abutment, he locked his tracks, bringing the forty-two ton war machine to a skidding halt. In the command hatch, the tank commander spun his turret in search of a target. Being a tanker, his favorite target was infantrymen.

As he looked for his enemy, he radioed for another of his armored brethren to join him in the hunt.

THE WHIP CRACK of the T-72's 125 mm high velocity gun was the sound of biblical doom to Hawkins. He'd always figured that he was going to hell, but damnation had come to him early in the form of a tank spitting flame. The HEAT warhead impacted the outcropping a millisecond later, sending jagged rock splinters flying like shrapnel. Getting hit by a chunk of flying rock could be as fatal as any bullet.

Regardless of his chosen profession, Hawkins wasn't the kind of man to go out of his way to look for trouble unless he absolutely had to. But this time, trouble had come looking for him, big time. If that tank kept coming, none of them would be walking away from the confrontation. Since he was the man with the RPG, it was up to him to try to stop that tanker's advance.

Before edging out around the side of his boulder, Hawkins made sure that the round was properly seated in the front of the launcher. Keeping low to remain as inconspicuous as possible, he lined up the RPG's sights on the front of the tank right below the driver's position, and fired.

Trailing dirty white smoke, the rocket streaked for the T-72. The 85 mm shaped charge warhead detonated with a bang and a gout of flame, and black smoke burst from the front slope of the tank's armor.

When the smoke cleared, there was a glowing red pockmark on the front armor, but that was all.

The whining sound of the turret turning toward him sent Hawkins back behind the boulder for cover. The ex-Ranger had come up against a lot of different opponents in his career, but slugging it out with a tank was a first for him. If he lived through this pissing contest, he intended to make sure that he never had to fight a tank again. The damned things were just too hard to kill.

The whip crack of the tank's main gun thundered, and almost instantaneously the projectile slammed into the rock in front of him. Dust filled the air and rock splinters whizzed past his head.

Coughing to clear his lungs, Hawkins fumbled to load another rocket into the RPG. This time, he'd try for the turret ring to see if he could at least disable the main gun.

He had to do something, or they were all going to die where they stood.

Stony Man Farm, Virginia

THE BIG SCREEN MONITORS in the Farm's Computer Room were switching from one spy satellite to the next, trying to find the best picture of what was unfolding in the Potemkin National Forest. "We have a real problem now," Aaron Kurtzman announced solemnly. "It looks like Gary had a detonator failure and the secondary charges didn't fire. The bridge is still standing."

"Radio them to pull back," Hal Brognola ordered.

"I'm not sure that they can."

"What do you mean?"

"They have a tank to deal with first," Kurtzman said. "One of them got across the bridge. If they try to run, they'll get chopped to pieces."

"Another tank's trying to cross the bridge," Hunt Wethers called out.

Brognola hoped against hope that the bridge had been damaged enough that it couldn't bear the weight of the T-72. But when an operation went to hell, hope was usually vain and that was the case this time.

"It made it," Weathers said. "Now they have to fight two of them."

Popping two antacid tablets, Brognola prayed to the gods of war for a miracle.

WITH THE LEAD T-72 concentrating on ferreting out Hawkins from behind his rock, Rafael Encizo was able to sneak around to the side with the other RPG launcher to try for a deflection shot. He had a healthy respect for tanks, but he had faced them before. The JS-IIIs of Castro's army had played hell with the brigade on the beach of the Bay of Pigs. He didn't discount the danger they represented, but he knew that they could be killed. A well-trained man with a good rocket launcher and a decent shot was more than a match for one of the metal monsters.

Once he had his position, he flipped up the sight, hoisted the launcher to his shoulder and stood to take his shot. The olive green tank was only a hundred yards away, well within the range of his weapon. He sighted on the gap between the top of the track and the road wheels. It was a small space to try to shoot through, but fortunately, this tank wasn't wearing its side skirts, which made his task a little easier. A tank's armor was always thinner on the sides, and it made a good kill point.

Taking his time, he waited until he had a steady

hold before he fired. The RPG round flew between the track and the road wheels and detonated against the side of the hull. The 85 mm shaped charge warhead turned into a half-inch diameter jet of molten metal and explosive gasses upon detonation. The superheated jet blasted through the side armor like a cutting torch, melting the steel as it went.

When it penetrated all the way into the interior, all hell broke loose. Most of the ammunition for the T-72's 125 mm main gun was stored in an autoloader under the breach and behind the driver's seat. The shaped charge blast hit one of the warheads and set it off.

Encizo was pleased to see the RPG score this time. After the initial detonation, there was a secondary explosion from inside the tank. The hatch covers blew open, emitting fireballs and chunks of what had been the tank's crew. The fuel tanks erupted an instant later, enveloping the back half of the tank in a boiling fireball. The stench of burning meat was strong over the smell of the diesel.

Loading another rocket into the front of his launcher, Encizo tried to get a clear shot at the second T-72, but was too late. When the first tank went up in flame, its partner went into reverse, backing up as fast at it could go across the span to the far end of the bridge. Turning in its tracks, it presented its thick frontal armor and brought its co-ax machine gun into play as well as the main gun.

WITH EVERYTHING HAPPENING so fast, Gary Manning double-checked his remote detonator to make sure that it was working properly and tried it once more. Again, the charges wouldn't fire. "I checked everything, Striker!" he shouted over the rattle of small-arms fire. "The detonators must be faulty!"

"Get out of there," Bolan ordered. "We'll cover you."

"Wait a minute guys," Hawkins called. "Give me a shot at it.

"Gary," he said, turning to the blaster, "are your secondaries connected with det cord?"

Det cord had to be the most helpful thing for a blaster since the invention of gunpowder. The explosive core of det cord was a plastic explosive that could be safely burned without detonating. However, when subjected to an explosive shock like that of a blasting cap, it, too, would explode, and the shock wave traveled down the cord at thousands of feet per second. If the demolition charges were connected with it, all he would have to do was blow one of them and the rest would go off as well.

"Yeah," Manning came back. "I used the standard wrap."

"Cover me," Hawkins said. "I'm going to try to set one of the charges off with a 40 mm."

Like most RDX explosives, Semtex was designed to be less sensitive to shock than dynamite, so it was safer to handle under field conditions. To sympathetically set off an RDX, it was more important for the shock to be fast than powerful, which meant a detonation of another charge of a fast explosive. The explosive core of a 40 mm grenade was C-4 plastique, and it detonated fast enough to propagate a sympathetic detonation in an RDX like Semtex.

One of the highlights of Hawkins's misspent youth had been the time he and a cousin had used their hunting rifles to detonate several sticks of old dynamite they had found at an abandoned quarry. While not an RDX, the dynamite contained nitroglycerine in a sawdust matrix, and the sticks were so old that the nitro was sweating out of them. Their light .22-caliber rifles had been enough to set them off. All he had to do was get a grenade close enough to Manning's secondary charges, and they would detonate like that old dynamite had.

BY NOW, ground troops had responded and were deploying along the other side of the gorge. They were the brigade's support troops instead of trained infantry, but there was nothing wrong with their marksmanship. AK rounds sang as they ricocheted off the rocks around the commandos. Under the cover of the tank fire, a squad of Russians was climbing down into the gorge.

Like all SVR officers, Yuri Belakov had endured several months of army infantry basic training before becoming an officer. He hadn't enjoyed it at the time, but once it was over, he had felt a sense of pride. He had completed the rigorous training and felt that he could handle himself on a battlefield. Since the Russian intelligence service didn't spend much time fighting conventional actions, though, he had put his infantry expertise in storage immediately after graduation.

Spotting the troops trying to make the end run on them, he suddenly remembered everything that the drill instructors had hammered into him so long ago. It was time for him to put his skills to work.

"We have a squad trying to flank us to the north," he called out over the com link. "I'm going after them."

"I'll cover you," Encizo replied.

Finding a new rock to shelter him, Belakov took a deep breath and started to fire at his countrymen.

OBLIVIOUS TO THE firefight raging above him, Hawkins climbed a few yards down the side of the chasm until he had a clear line of sight to the charges on the first pylon. The 40 mm grenade was designed to fly slowly through the air like a mortar round. Since its flight followed a ballistic arc, the launcher's sights were graduated to hit a target on the same level as the gunner. He was trying to hit a target twenty feet above him, so the sights were useless for direct firing. They could be used, however, to pick an imaginary aim point whose trajectory intersected the bridge.

His best chance was to aim so that the grenade was still on the upward half of its trajectory when it collided with the bridge. Taking a sight on a distinctive tree on the cliff beyond the bridge, he fired. The grenade flew right over the bridge and impacted on the cliff. Too high. Jacking another round into the launcher, he lowered his sights and fired again. This time it was too low.

"Get your ass out of there, T.J.," McCarter radioed. "They're bringing up a VLB. As soon as it's laid across the weakened area, we're going to be up to our asses in pissed-off tankers."

"Give me one more," Hawkins sent back. "I think I've got the hang of it now."

Using his reference point again, Hawkins carefully aimed and fired. This time the grenade arced out and hit a foot above the charges and a bit to the left. Again it was close, but no cigar.

"Dammit!" He ducked back and slid the launcher barrel forward to eject the empty case.

"T.J.!" McCarter called. "Get your ass out of there now! We're pulling out."

"I'm coming, I'm coming," Hawkins sent back as he stuffed another grenade into the launcher and locked the breech.

Sighting six inches lower than he had the shot before, he gave himself a little more windage, took a deep breath, let it out slowly and fired.

For a moment, he thought that round was going to miss too. From where he stood, it looked to be going high again. To his pure joy, he saw it hit the lower part of the exposed charge and detonate.

There was no thunderous explosion or balls of flame boiling up into the air. There weren't even any chunks of concrete flying out in all directions. Instead there was a series of sharp cracks, sounding more like a tank gun firing than an explosion. Puffs of brownish-gray smoke shot out from the junctures of the support girders as the linked secondary charges each detonated in turn, cutting another girder loose.

When the echoes of the explosions faded, the Stony Man warriors heard a deep groan. For a moment the bridge seemed to hang in the air. Then the weight of the superstructure bearing down on the now doubly weakened girders obeyed the laws of physics and took the path of least resistance. Since Manning had done a high-low offset cut, it took a moment for gravity to do the other half of the job for him, but gravity never failed.

The driver of the VLB vehicle tried to drop his span and back away, but he ran out of time. The roadbed dropped out from underneath him before he could uncouple his load. Slowly tumbling through the air, the thirty-three ton vehicle crashed into the gorge. It didn't bounce when it hit the rocks below.

The gorge was shrouded in dust and smoke as the western half of the bridge followed it into the chasm.

"T.J.!" McCarter called out. "Get out of there before the dust settles. They can't see you now."

"I'm on the way," Hawkins radioed back. "Cover me."

WITH NO MORE TANKS to shoot at, Encizo was using the last of their antitank rockets as artillery against the Russian troops Belakov was keeping busy. They weren't as effective as a mortar would have been, but they didn't have a mortar. After firing his last rocket, he took up his H & K to continue the battle.

He had just taken up a position beside the SVR officer when a ricocheting bullet tore into Belakov's thigh. Firing full-auto as he ran, he dashed across the broken ground to the wounded man.

"Belakov took a round in the leg," Encizo radioed as he tied a field dressing around the wound.

"Can he walk?" Bolan asked.

"With help."

"Start him back. We'll cover you."

WITH ENCIZO AND BELAKOV safely away and Hawkins back on top, the remainder of the team faded back into the forest behind them. The Russian fire didn't stop once they were under the trees. Even though the tanks didn't carry proximity-fuzed HE ammunition for air bursts, they still fired their contact-detonated HE round into the tops of the trees. The explosions not only sent shell fragments raining upon the fleeing men, but deadly splinters of the trees as well. There was no point in zigzagging. The Stony Man warriors could only keep going as fast as they could to get out of range.

When they finally reached their vehicles, they stopped long enough to take the dressing off Belakov's wound. "It's not bad," Hawkins said as he cleaned away the blood. "It went clean through. You'll be running the marathon again before the week is out."

"But I am not a runner," Belakov said, sounding confused.

"You'd better practice then, hadn't you?"

CHAPTER TWENTY-TWO

Stony Man Farm, Virginia

The monitors in the Computer Room were all linked to the recon satellites keeping watch over the battle for the bridge in the Potemkin forest. A satcom radio link was also in place, but Kurtzman couldn't intercept the com-link transmissions, so it was like watching a movie with the sound off. It was difficult for Price and the others to make sense of what they were seeing. No matter how many times they had gone through the drill, it still wasn't easy to sit thousands of miles away in complete safety while men they knew like brothers risked all.

While the satellite overwatch gave them much information they could send to the field units, it also brought them closer to the action and increased their sense of helplessness. They had seen the first set of demolition charges go off and had seen that the bridge had withstood them. But with the commandos fighting for their lives, they had known better than to radio for an explanation. They could only watch as the team continued the fight.

Then came the second set of explosions and what looked like the west end of the bridge collapsing.

"We have visual confirmation that the bridge is down," Hunt Wethers announced as he monitored the radar satellite sensors. "Those tanks aren't going to be leaving there for a long time."

A cheer broke out in the Computer Room, snapping the tension.

"Our guys are pulling back unopposed," Wethers continued as he took a quick report over the satcom radio. "Some of the tanks are firing into the woods from the edge of the gorge, but they're firing blind."

"Are there any casualties?" Barbara Price asked. She and Hal Brognola had been camped out in the Computer Room since the team had reached the forest, and the wait had been just as hard on them.

"The Russian picked up a bullet, but it's nothing serious. He's moving under his own power."

"I'm going to call the President," Brognola said. "And then I want everyone in the War Room for a conference call with Katz. I want to get this thing wrapped up as soon as possible. This has gone on long enough, and I want our people out of there before election day."

"You won't get any arguments from me on that," Price said. "If you'll remember, I wasn't exactly fond of this idea in the first place."

"I know, but we need to work out a way to tie up all the loose ends so the minister doesn't try to call in any more markers with the President. I don't want to have to go in there again anytime soon."

"I think our guys have done more than their share for Mother Russia," Price said. "Sooner or later, those people are going to have to learn to take care of their own problems."

"That's what we've been working for," Brognola said. "A chance for the Russian people to break free of the power brokers and make their democracy work for them. But Leoninski and Zerinov still have their hooks into too many of the people in government. They've brought governmental corruption to new heights, and we need to run them to ground and eliminate them before this will really be over."

"Let's get it done, then. I'm getting a little tired of hearing about this Lion guy and the general he has in his pocket. I'm also tired of having the President on our case about those people."

Brognola smiled.

"I'll see what I can do."

WHILE THE BLACKSUITS didn't have a "need to know" about the details of ongoing Stony Man missions, the grapevine between the War Room and the security force worked well, and this latest mission was no exception. Almost as soon as the bridge in the Potemkin National Forest came down, the blacksuits were talking about it.

"What's everybody in such a good mood about?" Jim Gordon asked his shift leader during the lunch break.

The man smiled broadly. "Apparently Striker and the boys really put it to the Russians again. Damn, a handful of guys taking out a tank brigade. That has to be some kind of a world record for brass balls. I'm an old Gulf War grunt myself, and I'd have loved to have been in on that one. Those Russian tanks in Iraq used to give me the shits, and I'd give anything to get some payback on those tin bastards.''

This wasn't the first time Gordon had heard about this mysterious Striker's doings. Exactly who he was, though, he hadn't learned yet, but his name kept coming up in conversation. From what he had been able to piece together, he was the leader of the commando unit, and a hero to the security force. The fact that this hero had somehow managed to neutralize a Russian army unit burned into Gordon's brain.

"Do you know what they did?" Gordon asked.

The shift leader downed the last of his sandwich before replying. "I don't have any idea. We don't have a need to know and all of that, but Striker's people have pulled off some unbelievable operations over the years. They're a real kick-ass bunch of guys.''

Gordon wasn't buying the story that only a few men had been able to destroy a tank brigade. That simply wasn't credible. But he did believe that the action arm of this organization had been targeted against the Russian army, and he felt it had to be connected with the upcoming election. Since one of the leading candidates was General Pavel Zerinov, the unit had to have been supporting him and it had been taken out to reduce his chances.

Unlike most of the Russians living in the Mother Country, Gordon knew the history of his homeland quite well, and normally he didn't like to see military officers involved in Russian politics. Generals thought with weapons, and he didn't want to see his country fall into another civil war. Too much of that had gone on already this century, and the Russian people had to stop killing one another. But from what he had been able to gather through the biased American media, Zerinov was the best hope to bring Russia back to what it had been before the disgraceful fall. At this point in time, a strong leader was the only hope to create a stronger Russia and if this organization was working against him, they had to be stopped.

The question was, how could he make any difference to an operation that was taking place half the world away? He was only one man, and he was surrounded by constantly vigilant enemies. As much as he wanted to take action, he knew that he couldn't chance it. His best course was to continue to try to find weaknesses in the organization and take his information to someone who would be able to help him seek revenge.

He had considered contacting the Russian Mafia and asking for their assistance. But he wasn't sure that he could trust them. From what he had learned of them during his time as a marshal, they were little more than street scum and were driven by greed like all of the other criminals he had encountered. He knew that he couldn't expect to find many of them who longed for the worker's paradise of the past.

It was obvious that he wouldn't be able to do anything to affect the operation against Zerinov. He was but one man, and he had learned about this organization much too late. But he vowed that he would do something to try to ensure that the people who ran this place would pay a price for meddling in things that weren't their concern.

BUCK GREENE HAD TAKEN Kurtzman's admonition to lay low to heart. Instead of prowling the Farm personally checking on each and every detail of the day's work, the security chief was camped out in the Computer Room. He had spent the morning sucking down Kurtzman's coffee and watching the raw feed from the surveillance cameras as it came in over the monitors.

"Aaron," he asked, "why is this feed so choppy? I know the cameras have a longer duration scan than this. It's like it starts a scan and then switches to another camera."

"That's just the miracle of cyberediting," Kurtzman explained. "The computer's recognizing our man Gordon and is sending only the tape segments that he appears in. That way we don't have to sit through hours of bullshit to get to our boy's activities."

"But he's not doing anything." Greene sounded extremely disappointed. Although he reviewed the tapes once a week, somehow he had expected this to be different.

"What did you expect?" Kurtzman asked. "If this guy is who we think he is, he's not going to be planting bombs when he's supposed to be doing his work. He's a real pro, and you've got to remember that he's damned near as American as you or I. He's not going to slip up and do something foreign when he thinks no one's watching."

"You're right," Greene agreed. "I guess I keep thinking of the VC infiltrators we used to get in Nam. We'd catch those bastards pacing off the distance from the gun pits to the perimeter or sketching the layout of the fuel depots. This time, I guess we're going to have to watch a lot of tape before we catch him off base."

"That's why I have a computer," Kurtzman said. "And that's why I told it to do that for us."

"How's that?"

"I worked up a program that will keep track of everything he does and tag anything that looks to be out of the ordinary compared to everything else. It will do the gross sorting, and we'll just have to look for the details."

"How'd you do that so fast?"

"I just modified a surveillance program I already had set up," Kurtzman replied. "All I had to do was to write in his personal ID characteristics so it can pick him out from all the other blacksuits. Then I have it scan for certain predesignated activities and tag them. It's easy enough to do once you have the main program set up.''

"So it will watch him for us?"

"Day and night," Kurtzman said. "And, after thinking about it, I've come to the conclusion that it might be best if you went back to your usual routine. Gordon's new around here, but he's been here long enough to have a good feel for how we do things. If he sees you disappear from your daily rounds, it might make him suspicious. Right now, we need to keep him as calm as we can. Raising his anxiety level is going to put him even more on guard.''

"You've got a point."

"But like I said before, don't focus on him and don't talk to any of the others about him. Just do your normal rounds like you always do."

"I guess I'll go back out there then."

"Just make sure you have a radio with you at all times," Kurtzman said. "The computer and I will keep watching this stuff, and I'll give you a call if I see anything that looks out of place."

"You see him doing anything out of line, and I'll be on him like white on rice."

JIM GORDON HAD the unmistakable feeling that he was being watched. It was so strong that he had to stop himself from stopping and turning. Even though he had been in enemy territory for fifteen years, he didn't have much real field experience as a spy. All he'd had to do was be the man whose name he had taken and to be careful about meeting anyone from his supposed past. It hadn't been the same as being an agent on unfamiliar enemy soil because he was as good an American as the next guy. Therefore, he didn't have the well-honed survival instincts of a real spy.

Nonetheless, as a marshal, he had learned to trust his gut instincts. And if he felt that he was being watched, he probably was. But if he was, the question was why?

Even though he'd had a scare about the Little Amerika lists being published, he didn't think that he had been found out. If the organization's leaders had any real suspicions about him, he'd have been taken in for questioning immediately rather than being allowed to remain free and a threat.

Also, he was certain that his fellow guards would have a hard time hiding their feelings if they suspected that he was bad. But he couldn't see that anything had changed in the way the other guards were treating him. They were still taking his money at the poker table, they were still eating their meals with him and loaning him boot polish when he ran out. If they thought he was an enemy agent, he'd have been taken out somewhere and shot.

The only thing he could see that was different was that he was being given boring, make-work duty assignments instead of being sent to different places each day to complete his indoctrination to the system. The security chief did seem to be keeping a close eye on him, that was true. But the chief did that with everyone, particularly the probationary blacksuits. Not much slipped by his constant scrutiny.

When he laid it out like that, he was confident that his name hadn't been connected with the Little Amerika list. Maybe he was being watched because of the gas-pump and power-line incidents. An organization like this one had to be professionally paranoid in order to exist. Maybe all of the other blacksuits felt this way too and had just learned to ignore it.

He couldn't afford to do that, however, and his self-imposed mission had just become even more dangerous. He was going to have to make sure that he was always where he was supposed to be, that he didn't have any more "accidents" and that his actions were completely above reproach. His name had come up twice so far, and he couldn't afford to have it come up again.

His plan to booby trap the diesel fuel tank would have to be put on hold. This was no time to be found with a stolen grenade in his pocket. He might feel safe enough later to try it, but he doubted it. Until the day he left this place, he was going to have to act as if he were on center stage with the entire world watching his every move.

This also meant that he needed to find another way to slip away if he felt he needed to. Without his planned diversion, though, it wasn't going to be easy. Simply taking off and running down the road wasn't going to work. If he was being watched as closely as he thought, he'd be gunned down before he took three steps.

That left the vehicles. There were a couple of high-powered Dodge Ram pickups that had been purposefully battered and left unwashed so they would look more like run-of-the-mill farm trucks. One of them would make a good getaway vehicle if he could disable the other one before he left.

The usual movie solution to take out a vehicle was to shoot out the tires. That tactic had worked well in the fifties, but with modern run-flat tires, it wasn't an option. A sharp jab in the radiator, however, was a simple but very effective solution. And it didn't require his doing anything more suspicious than having a sharp, sturdy implement around at all times. A pocketknife, a screw driver or even a sharp stick would do.

All he had to do now was find out where the keys were kept.

CHAPTER TWENTY-THREE

Moscow, Russia

Now that Zerinov's armored threat had been neutralized, it was time for the Stony Man warriors to put an end to the operation by tying up the loose ends in Moscow. When the team approached the city, Katzenelenbogen radioed them the location of the new safehouse hotel. After getting cleaned up and having a quick meal in the hotel dining room, Bolan and Phoenix Force joined Able Team for an after-dinner drink and tactical session.

"You did a good job on the bridge," Katz told Bolan. "The satellites confirm that enough of it is down that the whole thing's going to have to be rebuilt before the tanks can use it again. At least that much of Zerinov's program has been put on indefinite hold."

"Way to go, Gary!" Calvin James high-fived Manning from across the table.

The Canadian bowed.

"The other good news," Katz continued, "is that

there're three less Wolverines for us to worry about.''

''How'd you manage that?'' David McCarter asked. Though the Wolverines had yet to score against them, they had been a concern of his ever since Yuri Belakov announced that they'd been put in play.

''That was almost a freebie,'' Katz said. ''When we left the old safehouse, Gadgets left a couple of packages behind. We didn't do as well with them as I would have liked, but at least we cut the odds some. Those guys might have been good at what they did in Afghanistan, but they could use a few pointers in urban combat operations. They made a good entry, but they missed the booby traps.''

''What do you have planned next?'' Bolan asked.

''I've drafted a little program I think will wrap this up for us. First, we're going to concentrate on the weakest link: Leoninski. With him out of the way, his people will cease to be a factor, and we can concentrate on the general.''

''What about the surviving Wolverines?'' McCarter asked.

''We'll keep an eye out for them, of course, but I have started something with the Lion, and I want to keep the pressure on him. While you were gone, we stopped by his headquarters and left a few RPG calling cards.''

''We caught them completely by surprise,'' Schwarz added, grinning widely. ''I'd have loved to have seen Leoninski's face if he was in there when the RPGs started flying through his windows."

"You may get that chance yet," Katz said, "because here's what I have in mind…"

GENERAL PAVEL ZERINOV took the news from Potemkin Forest as well as could be expected. Following as it did on the heels of the Wolverines' ambush, it was an even stronger blow. He had already dispatched an engineer unit to the site to try to repair the bridge. From the reports he had received, it was severely damaged and it would be weeks before it could bear the weight of tanks again, more weeks than he had before the election.

This wasn't the first time that he had suffered a setback in a well-planned operation, and he wasn't out of the game yet. Flexibility was the greatest asset a military man could have, but he had to admit that with the brigade effectively lost to him, he had a serious problem.

Now that the tanks had been found, the shock effect they would have created on election day was lost. Lost along with it was the silent support of much of the Russian army. As long as it had looked like he was going to be successful, the other generals had been willing to sit and wait. Now that he had lost his big edge, they would start looking to their own interests. He hadn't had their open support before, but at least they hadn't come out against him. Now, he was hearing that some of them were thinking about taking a stance to oppose him.

Now more than ever, he would have to rely on Leoninski and his thugs to determine the outcome of the vote. Their methods, though, were blatantly corrupt, and, worst of all, expensive. Buying votes was neither subtle, nor cheap. Also, gangsters didn't have the brutal impact that a single forty-two-ton tank could have. The Russian people knew what armor represented—raw power. A tank didn't even have to fire its guns for its presence to be felt. When the armor had rolled before, it had put Boris Yeltsin in power and it would have seen him win the presidency as well.

With the situation as it was, Zerinov decided to move his CP to his country dacha. If the cards continued to turn against him, he didn't want to be trapped in the city. The Progressive Party apparatus would stay to run the campaign, and he would still fly out to make personal appearances, but he wanted room to maneuver if he had to.

He hadn't made plans to run yet, but he knew that a good general was always prepared for the worst.

VASILY LEBEDEV HAD BURIED his dead from the safehouse ambush and was moving on with renewed purpose. This was the second time the Americans had beaten him, but there wouldn't be a third.

Along with his surviving Wolverines, he had recruited a dozen veterans as reinforcements for his strike force and another two dozen as scouts. Scouting for a handful of the enemy in a city of millions wasn't an easy task. Fortunately, however, two of the Americans were ethnics and they would stand out in any crowd of native Russians. His extra eyes were already getting results.

Since one of the Yankee commandos was a black, he had been the obvious first target. Within hours, all over Moscow foreign blacks were being checked out and rejected as the one he was looking for. He also had other men looking for older Hispanic males. They weren't as easy to spot as the blacks because Russia still had contacts in South America, but they stood out.

As with any process of elimination, it was slow going but he was narrowing the field. If he was lucky, he'd get a lead in the first day or two, but it would take as long as it took. The next time he would know what he was sending his men into.

CALVIN JAMES FELT like he was a teenager again and had been caught in the wrong part of Chicago. Walking down what passed for Moscow's main street, he stood out as if he were wearing a flashing strobe light. Not only was he dressed in fashionable Western clothing, he was the only black he had seen all morning. Ninety percent of the passersby, both men and women, gave him more than a casual glance. More than a few quickly moved out of his way.

As he approached the ornate stone Metro subway station, a middle-aged man pushed himself away from the wall and walked toward him.

"Excuse me, mister," the Russian said, blocking his path, "do you have a cigarette for me?"

"Sorry," James said, shaking his head. "I don't smoke."

"Are you sure?"

James moved back half a step to give himself fighting room. "Yes, dammit, I'm sure. Get lost."

The Russian looked at him for a moment longer before melting back into the crowd.

"I think you just made contact, Calvin," Yuri Belakov's voice said over his earphone. "He was wearing a Veteran's Club pin."

"He also turned around ten yards behind you and is following you now," Carl Lyons added. "But don't worry, I'm on him."

"If I get killed doing this shit," James growled, "I'm going to come back and haunt you bastards."

"We've got you covered," Gary Manning said confidently. "Just keep moving toward the meeting place. It's down in the next block."

"I've got you in sight, Calvin," Rosario Blancanales called in next. "I'm thirty yards ahead at the corner of the Kit Kat Klub."

"I've got the sign," James radioed when he saw the flashing neon cat holding a champagne glass.

The Kit Kat Klub was one of Moscow's more famous champagne clubs, night spots that specialized in serving Russia's famed sparkling wine with the finest in feminine companionship on the side. The prices at these establishments were well beyond what ninety-five percent of the Muscovites could afford, so they were patronized by foreign business-men with generous expense accounts. The only Russians allowed in the doors were men who were connected to one of the crime syndicates. Since the Kit Kat was one of Leoninski's operations, most of the hoods loitering on the premises would be on his payroll.

Blancanales and James exchanged elaborate greetings on the sidewalk to joggle the memories of any watchers. When the bouncer heard them speaking English, he dusted off his limited vocabulary and invited them inside for a drink and to watch the show. His winking leer promised unspoken delights.

James and Blancanales stepped into the smoky club and were intercepted by a scantily clad waitress. "How about a table by the stage?" James asked.

The stage took up most of one wall and was brightly lighted so no detail of the world-class collection of dancing blondes and redheads would be missed. None of the girls looked to be much older than eighteen or nineteen, and they were just getting down to their G-strings to the accompaniment of classical disco tunes.

"Now I know where the seventies went," James said as the waitress led them to a table right in front of the stage. "They fled to Russia."

"You must admit, though," Blancanales said as a busty, long-haired blonde started doing bottomless squat-thrusts mere inches from his face, "this does give a whole new meaning to 'Staying Alive.'

That's got to be the best-looking BeeGee I ever saw.''

''I'm kind of partial to the redhead down on the left, myself,'' James said with a grin.

''How about a report?'' Katz's voice came in over their com links. ''You guys're supposed to be on the job.''

''Don't I wish,'' James said.

Now that the gyrating girls were down to the bare essentials, almost every eye in the place, Russian and foreigner alike, was focused on the stage.

''Well,'' Blancanales said, ''it looks like we have a mixture of the Russian women's Olympic gymnastic team and the Miss Universe finalists working out on the stage sans attire. The audience is about one-quarter thugs—you can tell them by the gold neck chains—and the rest are businessmen running up their expense accounts. You can spot the Americans by their bulging eyeballs. The Germans, French, et al, are taking this all pretty much in stride. We have a couple of guys giving us the eye, but nothing serious.''

''Keep your mikes hot so we'll know if something goes down.''

''That's not the only thing that's hot,'' James said. ''Can I be excused for half an hour or so?''

''We've got the back,'' Bolan broke in. ''Give us a moment, and we'll be inside.''

''Roger.''

With Lyons, Schwarz and Belakov hanging around the entrance and Bolan coming in the back with McCarter, Encizo and Manning, the Kit Kat Klub was surrounded.

"The girls are coming down onto the floor," Blancanales said. "This might be a good time to make your entrance. No one's going to be noticing much else for a while."

"On the way," Bolan said.

When James's redhead started his way, he pushed his chair back to get ready for the lap dance that was sure to come. To his shock, she bypassed him with barely a smile and zeroed in on the fat balding guy at the next table. When he saw the American hundred-dollar bill the man was waving, he understood why he had been stood up.

"We've got to get our expense account upped to cover situations like this," he muttered to Blancanales.

"We're in," Bolan said. "Get ready."

Blancanales pushed his chair back as well and cleared the edge of his jacket. Snapping open his briefcase, James put his hands on the MP-5 subgun inside.

Over the noise of the crowd, James heard a bit of a fuss at the front door and laid his hand on the pistol grip of his subgun. A moment later, Belakov walked in with Lyons and Schwarz flanking him. The two Able Team commandos had their MP-5s in their hands.

"This is a raid," Belakov shouted in Russian, then added in English, "everyone sit where you are and don't move."

One of the thugs at a side table rose to his feet and reached for a piece. From the back of the room, Bolan tripped the hammer of his silenced Beretta 93-R and drilled a trio of 9 mm rounds into his chest.

That show of force silenced the entire room.

"Just stay where you are and no one else will get hurt," Belakov said in Russian. "If you move, you will be shot."

As soon as the crowd was under control, James and Blancanales motioned for Belakov to join them at the bar. "Tell him that we want the money in the till," James told the SVR agent.

"Hand over the money," Belakov ordered the bartender.

When the man reached for something other than his cash register, James grabbed a bottle of champagne from the bar and slammed it against the side of the bartender's head. The man went down and stayed.

Reaching across the bar, James emptied the cash register and stuffed the currency into his briefcase. The overflow went into his pockets. Business was good at the Kit Kat Klub.

"Do you speak English?" Blancanales asked one of the hoods who was sitting motionless at the bar, his hands in plain sight.

The thug nodded. "A little."

"Tell your boss that he's finished in Moscow."

"Finished?"

"Done. Kaput. No more."

"*Da*. Finished."

"Make sure you tell him." James tapped him on the shoulder with the muzzle of his subgun.

The thug nodded, a surly expression on his face. "I will tell him."

With Bolan and his team covering the room, the others slipped past them and headed for the back door. Jack Grimaldi had pulled the team's van behind the club, and Katzenelenbogen had the doors open for them. As soon as the last man was in, Grimaldi stomped on the gas and sped down the alley. When he reached the street, he slipped in front of a bus and got lost in traffic.

"WE NEED TO GO BACK to that place when this gig is over," James said. "I think I've fallen in love."

"I don't think you can afford her, Calvin." Blancanales laughed. "Did you see that hundred-dollar bill that guy was waving at her? She zeroed in on him like she was a Sidewinder missile. Money talks and bullshit really walks in this town."

"I also need an advance on my pay."

"Now you're really dreaming."

"What's next?" McCarter asked Katz.

Katz looked at his list and the city map. "There's another club not too far from here we might drop in on. It's not as upscale as the Kit Kat, but it should be worth knocking over."

"What are we going to do with all the money we're collecting?" Hawkins asked.

"I thought we'd ask the minister if he could find

us a charity to donate it do. Maybe a home for retired hookers or politicians.''

"They're the same thing, aren't they?''

"It's called democracy.''

CHAPTER TWENTY-FOUR

Stony Man Farm, Virginia

Even though Jim Gordon had tried to reason out the situation he now found himself in, the feeling of being constantly watched was wearing at his nerves. Like it or not, he was beginning to think that he might not be able to stick it out until stand down. The normal shift rotation had two weeks left to run, and he just didn't think he could last that long. The stress was overwhelming him, and he was starting to make small but stupid mistakes. It hadn't been anything serious so far, but he was afraid that he was going to do something out of carelessness that would draw attention to himself again.

He still hadn't found the base's Achilles' heel yet and didn't want to leave until he did. He knew that once he left, the only way he would ever get back would be at the head of a strike force. There was nothing to be learned about the base from outside the perimeter fence. The only way he was going to find what he needed was to continue to be a black-suit for as long as possible.

AFTER DINNER that evening, he walked around the grounds for half an hour as he usually did before going into the blacksuit dayroom. He was starting to polish his boots yet again when one of the guards called out from the poker table. "Hey, Gordon, you got any money you want to lose tonight? Jackson puked out on me and we need a fourth."

He had sat out the last couple of games because his mind just hadn't been on it. Maybe it would be good for him to switch mental screens and think about something else for awhile.

"Sure," he replied. "I think I'm about ready for another lesson."

"You'd better watch that guy," Jackson called out from his bunk at the other end of the room. "He took all of my money and now he wants yours."

"I'm not taking his money," the card shark said, laughing. "He's paying me for the privilege of learning the game."

"I've heard that bullshit before."

The first hand Gordon was dealt was junk, and he folded without putting out a bet. The second hand that came to him was loaded, and he just couldn't think how to break it up so he wouldn't win. Screw it, he thought, even a loser had to win every now and then. He played the hand he had been given and won the small pot.

"Damn!" The last man in the game folded his hand and pushed the poker chips across the table. "That's one for the books. Our man Gordon finally hit the big time and won one. We'll have to tell the chief so he can save the tape of that one and give it to you.''

Gordon felt the adrenaline race through him. ''What tape?'' he asked.

The player pointed to the end of the room. Up on the wall by the alarm and the smoke detector was what had to be a small camera. If he had noticed it before, he had to have thought that it was part of the alarm system.

''Damned near everything we do around here is taped,'' another man explained. ''That's why we have to keep our games clean. Old Buck would have our ass in a sling if he caught one of us cheating.''

Gordon felt like he had been hit in the stomach with a baseball bat. If the tapes of their games were being reviewed by someone who knew poker, his ''losses'' would quickly be seen for what they were. Anyone watching his discards would see in a flash that he had been throwing away winning hands.

''You're saying that there are cameras all around here?''

''You bet your ass there are. Damned near every inch of this place is covered by some kind of video camera or other, even the orchard and the fields. That's the only way we can keep track of this place with so few guys. There's no way an intruder can get in here without being seen, either.''

Now Gordon knew why he had been feeling the way he had. Someone had been watching him at all times. Why it had taken him so long to notice it, he didn't know. The only question now was what he should do about it. He knew that if he begged out of the game now, the other players would know why he was doing it. The only thing he could do was to stay in the game, but play very carefully, knowing that his every discard would be scrutinized.

The adrenaline rush had put his mind back on his business. But, even playing poorly, the cards kept coming to him and by the end of the evening, he was still a couple of dollars ahead. Since this was a penny-ante game, it wasn't much, but it was the first time he had ended the evening ahead.

"Damn, Gordon, now I'm going to have to find myself another fish." The man who had talked him into playing grinned. "There's no point in playing with guys who beat me all the time. I can't make any stand-down money that way."

Gordon forced himself to relax. "I'm just trying to make back a little of what I lost before," he said. "I need some walking-around money, too."

"Where are you going to take your stand down?"

"I was thinking of going back to San Diego," Gordon said. "That was my last station as a marshal before I signed up for this gig."

"You ought to come down to Florida with me," the man suggested. "Three of us have a beach house in Tampa Bay we time-share, and the fishing's really great. We also do pretty well with the tourist girls this time of year. They get tired of the locals real quick because they won't buy them drinks. We've got room for one more if you'd like to join us."

"I appreciate the invitation," Gordon said, "but

I've got to pass this time. I need to finish up some business in San Diego. I got the job so quickly after the interview that I left a lot of loose ends out there I need to get wrapped up.'' He grinned. ''One of them's named Sylvia.''

''I understand those kind of wrap-ups. I've had to do one or two of those myself. Maybe next time.''

''I'll keep it in mind.''

''DAMN THAT WILKINS,'' Buck Greene said as he watched the tape of the poker game. ''He should have kept his mouth shut. Now that Gordon knows about the video cameras, he'll really be careful.''

''Did you watch his play tonight?'' Kurtzman asked. ''He was being very careful. He still played badly, but he wasn't so obvious about it and he stopped dumping his cards like he'd done before.''

''That's even more proof, isn't it?''

Kurtzman nodded. ''It's proof of something, that's for sure. I'm just not sure what, though.''

''Dammit, man,'' Greene exploded, ''what else can it be? The man's a goddamned Russian spy. You saw his name on the list. What more proof do you want?''

''I want to know what he's up to,'' Kurtzman said. ''You have to admit that he really hasn't done diddly so far.''

''Are you waiting for him to kill someone?'' Greene was practically yelling. ''Or do you want him to find a way to blow us all up? What in the hell is wrong with you?''

"Actually, this is a good opportunity to see just how good our defenses really are. We talk a good talk in the War Room and we've held off attacks from the outside. But this is the first time that someone's ever been working against us from the inside, and we don't know what he's found out about us. He might have found a weakness that none of us have seen."

He turned his wheelchair to face the chief. "We have enough right now to bring him in, yes. Actually we could have brought him in on a hell of a lot less than what we have. But I think this is too good a chance to pass up. Remember, we're on him night and day. He can't even take a leak out behind the machine shed without a camera watching to make sure he shakes it before he puts it back in his pants."

Greene shook his head. He knew that Kurtzman could be a hardheaded bastard, but this was being dangerously stubborn. "You realize that you're risking someone's life, don't you?" he demanded. "What if Barbara's out there and that guy decides to grab her and run? You know we couldn't shoot."

Now that his mind was racing, Greene let it all hang out. "What if he's been sent to kill Hal? What if he's waiting for Striker to get back to assassinate him? What if he decides that he wants—"

"I know all that," Kurtzman said, interrupting the chief's stream of vocalized fears. "But we're in the risk business around here, even Barbara. And we're taking a calculated risk with this. If we weren't on to him, I think we'd have a real problem, you're right. But we're watching him and we're going to keep watching him for a while.''

Buck Greene had been around Kurtzman long enough to know that he wasn't going to change his mind no matter what he said. "It's on your head, Aaron. Don't fuck up.''

Kurtzman looked him full in the face. "I don't plan to.''

THE FOLLOWING MORNING, when Gordon saw that he was the standby man for the day, he almost ran right then. He steadied himself when he realized that it was simply his turn in the normal rotation of duties. The standby man actually had a day off unless something happened to one of the work crews and he had to fill in.

"Hey, Gordon,'' Jennings, the shift leader, called out, "grab your hat and best boots. We're going to town.''

"Town?''

"Yeah, we go into town every now and then to buy something so the locals don't think that we're a secret government agency.''

"Right.''

Gordon followed the man out into the compound. "Grab the keys for the red Dodge,'' Jennings said, "and meet me at the truck.''

"Where do we keep the keys?''

"In the key box on the left wall of the garage.''

The key box turned out to be an old apple crate nailed to the wall with a number of tagged key rings hanging off more nails. It was authentically rural, but it wasn't a secure way to control vehicle keys.

Finding the tag marked Red Dodge he took it and walked down to the truck. A few minutes later, Jennings walked up with a tractor generator in his hand. "We've got to get this thing exchanged for a new one and pick up a tire that was repaired."

"That's all?"

"Actually we could fix both of them here, but, like I said, we have to keep the locals from talking about us by patronizing their businesses."

He opened the passenger door and laid the greasy generator on the rubber floor mat. "You drive."

"If I can remember how. It's been awhile."

Jennings laughed.

"I'M NOT SURE this is a good idea, Aaron," Buck Greene said as he watched the red Dodge pickup head for the gate leading to the highway.

"Relax," Kurtzman said. "This is another test of our boy's intentions. If he runs, I can have an APB on him before he gets a hundred yards."

"But he's out of surveillance range."

Kurtzman hit a key, and the scene on the monitor shifted to a view of the inside of the truck, complete with sound. It was being taken by a microcam, so the view was fish-eyed, but it covered both Jennings and Gordon.

"You're a sneaky little bastard, Bear." Greene shook his head in amazement. "I have to hand it to you."

"Aren't I just?" Kurtzman beamed. "I had Cowboy install the video pickup last night. "It's also being taped so we can go over it in detail later. For now, let's just watch and listen."

NEITHER MAN HAD MUCH to say for the first few miles, but that was all right with Gordon. Now that he was facing having to run, he was carefully noting the terrain and road networks in the area. Driving the route himself also helped him to memorize it and he paid particular attention to the signs directing traffic to places he might need to go. When he got back to the barracks, he'd try to locate a map if he could do it without attracting attention.

So far, Jennings hadn't said a word, and Gordon started to wonder if this trip was some kind of a test and decided to make conversation. "What's this 'Virginia is for lovers' crap I keep seeing?" he asked as they passed the second state tourism board sign in as many minutes. "Are you supposed to screw your brains out here?"

Jennings laughed. "That's just sucker bait to get Yankee tourists to come down here and spend their money."

"This is a pretty part of the country," Gordon said.

"It sure beats the hell out of Arkansas," Jennings said. "I was stationed there with the DEA, and it almost drove me bat-shit. That's a real armpit."

"If you want a real armpit, you ought to try L.A. All the guys in my unit prayed each night for the big one to hit so it would fall into the Pacific. We figured that we could get out and let the rest of the bastards drown.''

"Most of California's like that now, isn't it?''

"A lot of it is,'' Gordon agreed. "But there's still some real nice spots north of San Francisco and east of San Diego. The small towns aren't too bad, either. But any place like L.A. where you have so many people living on top of one another, it sucks.''

"I could never live like that,'' Jennings said. "And that's why I like this job so much. About the time I get fed up with being stuck out here in the boondocks, I get to go on stand down anywhere I want. If I want big city for a while, I can have it. If I really want to get away I can do that too.''

"That sounds good to me.''

They drove for a couple more miles in silence passing farms and woods. "How much farther to this town?''

"About ten more miles.''

KURTZMAN AND GREENE watched as Gordon pulled to a stop in the gravel parking lot in front of a farm implement company and got out. A few minutes later they came out carrying a box with a new generator inside. Back on the road, they drove a half a mile down to the auto shop and picked up the repaired tractor tire.

"Dammit,'' Greene said as they got back in the truck for the drive back to the Farm. "He's not doing anything.''

"He is taking careful note of the road signs," Kurtzman said. "That could be because he's in unfamiliar territory or it could be because he's mapping out his escape route."

"The only place he's going," Greene said, "is a federal prison."

CHAPTER TWENTY-FIVE

Moscow, Russia

Ex-Major Vasily Lebedev was forced to admire the Americans' latest move. On the surface, hitting night clubs would seem to have little military value, but it was causing an uproar among Leoninski's people. And if the Yankees' real goal was to prevent Zerinov from winning the election, it was very effective. Leoninski was screaming about the damage he was taking, and with the Mafia leader concentrating on protecting his financial interests, his men wouldn't be out convincing the voters to mark the right ballot.

Whoever was behind the Yankee operation had a good tactical mind. But, while his tactic was brilliant, it was somewhat predictable and that was always a mistake. If you knew where the enemy was going to attack, it was easy to defend that one target. In this case, there were several targets to guard, but the principle was the same, as was the solution to his dilemma—a mobile defense.

In its simplest terms, this meant keeping your reinforcements mobile instead of tying them down guarding any one spot. Since Moscow had a very good street network and Leoninski had no shortage of powerful cars in his stable, it was a natural solution to the problem. All he needed to do was to put the bulk of his forces in cars with radios. Some of them would be spotted close to likely targets and the others would be in position to go wherever the Yankees hit next.

As obvious as this was to Lebedev, though, it had taken awhile to hammer the concept into Leoninski's thick skull. Not only was he a hood with a criminal's narrow-minded mentality, he was a Georgian as well. Stalin had been a Georgian and look what he had done to Russia. Had it not been for his raging paranoia, the German invasion could have been stopped long before it was. When it came to paranoia, though, Stalin didn't have a thing on Leoninski. Now that he was the target of an operation, he didn't trust anyone.

The hardest part of implementing the plan had been getting the crime boss to agree to notify him when the Yankees were spotted. His Wolverines were more heavily armed than Leoninski's hoods, and they were experienced professional fighters. When the Yankees were cornered, they would be able to handle the situation without taking heavy casualties.

First, though, they had to be spotted.

THE WHITE VAN BRAKED to a halt a block away from the Blue Danube Bar for a quick recon. As with all of the other of Leoninski's establishments the Stony Man warriors had visited over the past two days, more than one man were standing in front. These three were wearing their long overcoats open, which meant they were packing.

"You ready?" Jack Grimaldi asked.

Carl Lyons snapped the last 12-gauge buckshot round into the magazine of his Street Sweeper and racked one into the chamber. "Ready."

"Let's do it," Schwarz said, raising his H&K.

"Here we go."

Grimaldi wasn't standing on the pedal like an L.A. gangbanger as he drove up to the club, as there was no point in announcing their intentions. Blancanales had the sliding door unlatched and snapped it open just as the van passed the corner of the building.

Lyons's 12-gauge thundered first, drilling double-aught buckshot into the chest of the first gunman, driving him back into the window. Schwarz's subgun chattered on full-auto, dumping almost a full magazine into the second guard and the windows before Lyons's shotgun took out the third man.

"That's it!" Lyons shouted, and Grimaldi hit the gas.

The purpose of the raids wasn't to conduct wholesale slaughter at Leoninski's establishments, just to keep him off balance. The more men he had to put on the street guarding his enterprises, the fewer he could use to harass Zerinov's opposition candidates and campaign workers.

"Damn," Schwarz said as Grimaldi powered away. "This is just like the Roaring Twenties. All we need are Tommy guns and snap brim fedoras. The Untouchables ride again."

"But we aren't busting booze," Blancanales pointed out. "So we're more like the Capone gang."

"It's almost the same."

Halfway down the next block, two Mercedes sedans with their lights out pulled out from the cross streets in front of the van, effectively blocking the road.

"Hang on!" Grimaldi shouted.

Cranking the wheel, he shifted into second and floored the gas. The van came up on two wheels and almost toppled over with the sudden turn, but Grimaldi fought the truck back down and sped away.

"They're coming after us," Lyons announced.

"I've got another one blocking the road ahead of us," Grimaldi said.

"Ram him," Lyons ordered.

Leaning out the passenger-side window, Lyons triggered his shotgun as fast as it could chamber the next round. When it ran dry, he pulled his .357 Colt Python and continued to fire.

Return fire from at least three AKs splattered the front of the van. One round punched through the windshield, showering Grimaldi with glass, but Lyons wasn't giving them time to aim well.

When the Russians saw that the van wasn't slow-ing, they scattered for cover. Lyons caught one in midstride and sent him sprawling against the curb with the last round in his Colt.

"Hang on!" Grimaldi yelled. Jerking the wheel at the last moment, he hit the rear of the Mercedes a glancing blow to try to knock it out of the way. The impact slammed the heavy sedan halfway around and forced it up onto the curb. As he drove past it, the steering wheel started to shudder in Grimaldi's hands.

"I think I broke something," he told Lyons. "It feels like the damned wheel is coming off."

"Keep on driving as long as you can. We still have those other two behind us."

"Striker says they're on the way," Schwarz reported, "but it'll take awhile before they can reach us."

"Find a place where we can make a last stand," Lyons said as he watched out the rearview mirror. "I don't think they're going to give it up this time."

Although the two sedans were keeping pace with them, they were hanging far back. They had learned that following the Americans too closely could earn them a 40 mm grenade in the face.

"I knew I should have gotten us a better vehicle," Grimaldi muttered as the shuddering of the front wheels got worse.

"Over on the left," Lyons called out. "That construction site."

The place Lyons had spotted was about as good a defensive position as they could ask for. The building under construction was modular, being put together from precast concrete slabs, some of which were as large as the floor space of the average Muscovite's apartment. Additionally it was surrounded by a chain-link fence that would help channel the bad guys.

Grimaldi fought to force the van to make the turn and was able to drive it through the gate right before the suspension collapsed.

"That's it, boys," he called out. "End of the line."

Grabbing their weapons and ammunition, the four men fled for the safety of the building shell.

LEONINSKI WAS MONITORING the radio in his office as he followed the chase on a city map. The best thing that had come out of his connection with the general was that he had been able to fully equip his people with military radios. That allowed him to keep some of his men in reserve and only move them when they were needed.

His men were telling him that the van that had been used in the attack on the Blue Danube appeared to have been damaged when it crashed through the roadblock, and that they were following it. A few minutes later, they reported that the Americans had crashed it at a building site and had taken refuge inside. Now that he had run the Yankees to ground, it was time to send everyone in to finish them off.

The general had wanted him to let Lebedev know if something like this happened, but he wasn't about to let that tin soldier in on his kill. Like the lion he was named for, he had run this prey to ground and he would make the kill himself. If all of the Americans weren't in this van, he would give the rest to Lebedev's Wolverines to finish. But these cowards were his.

After ordering all of his cars to converge on the construction site, he called down to the garage in the basement of his headquarters and ordered his driver to ready his car. On the way out of his office, he grabbed an AK-74 from the ready rack and pocketed extra loaded magazines for his Makarov pistol.

ONCE INSIDE THE SHELL of the building, Grimaldi and Able Team found positions to cover both the front and the back entrances in the fence. Grimaldi and Lyons took the ground-floor front side while Schwarz and Blancanales took the second floor. Depending on how many of the enemy were following them, they should be able to hold out until Bolan and Phoenix Force could come to their rescue.

They were barely inside the building when the first Mercedes sedan screeched to a halt behind their abandoned van. Four men packing AKs stormed out and took cover.

"Should we let them know that we're here, Ironman?" Schwarz radioed to Lyons.

Lyons let his shotgun do his talking. The 12-gauge roared, sending a load of buckshot into the side of the car. Two of the gunmen raced through the gate, firing their AKs on the run. Schwarz got one and Lyons took the other.

BY THE TIME Leoninski arrived at the construction site, two of his men lay dead on the ground halfway to the building and the rest were cowering behind their cars, trading shots with the Yankees.

Finding the man who was supposed to be in charge, he jerked him to his feet and slammed him against the Mercedes. "Why aren't you in there attacking the Americans?"

When the man stammered something about the enemy's firepower, Leoninski pulled the Makarov pistol from inside his coat, jammed the muzzle against the man's head and pulled the trigger. The man jerked with the impact of the slug in his brain and slumped to the ground.

"Are there any more of you who want to question me?" Leoninski shouted. "I want those Yankees dead!"

Now that their boss was on the scene, the Mafia troops recovered their courage and set up a heavy base of fire. A barrage of bullets drilled into the darkened building.

"Go! Go! Go!" Leoninski roared.

Under the covering fire of their comrades, a dozen gunmen rushed through the gate.

"WHERE THE HELL are the cops in this goddamned town?" Schwarz asked as he crouched behind a concrete slab. AK fire was ricocheting all around him, keeping his head down. "You'd think that someone would notice there's a full-fledged battle going on in their backyard."

"This isn't L.A.," Lyons replied. "These cops might wear funny uniforms, but they're smart enough to know that they don't want to get involved with something like this until it's over. They're not paid enough to get shot at."

Schwarz stuck the muzzle of his subgun around the corner of his slab and ripped off half a mag. "Phoenix had sure as hell better get involved before then."

KATZENELENBOGEN'S new safehouse hotel was across town from the construction site, and it took longer for Bolan and Phoenix Force to get there than he had figured. By the time they pulled up on the back side of the site, a raging battle was in full swing.

"Ironman, this is Striker," Bolan radioed to Carl Lyons. "We're coming up behind you."

"About time," Lyons came back. "We're up to our asses in assholes around here. We've got a couple dozen of them cornered."

"Just stay tight and keep your heads down."

Taking in the scene at a glance, Bolan sent Manning, James and Hawkins to the north side to try to break in and reinforce Able Team. He, Katzenelenbogen and Encizo would work their way around to hit the Mafia gunmen from the flank.

Manning had the night scope mounted on his

H&K long gun, and he put it to good use while Hawkins and James cut a hole in the fence. There was a little interference from the streetlights, but the night optics worked as advertised in the deep shadows. The bad guys were easy to spot because they were wearing long coats while Able Team was in American-style short jackets.

His first target was moving from one pile of construction material to the next, using all the cover he could find. From Manning's sight angle, though, it wasn't cover enough. He put the scope's crosshairs on him and squeezed the trigger. The 7.62 mm slug caught him low in the back and put him down.

He clicked on his throat mike. "One down on the north side."

"Gary," Hawkins radioed, "we're through the fence. Watch our flanks."

"Roger."

"Ironman," James radioed, "we're coming in from the north."

"Got you covered," Schwarz sent back.

With Manning scoping their path, the two commandos raced for the shelter of the building. "We're inside," Hawkins sent.

"Find a slab to hide behind and get to work," Lyons radioed back.

"We're on it."

LEONINSKI DIDN'T HAVE much night-combat experience, but he could count real well and he realized that he was seeing more muzzle-flashes than he had a moment before. The Americans had to have radioed for help and the rest of their fighters had joined them. That didn't matter to him, though. In fact he welcomed the chance to take them all down. He had radioed for more of his men to join him to finish them off.

When two sedans pulled up carrying a dozen men, he ordered them into the compound. One of the men got only a few yards inside the fence before he was taken down, and Leoninski grabbed his radio to call in even more reinforcements. Regardless of the cost, the Americans must die.

WITH THE EXTRA FIREPOWER of James and Hawkins in the building, the battle had reached a stalemate. Every time the Mafia gunmen tried to storm the place, they were beaten back with heavy losses. The Stony Man warriors had stopped counting their kills, but they were mounting.

While the bloodbath inside the fence was raging, Bolan, Encizo and Katz had worked their way around to the south side of the construction site. Almost a dozen Mercedes sedans blocked the street, and a cluster of men had taken cover behind them.

"That's got to be their command group," Katz pointed out. "Leoninski won't be inside the fence."

"Flash-bangs," Bolan ordered. "And then we take them all out."

The three men took flash-bang grenades from their harnesses and readied them. On Bolan's count of three, they armed the bombs and threw them behind the cars.

The sudden detonations and blinding flashes stunned the gunmen. Before they could recover, the three Stony Man warriors were on them, their weapons blazing.

Leoninski had had his face turned toward the building watching the assault, so he hadn't been blinded by the grenades. He saw the black-clad killers rushing toward them with death spitting in their hands. Swinging around his AK, he was shouting orders when he felt the first slugs drill deep into his chest.

His mouth filled with blood, and he crumpled to the ground.

SEEING THEIR LEADER go down, the surviving gunmen ran for their lives. If the Lion had been killed, there was no hope for any of them.

"Let them go," Katz radioed. "We need them to spread the news."

As soon as they had the field to themselves, the Able Team and Phoenix commandos gathered at the kill site. "That's Leoninski all right," Blancanales confirmed.

"One self-styled Lion down," Schwarz said. "Now all we have to do is take care of a general who should have stayed out of politics and we can all go home."

"And a few Wolverines," Katz said. "Don't forget about them."

CHAPTER TWENTY-SIX

Moscow, Russia

General Pavel Zerinov had mixed emotions about the death of Lion Leoninski and so many of his gunmen. He had been ashamed to have been forced into an alliance with the gangster, but it had been necessary. Leoninski's early death had saved him the trouble of having to stand the vulgar bastard up against a wall later and kill him himself. However, with his criminal empire leaderless now, he had lost the use of the Mafia manpower he had counted on to control the polling stations. Put that on top of having lost the armor, he was now in a position of having to beg for votes instead of showing his strength.

There was, however, more than one way to show his personal power. Even with many of the senior army officers withholding their support, he still had a large following among the more junior officers, the actual troop commanders. They were the men who were personally having to deal with the disintegration of the military, and they wanted to see their army brought back to its rightful position in the state. They might not be able to back him with their tanks, but he was confident that he could call upon their voices to support him.

Zerinov's Progressive Party organization had scheduled him to appear at what was being called a candidate forum in Moscow's main sports arena. There, he and the other candidates would hold a debate in front of an audience of thousands. He had shunned the usual candidate activities, but he relished this appearance. He had always been a man of great personal presence and he knew how to work a crowd.

The debate would be televised, which was even better for his purposes. Zerinov knew the power that the media, both domestic and foreign, could bring to bear on public opinion. The part CNN had played in bringing Yeltsin to power after the aborted coup of 1991 had brought that home to him loud and clear. If he could pack the bleachers with his army supporters, all in civilian clothing of course, he could turn this debate into a badly needed victory for the Progressive Party's cause.

He knew that his chances of winning the election had fallen dramatically, but he wasn't out of the running yet. As long as he was breathing, he would continue to fight. Picking up the phone, he started to place calls to the commanders of military units in the Moscow region. This was the time to call upon their support.

WHEN PAVEL ZERINOV arrived at the stadium early the next morning, he was wearing his old general's uniform with his medals from the Afghan war. The sun was shining, the weather spring-warm for a change, and he took the break in the weather as yet another sign of his luck changing. His phone calls to the lower-ranking army commanders the previous night had been successful. Almost all of them had been more than willing to send men to the rally. When he had issued his orders as to what he expected from these men, none of the officers had questioned them.

The stadium was the home of the Russian national soccer team, and the mood of the crowd was more like they had come to see a match rather than a political debate. He noted the number of younger men in the stands rather than the old women he had seen at earlier rallies. Many of them wore military-style haircuts, and they were staying together in groups. He smiled secretly; the sun had brought him luck.

When it came time for him to stand and be introduced, the audience rose en masse and started to chant his name. He stood at attention and let it wash over him.

Stony Man Farm, Virginia

WITH THE TIME DIFFERENCE between Stony Man Farm and Moscow, Jim Gordon was off duty and in the dayroom when the Moscow rally started. Since this was the biggest political event since Boris Yeltsin had taken office, CNN International had a full crew covering it, and CSPAN had preempted its regular programming to broadcast it live from start to finish. The cameras were rolling when the people started entering the stadium.

Gordon was stunned to see the pageantry of the Russian people after years of watching the carefully staged baby-kissing, hard-hat wearing, back-slapping photo ops of American political campaigns. Here were the Russian people coming out in strength to support their candidate, and their sincerity was plain to see. Unlike American voters who only got to choose between Tweedle Dee and Tweedle Dum with the end result being more of the same crap they'd lived with for decades, these people's future was on the line and they knew it. Their votes counted, and they desperately wanted to pick the right man to lead them.

He still couldn't get used to seeing the tricolor flag of the new Russian Republic, though, instead of the old hammer and sickle. There was the occasional red banner of the die-hard Communists in the crowd, but they were islands in a sea of the red, white and blue flags that had last flown under the czarist regime.

At least no one was wearing those idiotic straw hats that American political activists always wore at the Democratic and Republican Party rallies. He had always wanted to know why they wore such ridiculous headgear, but had been afraid to ask anyone. Certain things about American culture had to be taken on faith without asking too much about them. To question was to be seen as being foreign, and James T. Gordon had only survived by being as American as hot dogs, hamburgers and apple pie.

"You're sure interested in those Russians," one of the blacksuits said.

"Yeah," Gordon replied casually. "I took a couple of courses in Russian studies when I was in college. It was the thing to do back then."

"Back in the days of the good old evil empire," the guard said with a chuckle. "I've got to admit that it was real interesting back when we were standing eyeball to eyeball with the bastards waiting for the Big One to drop. Man, I sure as hell never expected them to fold as easily as they did. Our man Reagan was staring them down big time, but they blinked and now they're history."

The guard shook his head. "Hell, look at them now. They're just like all the rest of those half-assed countries. They can't even feed themselves. When you look back, it makes you wonder what in the hell we were so afraid of for so long. We could have kicked their sorry asses in a New York minute anytime we wanted to."

Gordon had to keep from throwing himself on the guard and beating him to death. Yes, Russians were having trouble feeding themselves now, but that was because the corrupt Capitalists who had taken over since the fall of communism were stealing food from the people. Under the old regime, that buffoon Yeltsin would have been taken out and shot. No matter what their faults had been, the Communists at least had been able to feed the population.

"Yeah," he said. "It makes you wonder, doesn't it?"

"And look at the poor bastards cheering for this guy with all the hero buttons on his chest," the blacksuit said when Zerinov was introduced. "All he's going to do is get them killed. He'll start trying to recapture their old empire, and then we'll have to jump in and kick their asses. From what I've been reading, their army's worse off than the rest of the country and that's saying a lot. Hungry soldiers don't fight for diddly."

The crowd was more than simply cheering for Zerinov—going berserk was more like it. The banners of the Progressive Party waved back and forth, and the chanting of his name echoed like cannon fire. The cameras zoomed in on the general's face as he stood at attention on the stage, soaking up the roar.

When he finally raised his hands for silence, the crowd hushed. A small cluster of people around a flag bearing the symbol of one of the smaller parties took up a chant, but it didn't spread. There was a brief flurry, all caught on film, as two dozen young men wearing short haircuts stormed this group and beat them into submission. When all was quiet again, Zerinov started to speak.

The speech was broadcast in Russian, and Gordon had to force himself to wait and listen to the English translation before reacting to what was being said.

"What's he saying?" the guard asked him.

"I don't know." Gordon turned to him with a frown on his face. "I don't speak Russian."

"The way you were listening, I thought you might have taken Russian with your Russian studies."

"No," Gordon stated, shaking his head, "I just took some Soviet history courses as electives to fill in a couple of slots on my schedule."

The moment that reply was out of his mouth, Gordon felt a stab of panic. As he had been repeatedly told by his Little Amerika instructors, only American Communists and journalists ever referred to citizens of the Soviet Union as Soviets. Regardless of their nationalities or ethnicity, the American people simply called them all Russians. His slip, though, could be explained by his college courses. Unless, of course, someone took the time to look up his university transcript. He had never dared to take a Russian studies course, nor the language. That would have marked him as a budding young leftist, and leftists weren't welcome in U.S. government service unless they worked for the State Department or the CIA.

It was stupid for him to have told such a transparent lie, but he had been caught off guard. The only saving grace was that he'd probably be out of here before anyone had a chance to go through his college transcripts.

His conversation with the blacksuit had taken his attention away from Zerinov's speech, and he was just wrapping up when he got back to it. When the general was done, he stood at attention again while the stadium roared his name.

The next candidate to speak was from a party Gordon had never heard of, the Social Reform Party. The name alone meant that they could be anything from raging socialists to free-market buccaneers. No sooner was the man announced than pockets of spectators started chanting Zerinov's name again. When the candidate tried to speak, the chanting grew louder.

The Social Reform Party members in the stands tried to outshout the Zerinov people, but weren't able to make themselves heard. A few of them took to using the poles of their banners as weapons, but that was a mistake. The Zerinov supporters had been waiting for the other side to make the first move, and when the first blow was stuck, they struck back hard.

Now their military origin was plain to see. Breaking up into ten-man squads, they rushed the Socialist Reform people and started busting heads. A few of the other minor party supporters decided to get into it, and they, too, were targeted by more of Zerinov's supporters. The stands quickly dissolved into a World Cup soccer match style free-for-all.

"Man," the blacksuit said, "those people sure know how to have fun. I haven't seen a fight like that since Brazil lost the World Cup to the Dutch."

Gordon was disgusted by what he saw. He was ashamed to see his countrymen acting that way. The

Russians were not a Third World nation, but they had lost their sense of who they were. More than ever he realized that only a man like Zerinov could bring them back to what they had been.

Moscow, Russia

PAVEL ZERINOV STOOD on the grandstand in the stadium and watched the brawl. He was careful not to smile as his military supporters swept the stands clean of the opposition. Knowing that this was going out to TV sets all over the world, he waited until order was restored.

"Comrades," he said when all was calm again, "we have seen today an example of the danger we Russians face in the coming years. We have seen hooliganism in action here, and we must guard against it. The Progressive Party is a party of law and order, and, as your president, I vow that I will see that personal interests never get in the way of the will of the people. If Russia is ever to become a great nation again, the good of the many must outweigh the selfish interests of the few."

When the stands burst out in cheers again, Zerinov was alone on the stage. The debate had been concluded the Russian way.

CNN INTERNATIONAL Service was running the highlights of the riot at the stadium at the top of each half-hour broadcast. Knowing a winner when they saw one, General Pavel Zerinov was being trumpeted as the man of the hour. The candidate that the people had come out to support was the one man who had been able to control the crowd in the stadium. Almost instantly, he had become the front-runner in the contest for control of Russia. In the name of media fairness, some of the other leading candidates were being interviewed, but they were coming off as whining losers.

Once more, a strong man had captured the attention of both the Russian people and the foreign press. It had been good enough to put Boris Yeltsin in office, and it looked like it would work for Zerinov this time. The way CNN was covering the story, Zerinov was a shoo-in to be the next president of the Russian Republic.

CHAPTER TWENTY-SEVEN

Moscow, Russia

"Okay," Bolan said as he snapped off the television in the Moscow hotel room. "We've seen what's going on, and I think it's time that we took this to the source. Taking down Leoninski was a good move, and it'll make a real difference for these people. But, so far, we've just been treating the symptoms and we need to deal with the disease."

"Are you talking about our friend the general?" David McCarter asked.

"Yes." Bolan nodded. "I know that earlier I said we should let the Russian people deal with him on election day, but that's obviously not going to work now. As we saw at the stadium today, even without his tanks, he still has enough force he can call upon to completely subvert the democratic process. I think the time has come for us to answer force with force again."

"That does seem to be the time-honored solution in Russian politics, doesn't it?" Katzenelenbogen asked.

"I'm afraid so."

"Do you want me to run this past Hal?" Katz asked.

"No." Bolan's tone of voice brooked no argument. "This time we do it the old-fashioned way. We call the shots, and we take the heat if it goes down wrong. If we get Hal involved, he'll have to talk to the President, who'll have to talk to the minister. And while they're talking it to death, Zerinov will have stolen the election. So far, we've tried to do this their way, and we haven't been able to take care of the problem. If we don't make a decisive move now, all of it will have been for nothing."

"That sounds about right to me," McCarter said. "The bloody Russians have never responded to anything except brute force in their entire history."

"We have the location of Zerinov's dacha, and I'm having Kurtzman send us aerial shots of it for the final planning. We'll go tonight."

"What's the opposition?"

"That's the question," Bolan admitted. "The latest Belakov was able to find out was that the general has a security guard of a couple of dozen men from his old command. I think we can expect them to be well armed and to know how to do their job."

"Can we expect to find any Wolverines lurking around there?"

"If we do," Bolan said, "we'll deal with them as well. I want to wrap this up tonight and be done with it."

"Until next time." McCarter wasn't smiling.

"With these people," Katz said, "there's always going to be a next time."

THE NEXT FEW HOURS were busy as the Stony Man warriors prepared for what they hoped would be their final mission in Russia. While they were busy with their gear, Katzenelenbogen contacted the Minister of the Interior and obtained the services of Yuri Belakov again without having to say why he was needed. The young SVR officer had recovered from his wound enough to be able to go with them again.

Belakov sat wide-eyed as Katz outlined what they intended to do once dark fell. "Does the minister know that you are planning to do this?" he asked.

"No," Katz replied, looking him straight in the eye, "he doesn't. And I don't want him to, either, because I'm not sure that he's up to signing off on this. The Russian people are struggling to become a democracy, but I think we all know what really has to be done to make it work for them. Your country can't afford to have General Zerinov in power."

Belakov swallowed hard but didn't run for the phone to call his boss. The Americans certainly weren't afraid to take drastic measures. But, so far, they had proved to have been very effective so he'd throw in with them again. If they failed, the worst that could happen would be that he'd die with them. And that might be better than trying to live through another military dictatorship.

"As I think you say, I am in." Belakov swallowed hard. "But God help us if this does not work."

ZERINOV WAS BASKING in the dramatic turnaround in his fortunes. His performance in the stadium had done him more good than two brigades of armor and a thousand Mafia thugs would have done. By the time he had returned to his second-floor study in his dacha, he already had a pile of phone messages congratulating him on having saved the day. Senior officers who had been sitting on the fence, now were firmly behind his candidacy. Even better, though, several of Moscow's most prominent Capitalists had called to pledge their financial support for the Progressive Party.

As he had learned, money was the key to politics and with Leoninski's support gone, outside rubles were vital if he was to keep up the momentum he now had going strong. The next week would be critical and it would take money to do what he had decided needed to be done.

Picking up his phone, he called to his command post on the first floor. A few minutes later, Major Vasily Lebedev was at the door to the study. "You wanted to see me, General?" he asked his commander.

"Take a seat, Major," the general said, gesturing to the overstuffed leather chair in front of his desk.

Lebedev walked in and sat.

"I cannot make it official yet," Zerinov said, "but I am promoting you to colonel and I want you to create a new presidential security organization of at least a thousand men for me. You will be free to call upon officers and men from the entire armed forces. I want you to build it around the core of your Wolverines, promote anyone who you think can do the job and, most importantly, who you can trust. As soon as this is over, you will have to move fast."

"To do what, sir?"

"To restore order to the political system," Zerinov said. "I have the support of most of the army now and over half of the air force. The navy doesn't count, and once we are in control, they will have no choice but to come around."

"What about the Ministry of the Interior and the SVR?" Lebedev asked.

"They will be your first targets, Major. On election night, you will move to secure their leadership. With them under control, the rest should be easy."

Lebedev wasn't old enough to remember the last great purge under Chairman Andropov, but he recognized what the words meant. Andropov had come up through the KGB and, when he came to power, he had cleaned house with the ruthless efficiency the old state security organization had been famous for. Zerinov was army, but he, too, knew the need to set his house in order. Had Yeltsin done that when he'd had a chance, maybe he would have been more successful.

"That may be messy," Lebedev said cautiously.

"You will be given enough manpower to do the job, and it will be up to the minister to see that things do not get out of hand. If they do, he will be brought in for treason."

The general laughed. "He will be shot for treason later anyway, but I can afford to let him think that he has gotten away with betraying Mother Russia for a few weeks. He brought those Americans in to subvert the election, and he will pay for that."

"Speaking of the Yankees," Lebedev said. "What do you want me to do about them?"

"Guard against them for now, and as soon as this is over, we will capture them and put them on trial. I am sure that CNN will cover that as well, and we will finally have America out of our internal affairs for good. Once I am president, there will be no more Americans in Russia unless I personally invite them in. And I will only do that if there is something in it that will make Russia stronger."

Lebedev knew how much American businessmen were doing to bring Russia into the modern world, but he knew better than to mention any of that to Zerinov. The general would need to secure his power base before he could spend much time thinking about modernizing the country.

"I will start making lists of the men I want for this new unit," he said.

"Good, get them to me as soon as you can."

"Yes, sir."

"And, Major..."

"This is all for Mother Russia."

"I understand, sir."

THE STONY MAN commandos were going for a full-court press on Pavel Zerinov. With Grimaldi, Katzenelenbogen and Belakov, that gave them twelve guns against perhaps three times that many. At least, though, they wouldn't be going up against prepared positions. The aerial photos had showed that Zerinov's dacha was still a simple country estate. It was a bit larger than most, to be sure, but it wasn't ringed with fortifications, bunkers or armored vehicles.

The SVR agent hadn't been able to get much updated intelligence about the opposition they could expect at the target. But since his stadium appearance, Zerinov was a rising star, and he now had the backing of several high-ranking generals. That could mean he might be getting additional security forces from military units, which was another reason that he had to be hit this night. The longer they waited, the more men he would be able to bring in.

Regardless of what they would be facing, though, this was a do-or-die operation. Zerinov had to be taken out, and they would only have one chance to do it.

"I have two sentries at the turnout in the road," Hawkins radioed to Katzenelenbogen, "and they're only armed with individual weapons."

The Stony Man warriors' ride in to their jump-off points had gone smoothly. Their ex-Mafia Mercedes carried the assault team that would come in the front, while the van carried the others to the river that ran behind the compound. Neither route had been guarded or blockaded. That was a hopeful sign to Katz. If the army was providing Zerinov's security, he would have expected to see at least sandbag bunkers with weapons or an armored car or two. Individual troops they could deal with.

"Take them out," he ordered.

"Roger."

Even though they were going in to eliminate Zerinov and his cadre of followers, they would try to do it with as little bloodshed as possible. The Russian troops guarding the dacha were merely following orders and, if possible, they could be neutralized without dying.

Hawkins and James moved in on the two-man outpost carefully, their night-vision goggles showing them the way through the spring growth in the fields. When they got within thirty yards of the sentries, they saw that they were wearing standard Russian army field uniforms. Had they been Wolverines, the commandos would have gone for silenced-weapon kills. Army troops they would try to subdue.

It took several long minutes before the two Phoenix Force commandos were able to crawl up to the sentries. Their night combat suits made them faint shadows in the dark, and their experience made them absolutely silent against the background noises of the countryside. They crossed the last few yards with their faces in the dirt. With a silent signal, the two commandos jumped up to take out their man.

Holding his sentry in a hammerlock with his forearm over the man's mouth, James slammed the butt of his Ka-bar fighting knife against the back of his head. The Russian instantly went limp, and James turned to help Hawkins subdue his man.

Hawkins had his hands full this time. The Russian was considerably bigger than he was, and the man was no stranger to unarmed combat. Had the ex-Ranger been trying to kill him, it would have been a simple task. James intervened and again hammered the butt of his knife against the base of the sentry's skull.

"Damn," Hawkins whispered as he reached down to slip a set of plastic riot cuffs over the man's wrists and slap a piece of military duct tape over his mouth. "I thought this one was going to take me."

"We're clear," James radioed Katz in a whisper.

"Hold there until we can join you."

Now that Hawkins and James had penetrated the outer ring of security, Katz, Manning and Belakov joined them to form the Anvil Team. Their job was to seek out and destroy the security outposts in their half of the area while blocking Zerinov from escaping.

Now that Katz and his Anvil Team had secured the road leading into the dacha, McCarter, Encizo and Bolan started their approach from the rear. As they moved, Lyons, Schwarz, Blancanales and Grimaldi kept a few dozen yards back in reserve. When the point trio had penetrated the security ring, they would join up with them to form the Hammer Team that would assault the house itself.

The point trio worked its way up from the riverbank they had followed after leaving the van a mile away. Again, as Katz had experienced with the frontal approach, they didn't encounter any security until they were within five hundred yards of the main house. The first sentry outpost was at the base of a large tree, and Bolan spotted them by their heat signature.

Catching McCarter's attention, Bolan drew his index finger across his sleeve to signal the need for a silent kill. McCarter nodded and crouched at the base of a tree to scan the grounds on either side of them. Finding that the outpost wasn't backed up, he signaled that he would take the man on the left.

Leaving Encizo to cover their backs, Bolan and McCarter moved out like shadows. They covered the open ground quickly but silently, swinging wide to come at the outpost from behind. Once they were in position a few yards away, Bolan clicked his com link to let Encizo know that they were making their move.

Drawing his Cold Steel Tanto fighting knife from his web belt, Bolan looked and saw that McCarter was also ready. Holding up three fingers, he counted down, and on three, rushed forward.

The Russian barely had time to hear the movement before Bolan was on top of him, the blade seeking his life. Clamping his left hand over the sentry's mouth, he snapped his head to the side and drove the chisel-pointed knife into the hollow of his neck at the same time.

The Russian gurgled as his blood poured into his lungs, and he was dead.

McCarter had taken his man out as well, and the two Stony Man warriors laid the bodies on the ground with their AKs beside them. Through night-vision goggles, they would look as if they had fallen asleep at their posts.

Bolan double-clicked his com link to let Katz know that they were inside the perimeter and were ready for the final approach. When the response came, he motioned for the others to follow him.

Encizo was getting to his feet when he caught a slight noise to his left and dived for cover again. The snap of a silenced rifle round sang past his head. He answered with a short burst of fire from his suppressed H&K before rolling to the left to get out of the line of fire.

"They've spotted us," he radioed.

The next flurry of fire was from an AK on full-auto as another outpost spotted the intruders.

CHAPTER TWENTY-EIGHT

Moscow, Russia

Pavel Zerinov was on the phone in his study making deals and giving promises to would-be supporters when he heard the first burst of automatic fire. Snatching up his handheld radio, he raced into the hall.

"Major Lebedev," he radioed, "we are under attack. It is the Americans."

"On the way," Lebedev called back from his security CP on the ground floor.

The Wolverine leader snatched up his folding-stock AK-74 and raced for the back door to the villa. He always led his men in person, and he had a score to settle with these Yankees. It was payback time, and he intended to get his share of it. He was confident in his ability to protect the general. He had the remainder of his Wolverine unit spread out in two-man teams, and the other sentries were from one of the elite guard regiments. These weren't recent draftees and they knew how to fight.

If the Yankees had come to play, he'd leave their bodies in the dirt.

NOW THAT THEY HAD BEEN discovered, the Stony Man commandos could only go into a run-and-gun scenario. The original assault plan was discarded. The night had turned into chaos, but that chaos could be put to work for them. With everyone firing at shadows, no one would be taking the time to practice proper night-combat, target-acquisition techniques.

When the Russians started to fire illumination flares, their night-vision goggles were rendered almost useless. They pushed them up on their heads and used them to find their targets. Rather than adding to the threat, the flickering light of the flares was another ally for the Stony Man warriors as it hid movement.

The Russian army troops were wearing day camouflage uniforms, and the browns and greens of the fabric could be seen plainly in the light of the flares. The Wolverines, however, were more difficult to spot wearing the new night-combat pattern of black and dark gray that had been designed for night light conditions.

Yuri Belakov saw a flash of reflected light from the corner of the dacha and dived for cover. Snapping his AK to his shoulder, he triggered off several short bursts in that direction. He remembered that his drill instructors had hammered into him that he had to aim low in night combat, and he was rewarded by hearing a cry of shock as his bullets struck home.

A return burst sang over his head, telling him that his opponent hadn't paid attention to his night-combat training. Rolling to the side, he dropped his night goggles back down over his eyes to look for the shooter in the shadows.

"I've got him," Grimaldi called out. "Second-floor window."

Belakov looked up just in time to see the window dissolve into glass shards. "You're clear now," Grimaldi sent. "Go!"

Belakov got to his feet and started to run.

LEBEDEV STEPPED outside into chaos. Night fighting was always chaotic, but this time it was working for the attackers. The damned Yankees were like ghosts as they worked their way toward the dacha. His men were firing, but they weren't making any difference because they couldn't see them. Even his night goggles weren't picking them up. The thought flashed across his mind that the Yankees might be wearing the new thermal radiation blocking uniforms he had read about. The damned Americans always seemed to have money to spend on things like that.

When three of his security teams didn't answer his calls, he had to conclude that they had fallen. He realized that he had made a serious tactical error; the Yankee commandos were good at their work. Seeing that the battle wasn't going his way, he radioed for the rest of the troops to pull in close to the main house for a final defense. The dacha was built like a blockhouse and could withstand any assault until reinforcements arrived.

By the time the Wolverines reported back to him, there were only five men left, and one of them was wounded.

WHEN BOLAN SAW the surviving Russians retreat into the house, he called Katz and the blocking team on the other side of the compound and ordered them to move in. Going room-to-room would require every gun.

Hawkins and James had the point again, and the ex-Ranger unleashed his M-16 M-203 rifle-grenade launcher combo while James covered him. The first two 40 mm grenades went through the front door. Switching to the second floor, he placed shots through the two windows above the entryway.

When a burst of gunfire came from behind the blown-in door, James sent a full magazine of 7.62 mm rounds through the opening. When he dropped back into cover to reload, Hawkins launched another grenade through it as well. Under their covering fire, the rest of the team had moved up and was ready to make its entry on command.

While Katz's team assaulted the front of the house, Bolan and McCarter made their move on the rear with Lyons and Schwarz backing them. Encizo, Blancanales and Belakov would fire suppressive fire from outside until Bolan and McCarter were inside. Then they would move up to make their entry.

This was a well-practiced routine for the paired entry team—boot the door, roll in a grenade and follow it with their weapons blazing. The covering fire and the thickness of the villa's walls kept them safe until they made their move. Hugging the side of the shattered door, Bolan counted down, and when McCarter booted the door, rolled a grenade inside.

The frager had barely crossed the threshold than the pair of them had the muzzles of their weapons around the sides of the door, emptying their magazines. Before stepping back to reload, the Briton lobbed another grenade.

By the time it detonated, Bolan was reloaded. He charged through the door, McCarter a split second behind him. With the door clear, Lyons and Schwarz charged in behind the lead pair.

When McCarter kicked in a door leading off the main hall, Bolan caught a glimpse of a figure stepping out from a room on the opposite side of the hallway. Dropping into a crouch, he fired a short burst at him. The Russian staggered as the 9 mm rounds took him in the chest. A folding-stock AK clattered to the floor beside him.

Bolan moved up to the man in black and gray cammies, kicked the AK away from his hand and moved on to clear the other side of the hallway.

ZERINOV WAS SHOUTING orders from the top of the stairs, an AK-74 ready in his hands. If he went down this night, he was going down fighting. He had put in a quick call to a supporter commanding the closest armored cavalry regiment, but it would be an hour before the first vehicles could reach him.

Meanwhile, Lyons and Schwarz had leapfrogged past McCarter and Bolan and reached the bottom of the ornate stairwell in time to run into AK fire from the top. For a few seconds, they traded shots covering each other, but the thick floor of the second story was soaking up fire as if it were armor plate, so shooting through it wasn't an option here. Trading fire with the bastard was tiresome, to say nothing of being dangerous and Lyons had enjoyed about all that he could stand.

Thumbing back the hammer of his Python, Lyons readied himself for a desperate move. "Cover me," he called out to Schwarz.

His teammate sent a burst of automatic fire up the stairwell as Lyons dived into the open, going into a tuck and roll as he hit the floor. He came out of the roll turned, and with the Colt on target in a two-handed grip.

When Zerinov stepped back out to return Schwarz's fire, he ran into Lyons's Python instead. The .357 Magnum slug took him in the chest and slammed him against the wall. His AK slipped from his suddenly nerveless hands, and he had a puzzled look on his face as he slid to the floor. His bid for power wasn't supposed to end this way.

When Zerinov went down, a voice called out from one of the upstairs room. "Yankees! We give up!"

"Come out with your hands up!" Lyons shouted. "And no guns."

"No guns," the Russian answered. "We give up."

Two young soldiers in Russian army uniforms slowly stepped into view, their hands high in the air.

In the front of the house, a brief flurry of fire ended with Katz transmitting an all clear.

VASILY LEBEDEV WAS STILL alive when Bolan approached him. He had taken two slugs in the chest and was breathing blood. From the major's pips on his shoulder boards and the snarling, fanged animal-head patch on the shoulder of his night camouflage uniform, Bolan surmised he was the leader of the Wolverines.

"Who are you?" the Russian asked in accented English as he faced the muzzle of Bolan's pistol.

"A soldier."

Lebedev tried to laugh, but coughed a bloody froth. "We are both soldiers," he gasped. "And look where it got us."

"But not all of us fight for the same thing," Bolan said. "Soldiers have to understand that the people get tired of war and want peace."

"Only the weak ones," Lebedev replied. "The general would have made Russians a great people again."

"The general is dead just like Leoninski."

"If he had not gotten involved with Leoninski,

we might have won. Leoninski was, how do you say, scum?"

Bolan didn't bother to agree with the man. "Do you want a doctor?" he asked.

"No." The Russian coughed. "Let me die. With my men gone, there is nothing left for me."

Bolan would honor that request. Now that Zerinov was dead, it would do no real good to put Lebedev on trial. Even though he had chosen the wrong side, he had followed orders. The Russian people didn't know of Zerinov's attempted coup, and what they didn't know wouldn't hurt them. They could still go to the polls with confidence that they were voting on their future. What that future would be, he had no idea, but at least it wouldn't be a renewed dictatorship.

"You did not tell me your name, soldier," the Russian said.

"No, I didn't."

Lebedev muttered something in Russian before saying clearly, "Give me grace, comrade."

Bolan was surprised to hear the Red Army veteran ask for a mercenary's grant of eternal peace. It was a time-honored tradition among warriors, but he hadn't known that the Soviets had followed the custom. It wasn't so much a battlefield execution as it was a release from pain.

"Go with God," the Executioner said as he triggered the mercy round.

Lebedev jerked with the impact of the slug and died.

When Bolan walked out, Katz and McCarter were waiting. "Are any of the Wolverines alive?" he asked.

McCarter shook his head. "There were two who might have made it, but they rolled over on their rifles and blew out their brains," he said, paraphrasing Kipling.

"They learned well in Afghanistan," Katz said.

"Too well," Bolan agreed.

Stony Man Farm, Virginia

WHEN THE MESSAGE CAME IN that Zerinov was dead, Hal Brognola walked over to the Computer Room coffeepot and poured himself a cup of Kurtzman's special brew. After all the Antacid tablets he'd been crunching the past couple of hours, a little battery acid would go a long way to bringing the PH level in his guts back to normal.

Barbara Price joined him and poured a more reasonable half cup of the scalding, oily brew. "We did it again," she said simply.

"Yes, we did," Brognola said. "We subverted a democratic nation's election process and took out the people's favorite candidate. Now we have to see what that will bring us instead. We may get worse than Zerinov before this is finished."

"As David likes to say, that's not too bloody likely, mate," she replied. "You and I both know that the combination of a ruthless general with ambitions of empire and the Mafia wasn't going to be good for anyone, much less the Russians."

He turned to face her squarely. "To be perfectly honest with you, I don't have the slightest idea what those people need and I don't think they really do either. The only thing we can do is to try to help stop them from making any real stupid mistakes until they can get it right. As someone famous said, 'freedom means the freedom to starve to death.'"

"Whoever he was, he must have been a Russian."

"If he was, though, he wasn't running for election. The Russian people don't want to hear that from their leaders.

"And," he said as he put down his cup, "speaking of leaders, I have one who is waiting to hear from me."

"Good luck," she said. "I'll call for the chopper, while you're getting your gear ready."

Russia

YURI BELAKOV WAS in a state of shock as he walked around the late general's dacha as the first streaks of dawn appeared in the sky. Even after the fight at the bridge, he hadn't been prepared for the bloodbath that had taken place here the previous night. He was also not sure how this was going to play with his boss, the minister. He knew damned good and well that it wasn't going to play well with the Russian press or the foreign media. Zerinov had been a winner in their eyes, and now he was dead at the hands of American commandos.

Katzenelenbogen didn't have to be a mind reader

to know what was going through Belakov's mind. As any Russian would do, he was desperately looking for a way to remove himself from what had happened here, and Katz didn't blame him one bit. Russian tradition wasn't kind to those who got involved with events of great political import. With the notable exception of Lenin, almost all of the other leaders of the Glorious Revolution had ended up with their backs against a wall facing the muzzles of a firing squad.

"Yuri…" Katz said.

The young Russian turned, and his face told the story.

"If I might make a suggestion," Katz said carefully as this wasn't the time to be giving the man any more orders, "you might want to get some of your SVR people over here to secure the general's papers."

When the Russian nodded, Katz continued. "You also might want to have someone look through the late Josef Leoninski's office as well. Proof that they conspired to subvert the election shouldn't be too hard to find. And don't forget the tank brigade hiding in Potemkin National Forest. Your minister has more than enough proof here to calm this down real fast. This was nothing more than a coup attempt that was successfully put down. If he takes that line, he'll get the credit for stopping it and be a hero."

"I will call him immediately." Belakov sounded relieved to see a way out of this mess. He had stepped a long way away from the instructions he had been given. And though he was convinced that he had done the right thing, he still wanted to save his career. Russia had a future again now, and he wanted to be a part of it.

"We'll also help you explain this," Katz said. "And if it comes down to it, we'll take you home with us."

"Thank you for the offer," the young Russian said, "but I need to stay here and help my country."

"Good man."

CHAPTER TWENTY-NINE

Stony Man Farm, Virginia

The CNN coverage of Pavel Zerinov's death was blaring from the dayroom TV set when Jim Gordon walked in that evening, and what he saw shocked him to the core. While no mention was made of any American involvement in the attack on the general's villa, it was apparent to him that it was the result of this secret organization's operation. He didn't see what else it could be. The other blacksuits sure as hell thought that it was, and they were talking about their hero "Striker" and his men again. Once more they had meddled in the Russian election, but this time they had killed one of the leading candidates.

He found it a fine irony that the Americans who prided themselves on their vaunted democracy weren't willing to let the Russian people elect the leader that they themselves wanted. He realized that he shouldn't have been surprised. That had been the bedrock of U.S. policy during the cold war years, and apparently nothing had changed. The Americans would allow the Russians to play at being a democracy as much as they liked as long as the almighty United States approved of the winners. It brought to mind memories of Allende, Diem and the other democratic leaders who had fallen afoul of American politics and had paid with their lives.

The Communists had controlled the leaders in their sphere of influence as well, but at least they had been open about deposing foreign leaders who didn't suit their purposes. They hadn't used secret mercenary units to assassinate them under the guise of promoting democracy.

"That's another one for your Russian history update," the guard he had discussed his background with the night before said. "Zerinov goes down with all the rest. Who do you think will win this thing now?"

"I don't have a clue," Gordon replied and, in fact, he didn't. He hadn't followed the election closely enough to even know the names of the other candidates.

"At least it won't be that bastard." The guard sounded very satisfied. "And good riddance. We don't need another war with the Russians."

Gordon held his tongue and let the man go on his way. His simple-minded, black-and-white assessment of the situation in Russia was so typical. The American public could only see the Russians as enemies or as a resource to be exploited for commercial gain. The pain and suffering of the people were of no concern to most Americans. And, as long as that was the case, men like Zerinov would step up and try to guide the Russian nation back to greatness.

Rather than watch anymore, Gordon picked up an entertainment magazine and retreated to his bunk. Snapping on his reading light, he pretended to be interested in the sex lives of the pampered rich and famous as he seethed over the assassination. He still had more than a week to go before rotation, but he wasn't sure that he could make it. The stress of knowing that he was under constant surveillance was unremitting. He had kept his behavior as clean as a choir boy's, but the knowledge that eyes were watching every breath he took was almost more than he could bear.

If he'd been working a normal civilian job, he would be able to get drunk on the weekends, drive up in the mountains or simply sleep all day to relieve the stress. But being a blacksuit was worse than being in prison. At least in prison he could hammer his fists against the wall without someone taking note of it.

On top of that, the news of Zerinov's death was ripping at his guts like a piranha. These people had robbed Russia of a much-needed leader, and they were going to get away with it cleanly because no one knew about it. The worst thing was that he knew what they had done, but there wasn't a damned thing he could do about it. Sure, he could get his weapon and kill a few of the blacksuits before he was gunned down, but he wasn't some suicidal postal worker.

Even if he started shooting, he would never be able to get into the farmhouse and wreak his vengeance on the people who were responsible for this outrage. All he would be able to do would be kill some of the guards, and they were simply working for a living. He wanted to kill the men who had done this thing, but they were still in Russia doing God only knew what.

As he had been trained to do so long ago in Mother Russia, Gordon went into a meditative state. Although the Communists had crushed religious faith in their empire, they had warmly embraced a number of other mental disciplines that required an equal unscientific fervor. In the intelligence services, transcendental meditation had become a part of their regular training program. When faced with a complex situation, KGB agents had been taught to seek solutions while in a meditative state.

As Gordon recited his mantra, he went deep in his mind to review everything he had learned since arriving at this secret installation. When he was done with this review, he would know what his next move should be.

AS HE HAD BEEN DOING for the past couple of evenings, Buck Greene was in the Computer Room with Aaron Kurtzman watching the video monitors.

"When are you finding time to sleep?" Kurtzman asked the security chief. It didn't take a rocket scientist to see that adding up the hours Greene spent supervising his blacksuits and watching the surveillance tapes came to more than a long day's work.

"I'm not," Greene growled. "As long as I've got an enemy agent on the grounds, I'm not supposed to be sleeping."

"Me and my staff can keep an eye on him," Kurtzman said. "Now that the Russian mission is over and the guys are coming home, we don't have anything else going on."

Greene shook his head. "I need to be here, Aaron. I appreciate the offer, but I have the watch."

Kurtzman looked up at the monitor showing Gordon lying on his bunk engrossed in a magazine. "You'd better get a cup of coffee then, because it looks like he's settled in for the evening. If you'd like, I can have the cook bring you a sandwich."

"I'll just stick with the coffee. If I eat too much, I'll get sleepy."

WHEN JIM GORDON BECAME alert again, the clock on the wall showed that only twenty-eight minutes had passed, but it had been time well-spent. He felt refreshed and ready for action. The disciplined trip through his subconscious had organized his thoughts and harnessed his emotions to the task at hand. After looking at the situation from all angles, it was apparent that the only way he was ever going to see vengeance visited upon these people was to escape at the first opportunity.

The key to his decision was the cold fact that he was the only man, not part of the organization, who knew what was taking place here. He alone knew the threat this bucolic little farm presented to the entire world. If they could assassinate a major Russian political figure with complete impunity, no one was safe. The world's governments needed to know what was being done here, and he was the only man who could pass on that information.

The second part of the equation was that he needed to get out as soon as he could. Every minute he remained was exposing himself unnecessarily to capture. He had everything he needed to know already, and risking himself in vain hope of finding the installation's Achilles' heel was exactly that— vain. He had to get out tonight.

The blacksuits were more alert at night, but even with their night-vision devices and heat sensors, the night was still a fleeing man's best cover. If he could get to the vehicle key box, he would take one of the pickups and disable the other one so he couldn't be followed. Once outside the perimeter, the United States was a big place to hide and he was confident that he could evade capture.

The blacksuits weren't confined to the barracks at night, but most of them stayed inside after dark unless they had duties on the grounds. Nonetheless, it wasn't completely unknown for someone to walk outside to take the night air, smoke a cigarette or just get away from his comrades for a few moments. He could do that, and hopefully no one would think anything of it.

He was very much aware of the video camera as

he got out of bed and opened his wall locker. Since it was a double-door military locker, the door blocked the view of the camera as he took his Beretta M-92 from its holster and stuffed it in his belt. Two spare magazines went into his front pocket. He shrugged on his jeans jacket, which covered the pistol, and put on his blacksuit cap before closing the locker.

On the way out of the barracks, he paused long enough to take two fragmentation grenades from the ready rack inside the door and slip them into his jacket pockets.

"GODDAMMIT," Greene said as he reached for his handheld radio, "he's making his run."

"All patrol units," he radioed as he ran from the room, "this is Control. Condition Zulu is now in effect. I say again Condition Zulu, intruder on the grounds. Locate probationary blacksuit James Gordon and take him into custody. Stop Gordon at all costs, but take him alive. I'll explain when it's over. Acknowledge in turn."

Kurtzman reached for the intercom button. "Barbara," he said when she clicked on, "Jim Gordon's making his move. He's armed and he's on the grounds."

"Can we stop him?"

"I don't know," he answered honestly.

"I'm coming down," she said.

SINCE ALL THE ALARMS at Stony Man were silent, Gordon had no way of knowing that his run for freedom had been noted the minute he walked out the door. Since he hadn't been assigned to night guard duty yet, he also didn't know that the teams were all patrolling the perimeter at that part of the shift and hadn't started to head back to cover the main house yet.

He did know, however, that the clock was running and he had no time to lose. Walking as if he had a purpose, but not running, he headed for the vehicle barn. On the way, he went past the fuel pumps and picked up the iron bar that was used to tighten down the fuel storage tank lid. It was three feet long and would do nicely for what he had in mind.

In the vehicle shed, he walked up to the first of the two pickups, stabbed the iron bar through the grille and felt it tear into the truck's radiator. The truck would still start and run, but it wouldn't run very long without coolant. Now he was committed.

Gordon walked to the key box and got the keys to the blue truck. Going over to the other Dodge, he opened the door and slipped inside the cab, keeping his head below the windshield as he rolled down both side windows. Putting the key in the ignition, he declutched, slipped the gearshift into first and raised his head just enough to check if the way was clear.

When he saw that he was alone, he took one of the grenades and, holding it securely in his left hand, pulled the pin. Sticking that arm out the window, he sat and twisted the key with his right hand. When the V-10 engine caught on the first rotation, he dropped the clutch, floored the gas and the powerful Dodge shot forward.

As he cleared the vehicle shed, he tossed the armed grenade over the top of the cab back inside. Snapping the wheel to the right, he powered through the turn to get lined up with the road just as the grenade exploded. The flash of the bomb lit up his rearview mirror, and he saw men running to cut him off.

He sped up and passed them at sixty miles an hour. A flurry of gunfire followed, but with the dust plume from the dirt road, most of it didn't score. Two rounds punched through the rear window on the passenger's side, but beyond splattering him with glass, did no harm.

When he saw the gate, he didn't even try to slow but crashed through it and kept going.

BUCK GREENE COULDN'T believe that Gordon had been able to simply get in the pickup and drive away like that. A squad in the second pickup was racing after him, but five miles out, they radioed that the engine was seriously overheating.

"Keep after him, dammit!" he radioed back.

"What's wrong?" Price asked.

"We've lost him," Greene reported. "The other pickup blew its engine trying to catch him."

"I already put out an APB with the state and county," Kurtzman replied.

Even though they knew that was the right thing

to do, both men also knew how futile it was. The county seat was better than an hour away and the state police didn't routinely patrol the rural roads. The chance of their running into him was very slim.

"You'd better get that out to everyone in the region," Price added. "With that truck under him, he'll be in the next state in little more than an hour."

"That's gone out as well," Kurtzman replied.

"Well, gentlemen," Barbara said. "I think I need to call Hal Brognola."

No one volunteered to make that call for her.

JIM GORDON HAD PLANNED to drive the pickup until the gas ran out, but one of the rounds that had been fired at him had hit a tire. Even though the Dodge was wearing military type run-flat tires, he could not risk a high-speed chase. His only chance was to ditch the truck now and continue on foot.

A dirt road led to a small beach that looked like a place where the local fishermen launched their boats. Stopping at the edge of the water, he switched off the headlights. When he opened the door to turn on the dome light to see if there was anything in the truck he might be able to use, he spotted a dusty John Deere baseball cap behind the seat. Leaving his blacksuit cap behind, he took it with him when he stepped out of the cab.

He quickly took off his jacket, shirt, boots and socks. After adding his billfold and his new cap to the pile along with his pistol and ammunition, he got back into the truck.

Shifting into first, he drove into the water feeling his way along the bottom. The river was a hundred yards wide, and he hoped deep enough to cover the top of the truck. The water was inside the cab when he felt the bottom take a steeper angle. Gunning the engine, the truck shot forward as the wheels fell into an unseen hole in the riverbed. As it headed under, he opened the door and stepped out for the short swim back to shore.

Shaking off the water, he quickly got back into his clothing and boots, putting his billfold in his shirt pocket so it wouldn't get wet. As much as he hated to do it, he took the Beretta pistol from his belt and the extra magazines from his pocket.

Having been a cop, he knew better than to risk being stopped with a piece. If he kept the weapon on him, he might be tempted to use it. Without it, he would have to depend on his wits to survive, but that would give him a better chance of making it. An armed man acted differently than a man without a gun to fall back on. He would take fewer chances and think everything over twice if he was unarmed. He threw the weapon as far out into the river as he could and sent the magazines after it.

Now he had to get to the nearest freeway. The walk would dry his jeans and keep him from getting too cold.

CHAPTER THIRTY

Stony Man Farm, Virginia

When he walked into Hal Brognola's office the next morning, Buck Greene was wearing what passed for a uniform around the Farm—a clean blue work shirt, well washed but pressed chino trousers and his best cowboy boots, polished to a high shine.

"What can I do for you, Buck?" Brognola asked.

"Mr. Brognola," Greene said formally, "I would like to tender my resignation effective immediately."

Brognola was surprised. The Gordon episode had been close, perhaps too close, but it was over now. The big Fed had put out a blanket capture-on-sight bulletin to every federal agency from the ATF to the National Park Service, as well as the police forces of all fifty states, Interpol and the intelligence services of the NATO nations. As well, Phoenix Force and Able Team were quietly working behind the scenes to track the man. Gordon was as good as dead.

"Please sit, Chief."

Greene sat stiffly.

"Why do you want to resign?"

"Well, sir," Greene said, "I really screwed the pooch big time on this one. I put the organization in danger by bringing Gordon in."

"And you think you should have caught him before you offered him the position, is that it?"

"Yes, sir." Greene nodded. "I failed to spot him in time, and now we've been compromised."

"You ran all the background checks on him just like you always do, right?"

Greene nodded again.

"You did, however, get onto him before he was here too long," Brognola reminded him. "And you and Kurtzman took your findings to Barbara. It's not your fault that she wanted you to let him run free so we could try to learn what he was doing here. In retrospect, we should have taken him into custody the minute you reported your first suspicions, but that's not your fault."

"I should have never let him in here in the first place. He's a damned Russian."

"He was born in Russia, yes. But he's more American than a lot of people who were born here because he studied so hard to become one of us."

"It doesn't matter."

"What's the real reason you want to quit?" Brognola asked.

Greene shook his head. "I just don't trust myself anymore. I screwed up big time and let this guy in. I'm afraid that I might make a mistake again."

Brognola knew that making mistakes went with the job description of being human. If he'd been required to pay for all of his mistakes, he'd have been dead a long time ago. In this business, making mistakes was nature's way of telling you to do something differently. And, if you were lucky, you survived. Those who learned from their mistakes were those who lived to make another, but different, one.

"Look, Buck. This guy slipped past you and, if you'd like, I'll dock you a month's pay or something like that. But since we have been penetrated, we have work to do right now and I need you to do it. I need to know exactly what this guy had access to, what he might have learned that someone could use against us. Whatever it is, we need to take care of it immediately. I need a thorough analysis of the whole security system to find our weaknesses. And, if you think that we need to scrap the whole damned thing and start over, do it. But I want it done ASAP.

"Then, since you're the one who found the flaw in our security force selection system, I want you to pinpoint the weaknesses there and fix them as well. You're right. We can't afford to have something like this happen again. We're too small to be able to absorb an enemy agent without risking the operation. To protect ourselves in the future, I need you to revamp our recruiting process. As a start, I suggest that you require complete medical records on all future recruits and have them thoroughly examined. Maybe a complete background check on an applicant's family is in order. You figure out what we need to do, and then you do it.''

"I'd like to put them all under chemical interrogation," Greene growled. "That way the bastards won't be able to hide from me."

"I'll take that under advisement," Brognola said. "But you have to remember that we sometimes get a bad reaction on that stuff. We don't want to brainburn a good man."

"I know," Greene admitted.

"And, Chief, after you've done all the damage control and have tightened things up, if you still want to resign, come back and talk to me about it."

Greene locked eyes with Brognola. "I might still do that."

"See me when this place is secure again."

"Yes, sir."

When Greene left, Brognola punched the intercom button connecting him to Barbara Price's office. His discussion with the security chief had been piped into her office, and she had overheard it.

"I'm glad he's staying," she said. "I don't know who we'd replace him with."

"He just needed to confess his sins," Brognola said. "He'll be around here until we shovel dirt in his face."

"Hal..."

"Yes?"

"What if Gordon tries to shop us? I know he picked up enough information to be worth a lot of money to the right people."

"That's a distinct possibility," he admitted. "And if he does, there's little we can do about it except to be even more vigilant than we've been in the past. I don't think that he learned enough to put us out of business, if that's what you mean. And these mountain roads are so complex maybe he'd never be able to find us exactly. But now that he's driven out of the area, he'll know the general location."

"I hate the thought of someone like him out there ready to expose us anytime he wants."

"I've got everybody in the business looking for him," Brognola said confidently. "Believe me, we'll get him."

"I sure as hell hope so," she said.

THE TRUCKER WAS CLIMBING into the cab of his eighteen wheeler at the truck stop outside Harrisburg when he saw a man approaching him. "You heading south, mister?" the man asked. "I sure could use a ride."

The trucker checked out the hitchhiker before replying. A person had to be careful nowadays about who he invited into his cab for a ride. If you made the wrong choice, it could be your last. The man looked like a farmhand, but his clothes were clean, he was freshly shaved and he didn't look like he was on the run from the law. "Where you headed?"

"Atlanta."

"I'm going to Charlotte. That's about halfway."

"Thanks."

Jim Gordon climbed into the passenger seat and settled in. "I sure appreciate this, mister."

"It's Bud, Bud Gates."

"I'm Jim White," Gordon answered without the slightest hesitation.

"You're traveling light," the trucker commented on his rider's lack of luggage. "What's in Atlanta?"

Gordon looked a little hesitant. "My little sister. She needs some help and I thought I'd look in on her."

The trucker caught the hesitance and figured that family matters weren't any of his business. His sister was probably knocked-up with no man in sight. "We'll be in Charlotte in three hours, and you shouldn't have any problem finding a ride to Atlanta from there."

"Great."

When the trucker pulled his rig out onto the freeway, Gordon leaned back in his seat and pretended to sleep. It had been some time since he had slept, and he easily could have dozed off, but his mind was racing. More than ever, he wished that he had a contact to debrief him. The information he had couldn't just stay with him.

He had failed to find a way to do any significant damage to the clandestine operation. But what he had learned might make it easier for the next man to destroy it. One way or the other, that secret installation had to be taken down.

As of today, ex-U.S. Marshal and ex-Blacksuit James T. Gordon was dead. He would change his name each time he picked up a new ride, but as soon as he reached California, he'd take up his alternate identity and start out again. It would be slow going at first, because his alter ego was a bit old and he'd have to invent a scenario that would cover the missing years. He'd begin by renewing his California driver's license, reopen his bank account, reapply for his lapsed credit cards and take it from there.

He was certain that he would be able to safely hide as Rick Mackin, but he wouldn't be able to look for work as a law-enforcement officer. That career field was out; his alternate ID wasn't strong enough to support an in-depth background check. But that didn't mean that he wouldn't be able to use his years behind a badge to his advantage. Having been a federal cop had taught him many skills that were marketable to the right people.

IN CHARLOTTE, he bid goodbye to the trucker at a truck stop on the interstate. As soon as the eighteen wheeler was back on the road, he headed into the gift shop. Before he started looking for his next ride, he wanted to change shirts and hats. Witnesses tended to remember the shirts and hats of the people they met.

After reoutfitting, he got something to eat before going back out in the parking lot to look for a truck with Texas or Arizona plates. If he could get to Phoenix, he'd be almost home free, but Tucson would be almost as good. He'd give each trucker he rode with a different phony destination and cover story so if they were interviewed, they couldn't give anything away.

When he spotted a cattle truck with a Lubbock, Texas, address painted on the door, he walked up to the driver. "You headed west, mister?"

In the Deathlands, power is the ultimate weapon....

JAMES AXLER

DEATHLANDS®

Gemini Rising

Ryan Cawdor comes home to West Virginia and his nephew Nathan, to whom Cawdor had entrusted the Cawdor barony. Waiting for Cawdor are two of his oldest enemies, ready to overtake the barony and the Cawdor name.

Unable to help an ailing Krysty Wroth, Cawdor must face this challenge to the future of the East Coast baronies on his own.

Book 1 in the Baronies Trilogy, three books that chronicle the strange attempts to unify the East Coast baronies—a bid for power in the midst of anarchy....

James Axler

OUTLANDERS™

NIGHT ETERNAL

Kane and his fellow warrior survivalists find themselves launched into an alternate reality where the nukecaust was averted—and the Archons have emerged as mankind's great benefactors.

The group sets out to help a small secret organization conduct a clandestine war against the forces of evil....

Book #2 in the new Lost Earth Saga, a trilogy that chronicles our heroes' paths through three very different alternate realities... where the struggle against the evil Archons goes on...

Desperate times call for desperate measures. Don't miss out on the action in these titles!

STONY MAN™